D1267920

Titles by Ginny Aiken

CANDY KISS
COUNTY FAIR
CRYSTAL MEMORIES

CRYSTAL MEMORIES

Ginny Aiken

JOVE BOOKS, NEW YORK

CRYSTAL MEMORIES

A Jove Book / published by arrangement with
the author

PRINTING HISTORY
Jove edition / October 1997

The Putnam Berkley World Wide Web site address is
http://www.berkley.com

ISBN: 0-515-12159-2

A JOVE BOOK®
Jove Books are published by The Berkley Publishing Group,
a member of Penguin Putnam, Inc.,
200 Madison Avenue, New York, New York 10016.
JOVE and the "J" design are trademarks
belonging to Jove Publications, Inc.

PRINTED IN THE UNITED STATES OF AMERICA

10 9 8 7 6 5 4 3 2 1

I'd like to thank the Winona County Historical Society for the research provided while I wrote this book. I'm especially indebted to Bruce, Ginger, and Marie, who answered endless questions with superhuman patience.

To everything there is a season, and a time to
every purpose under heaven: A time to be
born, and a time to die . . .
A time to love . . .

—Ecclesiastes 3: 1-2a, 8a

Prologue

"WHO IS HE?" Amelia Baldwin asked the young tour guide who was showing her and two co-workers through the old Opera House. Something about the face drawn in century-old oils evoked a response in her. His sadness touched Amelia's heart.

"The man in the painting is Michael Hayak," answered Wendy, "a patron of the Opera House around 1900. His wife died a few years after they married, and he raised their daughter while working the farm. As far as anyone knows, he never saw a production here, but his donations came until his death."

Upon entering the building, Amelia had felt an eerie kind of welcome, almost recognition, even though she'd never been to Winona or the Opera House before. She'd looked around the lobby, noted the nineteenth-century details that time had blurred, then tried to shake off the feeling of déjà vu. It had probably been caused by her fascination with the late 1800s. She loved vintage clothing, vaudeville, and century homes.

Amelia heard her companions' footsteps move off toward the stage, but she continued to study that face. Michael Hayak's poignant expression made her feel loss, loneliness, pain.

Shared anguish.

"Get with the program, Amelia," she muttered. "You're here to absorb the atmosphere of a turn-of-the-century theater, not to gape at some gorgeous dead guy."

With a final glance at the ornately framed painting, Amelia hurried after her boss and the guide. She hadn't come as a tourist. She'd been hired to costume a vaudeville revival at a recently restored theater on the outskirts of Chicago. She'd wanted that job in the worst way. "And unless you pay attention, you're going to lose that job," she told herself as she stepped onto the stage.

A chill ripped through her. Her hands went clammy. Mammoth moths dive-bombed in her stomach. Again she felt that weird sense of recognition.

But she'd never been here before.

Yet everything felt familiar, in a foggy way.

Slipping her damp hands into the pockets of her vintage lace-trimmed cotton skirt, Amelia approached center stage.

The structure resembled the theater back home in dimension and even the curtain set-up. It seemed many of these old auditoriums had been built from similar plans.

Looking out over the rows of seats, Amelia felt another cold shudder tear through her. An unusual thickness rose in her throat, and she brought her hand to her neck. The crisp lace collar of her violet Victorian shirtwaist rubbed against goosebumped skin.

This was bizarre. And she'd wasted enough time. Rosemary Pumphrey, her boss, had gone on to inspect the collection of authentic costumes they'd both come to see. Costumes were Amelia's responsibility.

Taking another step, she lost her footing and heard a loud *crack* beneath her feet.

Suddenly she plunged downward. . . .

Chapter 1

... THROUGH ENDLESS BLACKNESS.

Infinity stretched out around Amelia. As she realized this, a jackhammer began to pound at the base of her skull. She gasped from the pain, hurting more than she'd ever hurt before, then tried to open her eyes.

She whimpered, and a wave of hazy red pulsated in her head.

Breathing ached. Lifting her eyelids made her nauseous. For the moment, immobility would do just fine.

Since thinking seemed her only choice, she began to sort her memories of what had happened. She remembered entering the Opera House, and she'd never forget the portrait of that man ... Michael Hayak. Then she'd gone onto the stage. After that, things grew fuzzy, but she did remember the hideous scream of splintering wood.

She probably stepped on a rickety floorboard, fell, and hit her head. That would account for the raw ache, and a concussion would cause nausea and disorientation.

"H-help," she cried, but even through the accompanying

volley of pain, she knew the word had come out as a sand-papery croak.

At this rate, by the time she was found the set designer, the lighting expert, and Rosemary would be long gone from Winona. Although Amelia liked the old town well enough, the weird sensations she'd experienced since her arrival had her ready to return home.

She again tried to pry open her eyes. Once more the slic-ing throb stopped her. While the canvas behind her closed eyelids glowed demonic red, she fought down another wave of nausea.

Fine. She'd keep her eyes shut, but how long would she have to wait for someone to come by? Where was a Good Samaritan when you needed one?

Just her luck that no one seemed to be around. Of course, she was used to being alone. The foster care system offered an excellent education in loneliness.

She'd keep absolutely still. That seemed the only way to tolerate the pounding in her skull. The slightest movement brought back the queasiness and the threat of another blackout.

". . . Ain't seen 'er move yet," a man said.

Great. Now she even heard voices.

With or without voices, she felt worse than she'd ever felt before. Pain this bad probably meant she'd died.

Was she dead? If she was, had she been sent a country-style drawling angel? Why did such strange stuff always happen to her?

"She's breathing," a woman observed. Another angel, maybe?

"How can you be sure?"

"Why, her bosom— Herbert Weidel, you know perfectly well how I know she's still breathing! Quit staring at those pretty legs, you old coot, and find us a way to get her out of there."

"Where is there?" asked Amelia. After the expected bombardment of pain, she realized she still hadn't done more than murmur the words. Had her angels heard her measly sounds over their own argument?

Had they come to escort her to her final reward? And what kind of reward had she earned?

"There!" exclaimed the female. "You see? It's just like I told you, Herbert. She's not only breathing, but she's trying to talk. Poor child's hurt, and all you do is stare at her legs. Give her a hand."

Herbert wasn't a name Amelia attributed to angels, but then again, she'd never met a heavenly being before. And what about her legs?

"How'd'ye want me to do that, Pansy Pritchard? My arms ain't long enough to stretch down to th' ground."

Amelia chuckled at *that* name—then gagged as bile rushed up. Laughing was out of the question. Made sense. You shouldn't be irreverent on your way to Heaven.

"I don't know, but you're the one who's always babbling about how smart you are. This is as good a time as any to prove it."

More grumbling.

Figured. Only she would get stuck with a band of cranky angels. At least help was coming, even if she had no idea what form that help would take.

Millimeter by millimeter Amelia lifted her lids. Shapes floated somewhere above her. Although she still couldn't focus well, she assumed it was the angels she saw. Steeling herself against the lightheadedness that followed her efforts, and by sheer strength of will, she kept her eyes propped open. The unbearable thumping continued inside her skull.

Slowly the ethereal forms began to solidify. Amelia decided she could keep her eyes at half-mast and not go under again. Good. She was curious about her heavenly helpers. Then she began to perceive details of the beings from above.

Good grief! Who'd have thought angels were so different from humans? Heck, they were only floating heads with mouths near the top and eyes around where chins usually loiter! Although she'd heard two voices, there seemed to be at least five oddball cherubs staring at her.

Amelia blinked, trying to get a better view of her rescuers. Well, they'd be rescuers if they ever got around to helping her overcome the unpleasant residue from her recent demise.

"What . . . happened?" she asked, closing her eyes against the dizziness.

"See?" asked a new heavenly voice. "Pansy was right. She's trying to talk. How are we going to get her out?"

Out of where?

"Oh, stuff yore cacklin', Mildred!" retorted Herbert, the unlikely angel. "I know we gotta get her outta there, but I don't quite rightly know how we're gonna do it yet."

Just hurry, Amelia thought, hoping that when they finally got her out of *wherever,* she'd feel better.

When the vertigo abated, she opened her eyes. Instead of seeking her angels, though, Amelia checked to see if she was traveling on a cloud. That's how she'd always envisioned her approach to eternity.

When her eyes focused, however, the strangest sight swam into view. A pair of enormous, violet-cotton-covered mounds rose to nearly meet her chin. Were those . . . things . . . what she thought they were? And if they were, where did they come from?

Fighting another imminent faint, Amelia opened her eyes all the way. Damn! Those *were* Dolly Parton boobs springing up from her previously flat chest.

How'd they get so big? She'd occasionally wished for a curvier figure, but if Amelia knew one thing, she knew that wishing didn't necessarily make things so. If it did, she would have had a family, since that had been her fondest wish from as far back as she could remember.

Wiggling her fingers, she realized she could now command her body—her celestial body?—to move. Inch by excruciating inch, she brought her hand into her range of vision and found slender little fingers where long, sturdy ones had always been. She turned the hand one way, then the other, wriggled the dainty digits, then patted the uppermost curve of the inflated breasts. Sure *felt* real.

"She's moving!" cried Pansy Pritchard over Amelia's head. "See, Herbert? I *told* you she wasn't dead. Now, will you move along and find some way to help her out of that dirty hole?"

"Yeah, yeah. I'm goin', Pansy. Don't get yore bloomers all in a twist."

Again Amelia smiled at the strange speech of her angels, then went back to pondering the mysteries of the afterlife. A chest this cushiony could only come to her by miraculous means—diligent use of bust enhancers in magazine classified ads hadn't done it years ago.

This meant one got a brand-new body before arriving in Heaven. A body with all the accoutrements it had lacked in life. So be it.

When a suddenly sharper spasm at the back of her head caught her by surprise, she took her delicate little hand and gingerly patted the hurting area. Warm oozy dampness met her new fingers. Amelia brought the hand back into view and confirmed that the fluid was blood. A lot of it.

Could concussions follow you into the afterlife? And did you hallucinate when concussed? How about after you died? Hallucinations could explain the foreign body parts she saw, but she preferred the thought of a new and improved body for her eternal life. Amelia was pretty sure she'd died. This much blood had to mean the end of life. Besides, angels hovered overhead.

As she studied her bloody hand, she noticed dark strands stuck to the gore. If she didn't know better, she'd swear they were hairs, but hers weren't black, and as short as she wore her mousy-brown locks, they'd never come around her head like this.

Something strange had happened, and she meant to find out exactly what.

With superhuman effort, she propped both elbows against the rock-hard cloud she lay on, then struggled into a semi-sitting position. "What happened?" she asked again, thrilled to hear the words huskily murmured.

"Oh, Amelia, it's so good to see you moving around! We were worried about you!"

"Pansy?"

"Yes, it's me."

So there *were* angels named Pansy. "What happened? I mean before I arrived up here."

"Up here? No, no, Amelia. *We're* up here. *You're* down there."

"I'm down where?" she asked, afraid Pansy's response would conjure sulfurous, licking flames, a pitchfork, and horns.

"Under the stage floor, of course."

"The . . . stage floor?" Amelia concentrated on her vision and noticed that Pansy's face, together with those of about four other angels, wasn't hovering in the ether after all. The five upside-down faces ringed a circle of light in the dark expanse of what looked like the underside of oak floor-boards.

"Yes. You must have stepped through a weak spot on the stage. You're on the ground."

Ever so slowly, Amelia turned her face and found dark-ness, cobwebs, and hard-packed soil around her. "You mean . . . I'm not . . . dead?"

"Of course not! Although I think it was a near miss."

If she hadn't died . . . then who were Pansy, Herbert, and the others? "I'm not in Heaven? Or Hell? You aren't an-gels?"

"Amelia Baldwin, shame on you! A lady doesn't use such blasphemous language. You know very well you're in the Opera House."

Sibilant whispers played a background song for Pansy's reproof. How did Pansy know her name? And if she and her pals weren't angels, who were they?

Calling on the last of her will, Amelia pushed herself upright. Her new boobs ebbed somewhat, fireworks burst before her watering eyes, and the jackhammer detonated another salvo in her head. Since her scalp felt as if a split was imminent, she held on to it with her tiny new hands.

Through the roar in her temples, Amelia heard Pansy mutter, ". . . where that Herbert Weidel has taken himself off to this time."

"Well, you did tell him to get her out of there," Mildred responded.

Pansy countered, "He's sure taking his own sweet time figuring how to do it."

As the throbbing lessened, the gist of the argument registered. But before she could do anything, Amelia heard a round of exclamations.

"Now that's what we needed!" cried Pansy Pritchard.

"Hurry up," urged Mildred.

"I'm comin', I'm comin'," answered a panting Herbert.

Next thing Amelia knew, a shower of dust and debris rained down on her. An enormous crash at her side sent her lurching to her knees. A moan ripped from her throat at the renewed jab of the jackhammer.

"What? Now you're going to kill her?" asked Pansy.

Herbert snorted in disdain. "How didja want me to git her outta there if I don't git this ladder down to her?"

"Just be careful, Herbert Weidel."

"I know what I'm doin', ya cacklin' ol' hen."

"And who's got reason to be calling *who* old?"

"Bah," Herbert spat in response. Then through the narrow slit between her eyelids, Amelia saw the outline of a head block the miserly light that reached her prison.

"Hey! Amelia Baldwin! Can ya see the ladder, there?"

"Yes," she whispered, then cleared her throat and answered with more *oomph*. "I see it."

"Then git yoreself over to it, and see if ya can reach my hand."

Amelia was sure she'd never make it to the ladder. Not

that she had to go far or anything, but each slight movement seemed more difficult than the last. Still, it clearly offered the only way out of this hellhole, and she wasn't
staying down here any longer than she had to.

Tugging up her long skirt, Amelia crept inches toward
the ladder. Her knees complained. By the time she was
done, the rough ground would probably rub her legs raw.
But she had to get out.

She sucked in her breath, dropped her skirt, and resumed
her crawl to freedom. When she grabbed a rung on Herbert's wobbly wooden ladder, a rousing cheer sounded
from above.

"That's it!" called Pansy. "We'll have you out in no
time."

Amelia tried a weak smile, but it required too much effort, especially since she was trying to stand. Hand over
hand, she used the ladder for support, and soon found herself swaying on her feet.

"Take my hand," called Herbert.

Reaching blindly, Amelia sought the proffered help. She
waved back and forth over her head. Moments later she felt
the man's warm skin. Relief so strong it stole her breath
filled her at the contact. Herbert was too solid to be an
angel.

So she hadn't died.

Rung by rung she labored upward, and a couple of eons
later felt many more hands helping to lift her the rest of the
way.

Tears of gratitude and joy filled her eyes. "Thank you all
so much," she whispered through the lump in her throat.

"Well, now, child," answered Mildred in her no-
nonsense voice, "you did most of the work yourself."

"Hey!" cried Herbert. "I did plenny, myself."

"Quit tooting your horn, Herbert Weidel. The girl
dragged herself up. You only gave her a ladder to hold
onto."

"An' a helpin' hand, Pansy-Pants."

"Pansy-Pants? It's been decades since you and I finished school. Don't go calling a body childish names, Herbert. Not if you want to show the world that you're a smarter old codger than you were a kid."

"I ain't no older'n you," he muttered, then Amelia heard clipped footsteps departing.

"Herbert!" she called.

"Huh?"

"Thank you for your help. I couldn't have done it without your hand to hold onto. Thank you very, very much."

"Yore welcome, miss. So there, Pansy Pritchard. Girl knows what's what."

Pansy snorted. Or at least Amelia guessed it was Pansy.

By now, Amelia's tears had ended, and her brain had stopped turning cartwheels inside her skull. Tentatively she opened her eyes. Four women, all of a certain age, surrounded her, concern evident in their expressions. But it wasn't the women or their concern that caught Amelia's attention. It was their clothing that caused her to exclaim in pleasure and surprise.

They'd paired high lace collars and leg-o'-mutton sleeves with long, flaring skirts very much like her own. Amelia always wore Victorian-vintage clothing. Her "angels" must be actors rehearsing for a period production.

The show's wardrobe mistress knew her stuff. The clothes looked authentic and must have taken time, effort, and plenty of money to obtain. Amelia knew. She'd been tracking down and pricing antique garments for the vaudeville revival she'd been hired to costume.

"What play are you doing?" she asked.

"Play? No one's playing, Amelia. Herbert came to make sure everything was ready for tonight's performance, but he found you and ran to the street for help."

She must not be particularly coherent yet, Amelia thought. Either that, or Herbert, Pansy, Mildred, and the others were really getting into the spirit of things.

"Where's Rosemary?" she asked, wondering what had happened to her boss. "Did she already leave for Chicago?"

"Rosemary?"

"Who's Rosemary?"

"Chicago?"

The questions and puzzled looks told Amelia that Rosemary had probably left the Opera House. Would her boss leave town without Amelia? Wouldn't she wonder where Amelia was? She'd better hurry to the train station. Getting lost wasn't the best way to start a job.

"I'm all right now," she said, shaking her head. She regretted the movement immediately. With a grimace, she pushed herself to her knees, then carefully stood. "I'd better catch up with her before Rosemary leaves me behind."

Again her companions shook their heads and, exchanging looks that seemed to question her sanity, assisted her to a small flight of steps at the left-hand corner of the stage.

"You really should wait for the doctor before moving. That's a nasty gash on the back of your head. I believe it's still bleeding," said Pansy, a frown gathering her silver eyebrows.

Amelia knew Pansy was right, but she had to find her co-workers. She'd have her head looked at in Chicago. "I'll make sure to stop by the doctor's when I get home."

Her four rescuers stopped at the bottom of the steps. They glanced at each other, then stared at Amelia. "Oh, dear," murmured Mildred. "I think we'd better hurry and put her to bed. She's not making much sense, is she?"

Assenting murmurs followed. Amelia frowned. What were they talking about? Bed? She wasn't *that* bad off, and she made perfect sense. A knock on the head hadn't stolen her sanity. At least, she didn't think so.

"Yes, I have to go home. Immediately." At that, the four ladies smiled tentatively and assisted her down the aisle. Looking around, Amelia again noted the turn-of-the-century beauty of the theater. The sea of maroon seats rolled from the orchestra pit to the exit doors, and magnificent private boxes lined the right and left walls. A curved balcony with more maroon chairs hung over the ground floor, and the vaulted ceiling wore garlands of textured, gilded flowers.

The warm wood paneling made Amelia aware once again of the incomparable talents of nineteenth-century craftsmen. The auditorium was in amazingly good condition. She hadn't noticed the room when she'd first stepped onto the stage, but she remembered feeling saddened by the building's worn exterior as she approached earlier that morning.

As the women went from the auditorium to the lobby, Amelia made an effort to avoid the painting of Michael Hayak. Heck, her first look at the picture had made her so careless that she'd plunged through the floor of the stage! She didn't want to run the risk of getting run over by a car when she went outside. And future glimpses of Mr. Hayak might affect her as strongly as her first one had.

Pansy opened the front door for Amelia. The late summer sunshine blinded her momentarily. She closed her eyes and clenched her teeth against the throbbing in her head. Slow, deep breaths got her through the worst. Then she opened her eyes.

Her jaw dropped.

The street had turned into a packed-dirt strip where horse-drawn carriages and various kinds of buggies rolled by, kicking up clouds of dust. Instead of cement sidewalks, slabs of stone formed a walkway in front of the Opera House. And *everyone* wore period costumes.

"Oh!" she exclaimed. "It's a movie, right? The set director did a great job. You'd think the street always looked like this."

Picking up her pace, Amelia crossed the street and approached a horse and buggy tethered to a hitching post at the corner. Behind her, she caught the buzz of whispered consultations among her rescuing "angels." "What an

amazing job of reproducing the vehicles and the atmosphere of a turn-of-the-century town!"

"Well, it *is* the turn of the century," ventured Pansy.

"Yes, the next one," said Amelia, fingering the iron rim
on a buggy wheel. "Amazing workmanship. I wonder who
made it."

"Why, Amelia Baldwin, you know that's one of the
Nevius Livery's buggies. Mr. Benz does a lot of their
blacksmithing."

Those bewildered looks were beginning to rankle. Did
they think she'd memorized every last detail the tour guide
spouted? Besides, she didn't remember hearing a word
about iron workers during the brief drive to the Opera
House. This was really strange.

"Who's filming the movie?" she asked, hoping to change
the subject as she went on down the street.

"Filming?" asked Pansy.

"Movie?" added Mildred.

"What are you talking about?" demanded another one of
Amelia's "angels," while more puzzled stares came her
way.

She'd had it. It wasn't as if she'd spoken Swahili or anything. "I'm talking about the costumes, the buggies, the
horses, the dirt on the street! For heaven's sake, you don't
think you can keep something like the presence of a production company secret, do you?"

"Production . . . ?"

"Company . . . ?"

"Secret . . . ?"

"Amelia, dear," said Pansy, squaring her broad shoulders, "it's clear the blow to your head has had a rather serious effect on you. You're not making sense, and I think it
best for you to be abed."

With that, Pansy grasped Amelia's elbow and propelled her around the corner. At a near trot, they went toward the sun descending in the horizon. Unsure what to
do next, Amelia kept walking and continued admiring the

results of the film production's set crew. She soon caught sight of a man in a somber black suit and hat as he stepped out of a doorway up ahead. A sign identified the building as the W.L. NEVIUS & BROS. PALACE LIVERY, SALE, OMNIBUS, AND HACK STABLE. The faint musk of manure confirmed the proximity of horses.

As the man approached, something about him struck her as familiar. Strange. She didn't know anyone in Winona.

Then she noticed her four attendants had fallen silent. Totally silent.

Before her, the man paused. The brim of his hat shaded his face. "Excuse me," she murmured, trying to walk around him.

A chorus of comforting sounds rose from Pansy and friends. Then the man took off his hat.

Amelia gasped. It was—impossibly—the man in the portrait at the Opera House.

Michael Hayak.

Sky-blue eyes bored into hers, and she could have sworn that hate blazed in them. A hot shiver touched every bit of her body, stealing her breath. As she struggled to breathe, a stranger's name entered her mind unbidden.

"Christina . . ." she whispered.

"Gone," he responded, biting off the word, the set of his features grim. "We buried her this morning."

Chapter 2

BEFORE AMELIA REGAINED her composure, Michael Hayak shoved his hat back on his brown hair, and asked, "Where were you?"

"Me!" Amelia squeaked. "What do you mean, me?"

With a snort of disgust, he stepped past her and strode down the street.

Great! She'd walked into the middle of a movie set—nobody bothered to warn her about it ahead of time—and the protagonist mistook her for a member of the cast!

Amelia looked around, trying to find the cameras, but no matter how hard she stared, she saw no sign of the behind-the-scenes crew. The director must be one heck of a perfectionist. She'd read about them and their neurotic demands for authenticity.

Then she noticed the renewed silence of her escorts. A glance revealed they were staring at her, censorious expressions on all four faces. *Now* what had she done?

"Well?" she asked, sick of the hints, allusions, and unexplained assumptions. "What is it?"

Pansy lowered her gaze, grew red patches over her apple

cheeks, and wrung her hands. "He's right, you know. Katie spent hours crying for you. And Christina . . . well, Christina would have expected—and wanted—you there, too."

Katie? Who was Katie? And Christina—again. She was supposed to feel guilty about slighting them? How could she have slighted them? She didn't even know who they were!

Pulling away from Mildred, who'd sidled closer when *that man* had stomped past them, Amelia reclaimed control of the conversation. "Movie or no movie, I'm done here. I want to catch the first train to Chicago. I've had it with whatever's going on."

"But, Amelia, you weren't at Christina's funeral!" argued one of the two heretofore silent "angels." "You didn't even offer Michael a word of condolence just now. That was the least you could have done."

Nodding, Pansy pointed at Amelia's newly enlarged chest. "Esmée is right, missy. You assume certain responsibilities when you form a friendship, and death most certainly doesn't absolve you of those responsibilities. Especially *you*. Goodness knows, you *were* Christina's dearest friend."

"Me!" she cried again. "I don't know who you're talking about! Who *is* Christina?"

Withered little Esmée gasped.

Mildred hooted.

Pansy gaped.

The fourth "angel" rolled her eyes heavenward, then frowned formidably. "What on earth would make you say a thing like— Oh, Heavens to Betsy, the girl's got ammonia! Go fetch Dr. Wilhite. Tell him we need amnesia."

"Oh, Hannah Spitzer, you're talking backwards again," groaned Pansy. "You mean, she has *amnesia,* and Doc Willy might need *ammonia.*"

Tall, angular Hannah sniffed. "Well, Pansy, since you

knew what I meant all along, why don't *you* bustle to the doctor's office?"

Pansy squared her broad shoulders, looking like Amelia's idea of a drill sergeant. "Why, I'm returning the girl home, Hannah."

"I'll go," ventured a woman Amelia hadn't as yet noticed. Had she been there all along? Who cared? Amelia only wanted to go home.

But Pansy had yet to let go of her arm. "See, Hannah?" she crowed. "Melba knows what's what."

With an offended glare, Hannah turned her back on the others. "Oh, fine, Pansy! *You* take the girl home. Send Melba to do *your* bidding. *I* have better things to do with my time than snap to your orders." Iron-gray head high, she stomped off. Melba faded away.

"So there!" added Pansy, mimicking Hannah's affronted tone.

Amelia watched the exchange, fighting the urge to laugh since she had to persuade this gaggle of misguided geese to take her to the train station. The matter of mistaken identity, dead friends, mysterious man, and movie sets had distracted her long enough.

"The train, ladies," she stated, giving her remaining "angels" her sternest look.

Pansy marched up, wrapped a cannon-solid arm around Amelia's shoulders, and again marshaled her off. In the direction Pansy wanted her to go, of course. But Amelia had reached her breaking point. She dug in her heels. "Where are you taking me?"

Pansy paused and *tsk-tsk*ed. "Home, of course."

"But I need to catch the train to go home!"

Pansy frowned. "Perhaps Hannah was right, after all. You know perfectly well that you do not need to catch a train to go home. Home is only a matter of blocks away."

The whack on the head couldn't have scrambled her brain that much. What was going on here? Amelia surreptitiously pinched herself. It hurt.

Okay. She wasn't sleeping. She'd already verified that she hadn't died, and she knew she didn't live a few blocks away from where they stood. She lived in Chicago, and Chicago wasn't here. "Look, ladies. You probably have lots to do. So do I. Now, give me directions to the train station, and we can all get back to business."

"That's precisely what I've been trying to tell you," Pansy said with a wealth of patience. "It's my responsibility to bring you home, safe and sound."

Amelia was no longer amused. She battled rising panic. "Don't you understand? I have to get to Chicago. I live there. To get there I need to drive, fly, or take a train. Now, which is it going to be?"

And the "angels" chimed, "Fly?"

Amelia frowned. "Is there an airport nearby?"

The "angels" exchanged raised-eyebrow looks. "What's an airport?" asked Mildred.

Amelia's eyes widened. Her jaw dropped. "Aren't you carrying this historical movie thing a bit too far?"

The seraphim chorused, "Movie?"

While they'd argued, Pansy hadn't allowed their pace to slow. Amelia had no idea where she was—even though she could see they'd followed the setting sun. She cast a look around. No cars, no neon signs, no teenagers hanging out with blaring boom-boxes. She'd seen all those on her way into town.

She flirted with a wild idea. "Nah." It was impossible.

No matter how much she'd always wished it could happen, time-travel remained the stuff of writers, dreamers, and sci-fi buffs. She knew better than to think she'd fallen through the stage floor of the Winona Opera House and into its earlier days.

And yet . . . the strange, impenetrable blackness, that eternal nothingness she'd crossed before she came to, could be explained as a near-death—or would it be near-life?—experience. Couldn't it?

No. A near-death experience didn't explain how the "angels" knew her name and where she supposedly lived. Nor did it provide her with a reason for their accusations. How could she have failed a dead woman she didn't know?

They weren't dealing with a case of mistaken identity. They'd called her Amelia Baldwin all along.

Maybe she'd finally gone nuts. She'd always fantasized about life in Victorian times. Maybe she was experiencing delusions caused by her longing for another time, since she'd never felt quite at home in her own.

Rampant psychosis would explain how these strangers knew her name. Figments of her warped imagination would certainly be familiar with her.

The viselike grip of Pansy's powerful fingers brought that train of thought to a stop. Those fingers were no figment. "Ease up, Pansy. You're hurting me."

"Oh!" she cried, "I'm ever so sorry. But, see? We're here. You can just take yourself right to bed." Turning to her troops, she began barking orders. "Mildred, brew her a cup of tea. Esmée, find blankets and all the pillows in the house." The military commands then homed in on Amelia. "Go on up. I shall help you undress and tuck you right into that bed."

Help her *undress?* And pigs weren't flying by yet? *Never.*

Amelia took a fortifying lungful of air. "No," she said. "Mildred will *not* make me tea. Esmée will *not* find blankets and pillows for me. And there's *no way* in He—" She came to a screeching halt. Forcing herself to sound calm, she went on. "No, Pansy. You will not undress me."

That had felt great! Then, since she was on a roll, "Besides, who are you planning to foist me off on? Who lives here?"

More of Pansy's *tsk-tsk*ing came as she tried to shove Amelia to the front door of the house Mildred had barged into. Fortunately the spinning in Amelia's head had abated somewhat, and her strength was returning. She stood her ground.

"Amelia, dear." Pansy sounded as if she were speaking to a child or someone with the IQ of a pet rock.

Amelia held up her free hand palm out. "Stop right there, Pansy. Whose house is this? Why did you drag me here? How do you know my name? Especially since I've never set eyes on you before today. And I *really* want to know what that Christina and Katie business with . . . Michael Hayak was about."

Pansy gasped. She patted her well-upholstered bosom and offered more sympathetic noises. A somber expression finally blanketed her face. "You aren't poking fun at me, are you, Amelia?"

"Not in the least."

"You don't remember seeing me before you came to under the stage?"

"Nobody could forget meeting you."

"Why, thank you! What a lovely thing to say."

Amelia didn't have the heart to tell the older woman that she hadn't meant her words as a compliment. But as long as she had the drill sergeant mollified, Amelia was going on reconnaissance. "You're welcome, I'm sure. Anyway, why don't you start by telling me how you know me."

"Of course," Pansy said, looking as if the conversation was anything but a matter of course. "I'll tell you, but you really must rest. And that nasty cut needs tending. You wouldn't want it to go afoul, now would you? Come, come. Let's sit in the parlor, and I'll tell you whatever you want."

They climbed the steps to the black-painted door and entered the house. As Amelia's eyes adjusted to the sunset-shadowed room, she smiled in delight. Plum and gray upholstery covered a mahogany-trimmed sofa and armchair. A floral carpet in complementing colors cushioned her steps. Leaded-glass windows filtered the evening light, and a marble hearth invited one's approach. "How lovely!"

Pansy shook her head, but merely said, "You've always had exquisite taste."

Amelia darted an accusatory glare at her companion. "So tell me about my good taste."

"Very well." Pansy settled into the overstuffed armchair. "I've known you all your life. Your mother and father were members of St. Joseph's parish, just like Mr. Pritchard and I are."

As an orphan, even *she* didn't know her parents. "What exactly do you mean by 'all my life'?"

"Why, Amelia, we were present at your baptism!"

Since the sisters had her baptized shortly after she arrived at the Home, Amelia sincerely doubted Pansy had been around. "When was that?"

"Amelia Baldwin! Do you really not recall anything about yourself?"

Pausing for a moment, she considered the question. A wry chuckle accompanied her thoughts. "I *don't* know you or the others. I *don't* remember this house. I *didn't* recognize any of the streets we crossed getting here. And I certainly *didn't* recognize the man who accused me of missing a burial."

Well, that last hadn't been squeaky-clean right. She'd recognized Michael Hayak from the portrait in the lobby of the Opera House. And she'd seen *that* before she ever set foot on the stage.

For a few minutes, Pansy sat, obviously stunned. No actress dead or alive could have feigned the bewilderment on her stolid features.

Am I losing my mind? Amelia wondered.

As an explanation, amnesia didn't work. She remembered being hired to work on the vaudeville revival. She remembered Rosemary Pumphrey. She remembered Chicago, the orphanage, and the foster homes where she'd grown up. She remembered standing in the check-out line at her local grocery store, waiting for the electronic scanner to read her automatic banking card. She even remembered the train ride into Winona. Maybe she had some kind of selective amnesia. . . .

No way! She remembered the Beatles, the Rolling Stones, Dolly Parton, and the Smashing Pumpkins. Presidents Reagan, Bush, and Clinton. And she'd never forget her first evocative glimpse of Michael Hayak. The Victorian time-warp stuff had to be a form of hallucination. Only someone with a serious mental disturbance could come up with something this impossible.

Although she'd never thought herself deranged, she'd better get into counseling *now*. Whenever "now" was. How long had she lain unconscious under the stage floor? She'd entered the Opera House in the morning, and now the sun was setting. She'd been unconscious that long?

"Could you please tell me what time it is?" she asked.

Pansy breathed a bit easier. "This I can readily do." She pulled a scroll-embossed watch from the pocket on the bodice of her russet dress and popped its lid. "Six o'clock."

"I was out for the better part of a day?"

Pansy pleated her eyebrows. Her gaze raked Amelia. "Perhaps. But that doesn't explain where you've been since Friday."

"*What!* Friday? Two days ago?"

A nod answered her questions. From the corner of her eye, Amelia caught Mildred and Esmée avidly following the conversation.

"Yes, Amelia Baldwin. You ran out of Christina's bedroom on Friday, and nobody has seen you since."

"I've never even *been* in Christina's bedroom—" She cut off that line of reasoning since none of her listeners were buying it. "Never mind. Today *is* Monday, right?"

When Pansy and the others nodded, Amelia sat back against the sofa she'd perched on. At least they agreed on something.

A sudden thought stole Amelia's breath. "What year is this?" she asked before she could stop the words, before she could remind herself that the question was worse than ludicrous.

With a resigned shake of her head, Pansy responded, "We've turned the century, of course. It's 1900."

How could she? Michael asked himself as he paced the blocks to Mrs. Tomicek's home. How could Amelia stand there, pretending surprise at his question?

"Me!" she'd squeaked, sounding innocent, blameless. *"What do you mean, me?"*

How could a person forget that her closest friend lay dying? That the dying friend counted on her to care for the child who would soon be motherless? How could she forget she'd promised to help the future widower with that child?

What had made Amelia Baldwin vanish moments before Christina labored over her last breath?

Michael's anger collided with his grief. She'd promised—all three of them—to be there when the time came. Yet Christina's last utterance had been a plea for Amelia's presence. Amelia, who couldn't be found.

Where had she been when Katie had called for 'Melia? When she'd needed loving arms to hold her after her mama no longer responded to her cries? When Katie's father reeled under the pain of watching his wife die?

Where had Amelia been when he'd needed her?

Finding himself in front of Mrs. Tomicek's door, Michael ran a hand over his forehead, his eyes, knowing Katie shouldn't see the ravages grief and guilt had wrought on her papa's face.

Taking a deep breath, he knocked. Moments later, Mrs. Tomicek let him in. "Did you find her?"

Michael's lip curled in contempt. "That I did."

"And . . . ?" asked the widow who'd offered to watch Katie while Michael buried his wife.

He shrugged. "And nothing."

"Did you ask her where she'd been? Did you ask why she didn't come to the viewing, the funeral Mass?"

"Yes." And she'd looked stunned by his question, a patently false innocent look in her green eyes.

"Well, then, Michael, what did the girl say?" Mrs. Tom demanded, obviously losing her patience. Michael knew her question wasn't prompted by morbid interest. Mrs. Tomicek cared.

It didn't make the truth any easier to take. "Nothing."

"What do you mean, nothing? Did she refuse to speak with you?"

Just then, from the door in the rear wall of Mrs. Tomicek's parlor, the sound of little feet caught his attention. "Katie," he whispered, his voice catching. Poor child likely thought everyone who mattered had abandoned her.

Michael knelt and opened his arms wide. Giggling with pleasure, his two-year-old daughter flung herself at him. "Papa, Papa! Kiss Katie!"

The warmth of her round little body seeped into him, and the knot of ice that had replaced his gut began to melt. A child this young was nothing but a gift. All she asked for were the basic human necessities and tenderness, love.

The love he could furnish. It was Katie's other needs he didn't know how he would supply now that Christina was gone and Amelia had proved false-hearted.

Katie patted his cheeks. "Papa, kiss?" He obliged.

"Michael," said Mrs. Tomicek, "you haven't answered my questions."

Mrs. Tom had been his mother's crony, the two of them always chatting—gossiping, really—sharing sewing patterns, recipes, and watching each other's children when the need arose. She wouldn't soon forget how Amelia Baldwin had failed Michael and Katie Hayak in their moment of direst need.

"She squealed like a cat's fresh-caught dinner. '*Me? What do you mean, me?*'"

"And that was all?"

"Yes, Mrs. Tom. That was all."

Mrs. Tomicek frowned. "How strange. That doesn't sound like the Amelia Baldwin I know."

"Doesn't sound like the one I thought I knew, either."

Michael twirled one of Katie's honey-gold curls around his index finger.

"Did you ask what she meant?"

He remembered the sense of betrayal he'd felt as he stood before Amelia. "I couldn't stomach the sight of her. Not after she abandoned Christina and Katie. Especially since she acted so innocent and surprised."

Mrs. Tom wrung her hands, then nervously fluttered them in the air. "Shouldn't you have said—"

"What?" he asked, cutting off the question. "Should I have begged her to come and help us?" Michael shook his head. Katie wrapped her chubby arms around his neck.

"Maybe she didn't know Christina had died—"

"How could she not have known? She'd spent the better part of the night at Christina's bedside, wondering if each breath would be the last. I know. I sat there, too."

But as Michael argued vehemently, a damning vision darted through his mind. If only he hadn't lost control. If only he hadn't touched—"

No. That couldn't have mattered. She'd promised to be there. For Christina. And Katie. Michael's blunder couldn't have—shouldn't have—mattered.

Why? Why did she run from the farmhouse? Why didn't she answer when he knocked at her door till his knuckles turned raw? Why had she chosen to miss her friend's funeral?

No matter how often he considered the events of the past three days, no answer came. Nothing explained Amelia's behavior. But regardless of her reprehensible actions and her fickle nature, Michael intended to find out why she'd abandoned them.

He'd get his answers.

For Christina's sake. For Katie's sake.

For his sake, too.

When Katie's bright blue eyes gave up the fight for wakefulness later that night, Michael breathed a sigh of relief.

He'd rocked her, hoping she'd sleep, but she'd refused to close those eyes. Each time she did, the crying resumed. Then he'd dried her tears, offering clumsy comfort.

As he lay his precious doll-child on her bed, his first real smile in days warmed his heart. Yes, Christina was gone. But he had Katie. And somehow they would make it through.

Treading silently, he went downstairs. He still couldn't face entering the room where Christina had died. The room where he and Amelia had kept a vigil for days.

In the parlor, he stretched, hearing the bones in his back crack from stiffness. He'd held Katie for hours. Shaking out a blanket folded over the arm of the sofa, he collapsed and covered himself. Perhaps exhaustion would grant him sleep.

But the moment he closed his eyes, Amelia stole into his thoughts. He'd never suspected she possessed such acting talents. He could almost swear that her shock at his question earlier in the evening had come from the innocence on her features. He could almost believe the bewilderment in her beautiful green eyes.

Almost. But the past two years remained vivid in Michael's memory. Amelia and Christina had been the closest of friends. And Michael had encouraged their friendship, even though there were those in town who turned up their noses at the thought of his wife befriending a woman who consorted with vaudevillians.

Michael had never seen signs of inappropriate behavior in Amelia, and he'd given little heed to malicious whisperings. Now he had to wonder. Was she so superficial that she couldn't face the reality of death? Was she frightened by Christina's passing?

Or was it you *she ran away from?* taunted his conscience.

Michael's eyes popped open. He sat up. That was one train of thought he wasn't about to take a ride on.

Abruptly he stood and headed for the kitchen. Maybe

something full of fire would help. Something that would sear right through him, bring him the blessed peace of oblivion. How much could a man bear?

He'd spent the past two years seeking the finest medical care money could buy. They'd all said the same thing. Christina's heart was weak, a little more life would leave her each day. Nothing could heal her defective heart.

And so, Christina's delicate blond beauty faded, her lips turning gray with time. She'd fought for each breath to the very end, her blue eyes open wide, staring at their beloved daughter, asleep in his arms.

Amelia had sat beside his wife, holding her hand, promising to love Katie as if the child were Amelia's own. Christina had stopped all of Amelia's feeble protestations, her useless words of hope for Christina's recovery.

Perhaps her betrayal stemmed from that. Perhaps Amelia couldn't cope with the responsibility she'd accepted.

The cause didn't matter. Not really. Only the promise she'd broken mattered. She'd turned her back on them.

Out of the dark, the sound of a sob stole the hope he'd had for the night. *Not again.* Dear God, hadn't the child suffered enough without a mother for the better part of her life? Wasn't it enough that the only other woman Katie loved had walked away from her?

"Mama!" Katie cried. "Mama, come!" Heartrending sobs followed.

Michael took the stairs two at a time. Seconds later, he held his baby again, patting her heaving back, feeling her misery seep through the cotton of his shirt. In a hushed tone, he crooned an old lullaby his mother had sung to him.

In Christina's maple rocker, he began yet another vigil. This time, however, he knew that time would bring the healing denied his wife.

But he'd never forgive Amelia for what she'd done. Never.

Chapter 3

AMELIA WAS ALMOST scared.

Mostly she was fascinated, enchanted, thrilled. From all indications, she had traveled through time. It was the only explanation that made any sense.

She chuckled. If anyone could hear her thoughts they would hustle her to the nearest psychiatric ward. But despite the outrageousness of her theory, careful examination of the evidence led her to believe the unbelievable.

She'd traveled through time.

After her "angels" left last night, Amelia had spent hours exploring the small house the women had sworn belonged to her. Her late parents had left it to her, or so they said.

Although nothing about the home was luxurious, it was comfortable and attractively put together. A profusion of Victoriana gave the house a cluttered look, but that decorating excess distinctly represented the turn of the century. The *last* century.

She'd found that the garments in the cherry-wood wardrobe fit. They were the kind of clothes she would have bought herself in a future Chicago life. As she'd opened the

door of the piece of furniture, she'd felt a tiny hitch of
recognition in the pit of her stomach, almost as if she'd
opened this door before. The honeysuckle fragrance that
wafted out was somehow familiar, too, reminiscent of the
cologne she'd used for years. Yes, in that past—or future?—life.

Yet another thing to puzzle Amelia.

After all, she had this new, improved figure—smaller
and curvier, more voluptuous—and the clothes to go with
it. At the same time, she clearly remembered the slim, almost boyish shape she'd sported back in Chicago. She'd
yet to hear of someone trading in a less desirable appearance when they took a train out of town, unless they were
on their way to visit a plastic surgeon. As far as Amelia
knew, there were no plastic surgeons in 1900.

Stretching on the cloud-soft bed, she decided she'd better
get dressed. Who knew what today would hold? What new
delights would she encounter? Who would she meet next?

Excitement rippled through her middle. Michael Hayak's
face flitted momentarily through her thoughts. He was the
most attractive man Amelia had ever seen—in *either* lifetime. Certainly the only one who'd affected her so strongly.
Too bad he seemed to detest her.

As Amelia removed her lace-frosted cotton nightgown,
she caught sight of her profile in the mirror above a delicate
cherry-wood washstand. It would take a while to get used
to her new breasts. The white globes, tipped in soft rose,
looked nothing like the slight mounds she'd once had.

Curious, she measured their weight in her cupped hands.
They were warm and firm, and yes, much more than a
mouthful. Thank goodness once she'd removed the stifling
corset, their projection had subsided considerably. She then
smoothed her hands down silky, never-tanned white skin,
marking the flatness of her belly, the generous fullness of
her hips. An hourglass figure, to be sure.

She wondered if she'd fit the clothes in the wardrobe
without having to put up with the torture of a corset. She

turned a critical eye to the image in the mirror. Her new waist was certainly trimmer than her old one, and the cut of most turn-of-the-century fashions should accommodate her rounded hips and buttocks.

Turning, she inspected the froth of midnight waves cascading down her back. They were exactly what she'd always wished for. Catching the thick mass in her hands, she pulled it over a shoulder. Then she got a good look at her augmented rear cheeks. If nothing else, she certainly offered a man something to hold onto through the night!

After a last look, Amelia decided she preferred this body to her old one. The outfits in the wardrobe were as quintessentially feminine as her new look.

Going for clean clothes, she heard children laughing. With a glance out her bedroom window, she saw two boys playing marbles in the postage-stamp–sized yard of the house next door. As she watched, she heard a vehicle rattle down the street. She hurriedly hugged a lace curtain to her bare chest, craned her neck out the window, and saw Michael Hayak tying a horse's reins to the hitching post in front of her new home.

He patted the horse's withers, then strode up the short walk to her front door. Dropping her inadequate cover, Amelia hurried to dress. Then she heard knocking at the door. "Just a moment, please!"

Dispensing with the corset, she donned a dainty camisole and chose an emerald-colored dress. With a prayer, she pulled it down over her head, and smiled when it settled over her body. She didn't need the killer corset after all.

She ran to the front door, yanking it away from Michael's descending fist.

For a moment, both stood frozen in place. Her gaze met his. A shiver shook her and she caught her breath. Flames of anger shot from the deep blue depths, but something else burned there, too. That something touched her, making her nerve endings stand at attention. Its heat caused a spasm of

awareness to warm private parts of her body, shocking her
with the strength of her response.

Amelia wasn't up to examining that response.

"May I help you?" she asked, inwardly cursing her shaky
voice.

A muscle in his jaw twitched. If anything, his eyes grew
more turbulent, and his brow furrowed into a scowl. "I
doubt it," he spat, then turned on his heel.

"Hey!" Amelia yelled at his broad, retreating back. She'd
had it with his attitude. She'd done nothing wrong. A person couldn't miss a funeral she didn't know about. "You're
the one who came calling. What did you want?"

As she watched, he pulled a small crate from the wag-
onbed. "Since you won't be spending any more time at the
farm," he said, "I see no reason to keep your things there."
He heaved the crate on the floor by Amelia's bare feet.

With her temper rising to meet his, she opted for a tried
and true approach. Communication. "What farm?"

He sent her another murderous look, but withheld comment. He tugged the horse's reins free of the hitching post,
swung his lean frame into the wagon, and started the horse
on its way down the street.

"Damn him!" What right did he have to treat her like
that? This had to involve more than a missed funeral.
Something else had to be bothering Michael Hayak.

If only she knew what he held against her, but even if
she knew what she'd done to earn this shabby treatment,
how could he hold her accountable for something Amelia—
the 1900 Amelia—had failed to do? Who had the 1900
Amelia been? What had she done to inspire the rage and
apparent hatred in Michael Hayak's eyes?

Refusing to let the man spoil her first day in Victorian
times, Amelia bent to the crate, gave it a shove, and pushed
it inside the house. The lid bounced loose, and she took it
off. What she found made her catch her breath. The most
amazing assortment of satins, silks, velvets, and brocades

met her gaze. They were richly trimmed with leather, fur, hand-tatted lace, and a rainbow of ribbons.

Unable to resist her curiosity, she eased a dress from the box. It was obviously not hers. Two of the new and improved Amelia Baldwin could comfortably get in it. Whose clothes were these? And why had Michael Hayak had them at his farm? Why would he bring someone else's clothes to her?

Frustrated, she caught the curtain of hair that trailed down her back and began braiding it. She couldn't run around with that mane loose. If nothing else, it was a nuisance, blocking her view every time she shifted position. As she wove the strands into a thick rope, she walked down the center of the shotgun-style house and arrived in the kitchen at the rear.

She desperately needed the drink of the gods. "Java."

But as she rummaged around, she found Mother Hubbard-bare cupboards. Didn't people eat in the past? She opened another cabinet and jumped back when a canister tumbled out, its cover flying open in midair. A cloud of what had to be flour surrounded her. Waving the stuff away from her eyes, Amelia sneezed.

Yes, she was definitely in the past. Either that or Hell. No frozen entrées in sight, and as the "angels" escorted her home last evening, she'd seen no golden arches. If she wanted to eat, it looked as if she'd have to chance her own cooking.

To cook, however, one had to have groceries. A trip to the mercantile was in order. Amelia went to a door in the side wall of the kitchen, reached into the dim closet, and pulled out a large wicker shopping basket.

Then she gasped. How had she known where to go? How had she known there would be a basket in that closet? And how could the notion of a mercantile cross her twentieth-century mind?

Heck, how could the notion of a notion even enter her thoughts? She'd never used *that* word in her life!

Her stomach clenched, and sudden shivers rocked her. She could almost handle traveling through time. But how could she explain her instinctive solution to a set of circumstances that belonged strictly to the time she was visiting? A time presumably foreign to her?

Would a cosmic, collective memory do that? Good grief, she even sounded New Age! This had bypassed scary and was zooming straight for spooky.

Using the large, mottled-brass key she found on a hook in the entrance of the cottage, Amelia locked the front door. She walked to the street, then glanced at the small house she'd just left. After the eerie episode in the kitchen, she'd rushed upstairs, grabbed shoes and a small handbag, and fled. A cowardly action, but the one she'd taken.

Now she planned to find the mercantile—even though she had no idea where one might be, probably wouldn't recognize it if she walked right into it, and didn't even have a penny to pay for the bare necessities.

Standing by the hitching post, she looked up and down the street, wondering which direction would lead her to her goal: food.

"Good morning, Amelia!" called a woman sweeping leaves in front of the house two doors to Amelia's left.

"Good morning, Mrs. Connol . . . ly . . ." Amelia let the syllable slip from her lips. The woman smiled and nodded, then went back to her work.

How had she known the neighbor's name? The "angels" were—presumably—the only people she knew in town. Besides Michael Hayak, of course.

As fear began to bubble again, Amelia set off in an easterly direction so she'd be able to come home by following the sun, and picked up her pace to escape the questions rioting in her mind. She didn't want to think about the strange things that were happening to her; she didn't want to think about anything right now.

"Wrong," she muttered as her stomach's gurgling called her a liar. Her stomach, at least, wanted to think about food.

A few blocks later, the small neat homes gave way to various business enterprises. Storefronts became the structures of choice on either side of the street, and to her left she saw the heavier traffic of a broader, parallel thoroughfare.

She turned in that direction. Moments later, she stood on a busy corner under a street sign that proclaimed this to be W. Third St. A plaque over the front entrance of the cream-colored brick building before her identified it as the Schlitz Hotel. For a moment she wondered if it had anything to do with Schlitz beer, but then caught herself, and returned to her original task.

She looked to the east and the west, trying to decide where she'd find food. Trying *not* to notice that the vehicles were still horse-drawn and the fashions vintage Victorian.

Watching the folks on either side of her, she crossed the busy street and proceeded eastward. Before too long, she came to a store whose packed display shelf verified the claim of the gold letters on the window glass. Smyser's Mercantile carried a plethora of items Amelia imagined a Victorian household would need.

Washboards, enameled basins, a coffee grinder, hats, bolts of fabric, and a box filled with paper-wrapped cakes of soap rubbed shoulders behind the gleaming-clean glass. An odd scent escaped through the door, hinting of spices, the snap of pickle juice, a liberal dose of dust, and the tang of leather goods.

Amelia's curiosity kicked into action. She'd always wondered about stores in the late nineteenth century. Her heart sped up. She was about to experience one firsthand!

Feeling better than she had since Michael Hayak arrived at her house, Amelia took the steps into the store. It was dark inside, and her eyes took their time to adjust to the lack of light. When they focused, they popped open. Floor-

to-ceiling shelves lined the walls, displaying the most phe-
nomenal assortment of items.

Shoes, hats, and tin pails filled one rack. Lethal-looking
razors and leather strops, hammers, saws, and medical po-
tions of all sorts lined the next. Cans of Richardson & Rob-
bins's Plum Pudding, Boston Baked Beans, Eagle Brand
Condensed Milk, and boxes of Enoch Morgan's Sons
House Sapolio soap were piled one on the other, while
matching narrow boxes labeled Men's Rainbow Balbriggan
Undershirts and Drawers ranged yet another. Two by two,
down the middle of the large room, tables bore bolts of fabric in every color and weave. Like clusters of ripe, purple
grapes ready to pick from the vine, black-and-white mot-
tled enamel cookware hung from hooks in beams that criss-
crossed overhead.

Amelia clasped her hands at bosom height and turned
slow circles, devouring every detail. "Wow!" she whispered reverently. A curious finger ran over a bolt of denim,
then tested the soft comfort of a roll of cotton flannel. Both
felt very, very real.

A woman's chatter and the clink of coins caught
Amelia's attention. At the back of the room, a counter held
jars of multicolored candy sticks, a gleaming black cash
register, and various stacks of paper. On the floor, right in
front of the counter, barrels stood like sentinels, probably
filled with the pickles she'd smelled. There seemed to be
too many barrels to contain only pickles, though, so who
knew what other treasures hid in those marvelous casks!

Approaching the counter, she spied the talkative clerk, a
plump matron whose knot of silver hair bristled with pen-
cils. Her movements were quick, spare, and, from what
Amelia could see, precisely efficient.

The woman looked up and saw her standing by the
counter. "I've had your order packed and waiting since Friday," she chided Amelia. "You never came as you'd said
you would." The frown on the grocer's brow told Amelia

that not only was her absence unacceptable, but probably uncharacteristic, too.

Before she could formulate an answer, the lady went on. "I stored your fresh food in the icebox, and it should still be fine. Where have you been?"

"Not at Christina's funeral," responded Michael Hayak.

Amelia stiffened at the sound of his critical voice. Where had he come from? And why couldn't she go anywhere without coming smack up against him and his attitude? She'd had enough of that.

Spinning around, she slammed her basket onto the counter, then faced her private judge and jury rolled into one. "Okay," she said, fighting to control her irritation. "That's twice you've mentioned Christina and her funeral. I'm as laid back as they come"—the clerk's eyes frogged out at the twentieth-century slang—"but your accusations are ridiculous. I don't know Christina, and I had no idea I was expected at her funeral. I doubt I was even around for it." As an afterthought she added, "I'm sorry she's dead."

Again the muscle in Michael's cheek twitched. Brown eyebrows crashed over the bridge of his nose. "You actually think someone will believe such horsesh—"

"Michael!" warned the store clerk.

Mr. Hayak swallowed hard, took nose-flaring breaths, straightened his already erect posture. "Pardon me, Mrs. Smyser." After his perfunctory apology, he again leveled his laser gaze on Amelia. "I heard tell you developed amnesia from the fall through the Opera House stage floor, but I can't believe you could forget a promise you'd just made to your closest friend. Or the responsibility you so recently assumed."

"Closest friend?" she echoed. Frustration climbed higher still. If this man didn't buy the amnesia theory, he'd pitch a fit if she tried the hypothesis of time-travel on him. "Humor me," she suggested, hanging onto the tail end of her patience. "Tell me who Christina is or was. Tell me when she died and when I was supposed to attend her funeral. And please, illuminate me on this responsibility you're suggesting I took on."

He offered the expletive he'd held back. Mrs. Smyser clucked a reprimand. Amelia winced at the virulence in Michael Hayak's voice, but he gave her no chance to diffuse the charged atmosphere.

Pacing, he shoved a hand through his thick brown mane, reminding Amelia of a caged lion she'd once seen at the Chicago Zoo. "This is ridiculous!" he finally said. "If you have nothing better to do than discuss your supposedly lost memory, then fine. Find someone else to indulge you, Miss Baldwin. Unlike you, I take responsibility most seriously. Especially when it comes to my daughter."

That did it. "You pompous buffoon! I demand you refrain from spouting any further balderdash this very instant. I don't know you. I don't know Christina. I'm frightfully sorry about the funeral, and I've never had the pleasure of making your daughter's acquaintance."

Amelia suddenly paused to take a breath. Had she really said all that? Called him a pompous buffoon? And *balderdash*? What kind of word was balderdash?

Questions doused her anger. Amelia had meant every word she hurled at Michael Hayak, but the words had been someone else's. And why had she said that knowing his daughter would be a pleasure? Why word her thought that way? She should have said, "I've never met your daughter."

Come to think of it, her little speech sounded amazingly like what one of the Victorians she'd met since yesterday would say. But she wasn't one of them. Maybe archaic speech patterns were contagious.

Cramming his brown hat on his brown head, Michael Hayak graced her with another of his caustic glares and, shouldering a fat sack, strode through the store. At the doorway, he shot back, "I have no time for a foolish woman."

Then he left.

Silence filled the room. Amelia's heart beat hard and fast. Indignation burned in her stomach, and embarrassment heated her cheeks. "Chauvinist pig!" she muttered. A couple of stunned gasps around her punctuated her words. At that moment, and only then, she felt the perusal of several pairs of curious eyes. Michael Hayak's temper tantrum had made Amelia the center of attention. Everyone in the store gawked at her as if she were a *Star Trek* alien.

"How much do I owe?" she asked, for the first time wondering how she would pay for her groceries. The thought of slinking away also crossed her mind.

But the woman behind the counter shook her head before Amelia slunk in earnest. "It's not the end of the month yet. I put it on your account."

"Oh. I . . . I didn't know."

Faded blue eyes appraised her. "Amnesia?"

Amelia straightened her shoulders. "Apparently so."

"But you know your own name, don't you?"

"I'm Amelia Baldwin. Of that, I'm sure."

The porcupine on the grocer's head bobbed once. "Then you don't know who I am, do you?"

"'Fraid not."

"I'm Hilda Smyser, child. And you're going to need help."

A spark of hope sprang up inside Amelia. A friend perhaps? "How do you figure?"

From the corner of her eye, Amelia saw a burly redheaded man shake his head and roll his eyes. He'd already made up his mind about her—she was bonkers.

A glance at Mrs. Smyser told Amelia she still had a chance with the kind lady. "What sort of help do you think I need?"

"Someone's going to have to introduce you to neighbors and teach you what you've obviously forgotten."

Amelia tried a tentative smile. "Then you don't think I'm . . . insane? Irresponsible?"

"I don't think so. Something happened to you, especially if a body goes by what Pansy says."

Amelia groaned. Then she chuckled. A ripple of laughter sped around the room, and the various shoppers who'd stopped their activity to witness the more interesting scene Amelia and Michael enacted returned to their earlier endeavors.

Mrs. Smyser let out a belly laugh. "I know, I know. A body takes Pansy Pritchard with a grain of salt."

The mere mention of Pansy zapped Amelia's mind back to the moment she'd come to under the stage floor. And from there, it was only a matter of an image fleeting through her memory to return to the man who'd just left. "Then why, if you can accept me and hold your judgment, does that man look at me as if he wished I were the one who'd died instead of Christina? Whoever she may be."

A gasp from behind her told Amelia someone found her question disturbing. So be it. She needed answers.

"He probably *does* wish it had been you, or at least anybody but Christina," Mrs. Smyser answered, then stuck another pencil into her hairy pencil-holder as she rounded the counter. "Fred!" she called toward the back of the building, "tend the store. There's something I must do."

With easy motions, the grocer stripped off her pristine white apron and picked up Amelia's basket, now filled with food. As if the sight of potential provisions had jostled her appetite awake, her stomach made its presence known, emitting a loud grumble. She blushed. This Victorian business was a lot more mortifying than her 1990s life had been.

"Did you eat yet?" asked Mrs. Smyser.

"Aside from a canister of flour, I found nothing edible in my kitchen this morning."

"You hadn't been eating there for a long time."

Huh? "Where had I been eating?"

"Why, at the Hayak farm, of course!" Mrs. Smyser

shook her head. "Did you at least remember anything about the kitchen?"

"Just that I'd find this basket in the closet."

"How do you intend to prepare yourself a meal, then?"

"With a lot of prayer?"

"Oh, my! We have our work cut out for us."

Once again Amelia found herself propelled westward, this time with the hope of appeased hunger and answered questions leading the way.

She'd gotten food.

She'd gotten answers.

But those answers had only led to more questions.

Now she knew Christina had been Michael Hayak's wife. She died Friday morning an hour after Amelia Baldwin—the 1900 Amelia Baldwin—left the Hayak farm. The 1900 Amelia had been Christina's best friend, and *that* Amelia had spent the last two years mothering the Hayaks' toddler and nursing Christina as her failing heart gave up its grasp on life.

Yes, it was very sad. Amelia had played no part in that tragedy, but how on earth could she prove it?

If Michael and the rest of the people of Winona didn't buy the simple amnesia explanation, they'd probably burn her at the stake if she suggested time-travel instead. Goodness knows, she had a hard enough time believing it herself, and she was living it.

They were judging her by another woman's actions since she'd somehow wound up taking over that woman's life. And from what Mrs. Smyser had revealed, Amelia had been viewed with a tinge of mistrust because she'd befriended a number of vaudeville artists who came into town to perform at the Opera House. Now her alleged betrayal of her best friend's family would probably brand her an outcast.

So why had she—the 1990s Amelia—been brought to this century? She'd always imagined a new life would give you the niceties you'd lacked in your previous existence. While a great body was nice, it didn't make up for the family she'd always longed for. . . .

The way she saw it, this life looked lonelier and more dismal than her other one. So why was she here?

A sudden knocking at her front door startled her out of her maudlin thoughts, causing the tears that had formed to spill down her cheeks. "Coming," she called, then rubbed her damp face with the generous puff of her leg-o'-mutton sleeves.

Nothing would have prepared her for what she found on her front stoop. Taller than a mountain and fiercer than that poor lion at the Chicago Zoo, Michael Hayak raked her with yet another seering glare. Then Amelia noticed the child he held in the crook of one arm.

Honey-gold curls ringed a round face that blazed fire-engine red at the moment. Squinched-shut eyes pruned up what might otherwise be an angelic face, while rosy lips stretched cavernously to emit ear-shattering, mad-as-hell banshee shrieks. Little feet in sturdy black shoes kicked dangerously close to choice parts of Michael's anatomy.

When a scuffed black toe connected, Amelia winced, and Michael moaned. With no warning, he thrust the child at Amelia. "Here. It's harvest time. I must bring in the grain."

Shocked, Amelia responded instinctively, holding the child at a safe distance. Questions, demands, phrases, and words jumbled in her mind. But not a one came to her rescue.

Mr. Michael Hayak went on. "You helped Christina with her and you promised to watch her after Christina died. Well, she's dead, and I have a harvest to see to, so you may as well keep Katie while I work."

Holding the child as if she held a venomous serpent, Amelia felt the wildest urge to join the child's protest.

"NOOOOOOOO!" bellowed Katie Hayak.

Noooooooo! silently echoed Amelia Baldwin.

Chapter 4

To HER DISMAY, Michael spun on his heel and stomped off to his wagon. Damn, but he did that dismissal thing well!

Ears ringing from the screams of the child she held, Amelia stood Katie upright at her side and closed the front door.

Mistake! If anything, the girl's screaming seemed worse when trapped in the confines of the small parlor. "Time to stop," Amelia suggested in a serious though not unkind voice.

Her words had no effect. Unless one considered Katie's increased decibel level a direct result of Amelia's effort.

Would Katie be stunned silent if Amelia joined in her bellowing? Maybe, but Amelia doubted that sinking to the tantrum level was good for maintaining an air of authority. And she had to remain in control for . . . who knew how long Michael would be gone before picking up his daughter?

How would she cope with a grieving toddler? A confused baby?

Confused? Heck, Amelia's head was spinning even though at twenty-eight she'd left babyhood a long time ago. Unfortunately, during all those years she'd racked up no experience with children. None. Zip. Nada.

"Okay, Amelia. If you were this child what would *you* most like right about now?" she asked herself, hoping logic might help.

She found the answer in her heart.

Kneeling before the weeping child, Amelia whispered gentle words, soothing sounds, then opened her arms. Katie's wailing continued, but as a huge hiccup made her pause, the child saw the offer of comfort, and her eyes widened.

A chubby fist pressed reddened lips. Sobs racked rounded shoulders. Gasps puffed out. The shrieking mercifully stopped.

Amelia increased her efforts, only to have Katie back up as she approached and renew her bellowing, albeit decibels lower than it had been.

"Patience," she murmured, afraid she might have spent her entire allotment on the girl's unreasonable father.

Inch by inch, tear by sob, the battle for the two-foot distance between them and the future of her sense of hearing was won. Sitting on the floor, Amelia closed her arms around the warm, damp-faced little girl. In silence, she rocked on her hips as Katie's sobs lessened then turned into long, ragged sighs. She counted her first round with the child a success when long brown eyelashes fluttered down to rest on tear-reddened cheeks.

Carefully Amelia laid the child on her bed. After tiptoeing from the bedroom, she dropped onto the sofa in the parlor. Her shoulders felt tight and sore. After a few neck rolls and deep, cleansing breaths, she felt better.

And . . . what? What should she do next?

Mrs. Smyser had helped her store her purchases and had prepared a meal of ham, biscuits, and canned stewed tomatoes. Amelia had watched every step of the preparation, try-

ing to memorize them for future reproduction. But she was
full now and not yet ready to tackle cooking. Not until she
absolutely had to.

She remembered the trunks in the small bedroom across
from hers. Mrs. Smyser had called it her sewing room.
She'd also said Amelia supported herself with her dressmaking skills.

At least she wouldn't have to learn that from scratch.
She'd majored in Theatrical Design and Costuming, and
sewing came as second nature to her.

Curiosity knocked, and she homed in on the trunks. Did
Amelia—the 1900 Amelia—have many customers? How
quickly did she complete a garment? Amelia cast a suspicious glance at the sewing machine, spied the treadle, and
groaned. If her visit to Victorian times lasted long, she
would miss her electronic, commercial-grade sewing machine.

As she suspected, the trunks contained garments in various stages of completion, a small piece of paper attached to
each with measurements and a description of what the customer wanted. For the most part, the instructions detailed
techniques Amelia had long ago mastered.

A knock at her front door interrupted her search. Hurrying to respond, she skidded to a stop at the thought that
Michael Hayak might have returned. Then she remembered
the determination in his stride as he left his child with her.
He had harvesting to do, he'd said, and Amelia suspected
there would be no holding him back from his work.

On her front stoop stood a stranger, a woman in her mid-
thirties, clutching a bolt of ice-blue satin. "Hello, Amelia,"
she said. "I'm awfully sorry I'm late. I had another go-
round with Cookie. The woman is the most marvelous
cook, but I can't seem to persuade her that we don't require
seven-course meals every night."

Amelia stood back as the attractive blonde swept into her
house. Cookie? The woman had a cook? And she complained? Amelia rolled her eyes. Heck, even if she ended

up in the Guinness Book as the fattest woman in the world, she'd happily chow down what someone else had cooked!

The blonde dropped her fabric on Amelia's sofa. "Silly, isn't it?"

Amelia nodded, agreeing, but for a different reason. She approached the beautiful bolt of cloth. "Uhm . . . what's this for?" she asked, wary of what such an exquisitely dressed woman might want.

A frown rippled the otherwise smooth forehead. "*You* know. We discussed the gown last week."

Uh-oh, amnesia time again. "Humor me," she said, "I had a fall, hit my head, and I seem to have forgotten everything but my name."

"I'd heard that, but I didn't want to believe it. So it's true, then?"

Amelia lifted a shoulder. "As far as I can tell."

"Do you remember how to sew?"

The question stung Amelia's professional pride. "Well, of course! I spent enough years in school and as an apprentice."

"Apprentice?" asked the blonde, a look of bewilderment on her pretty features. "I didn't realize Snow's Dressmaking College required an apprenticeship for its students."

Well, maybe in 1900 she wouldn't have done an apprenticeship, but Amelia could reassure her customer in one regard. "Trust me on this, I can sew. I might not know— *remember* your name, but I can make anything you want with this satin moiré."

Skepticism raised a golden brow. "How about my measurements? Do you also know those?"

"Uhm . . . not exactly." Since it seemed her 1900 counterpart sewed on a regular basis for this woman, she probably had those measurements noted down somewhere, but where would that other Amelia have kept her business information? The new and improved Amelia had a lot of rummaging to do before she felt ready to tackle this new career. "We can take them again. It'll only be a minute."

"Very well," said the blonde, sounding uncertain.

After finding a faded cotton tape measure in one of the drawers of the sewing machine cabinet, Amelia asked the woman to describe the ball gown she had in mind. Although she didn't know where she'd get the fancy trimmings her customer wanted, Amelia swore she'd construct her most spectacular creation. Her professionalism was at stake. She couldn't afford to lose her best customer.

She jotted down the figures on a scrap of paper, stood, and tucked her pencil behind her ear. "I think we have all we need, Mrs. Stoltz. You can plan on a fitting in ten days' time."

Suddenly Amelia realized what she'd said. And what she'd known. Mrs. Stoltz was Amelia Baldwin's best customer. But how had *she* known that? Even the woman's name.

She felt a chill. She shivered. Her stomach knotted.

Then she heard Mrs. Stoltz. ". . . if I hadn't seen you put that pencil behind your ear, I would have vowed someone else was living in your body." Then she chuckled, shaking her head at the absurdity of her words. "You can count on me in the afternoon. Most likely around one o'clock."

Amelia nodded, trying to stay calm, but her hands shook so much that she dropped her measuring tape. Bending to pick it up, she didn't notice when Mrs. Stoltz did the same, and they bumped heads. "I'm so sorry," she murmured.

Mrs. Stoltz waved the apology aside. "It was nothing. Perhaps another knock on the head will bring back what you've forgotten."

"May . . . be," Amelia said in a hollow voice.

"Are you sure you're all right?"

No. "Of course, of course. Here," she added, opening the door for Mrs. Stoltz, "I'd hate to make you late."

Again the blond brows rose. Amelia's poorly disguised dismissal hadn't gone unnoticed.

"Of course, Amelia. Oh, and don't work too hard. That fall seems to have done a dreadful lot of harm."

You don't know the half of it! Amelia withheld the snappy comeback, glad to be rid of the woman. Actually, if her situation weren't so implausible, she'd probably have enjoyed Mrs. Stoltz's company. But as things stood, she dreaded speaking. She knew what Victorians did with their mentally ill, and she didn't intend to experience it firsthand.

Breathing a sigh of relief, she ran back to the sewing room, refusing to think about her brief flash of . . . what? Memory?

No. She couldn't remember things she didn't know. But it sure felt like déjà vu to her.

In another drawer of the sewing cabinet, she found a black book full of measurements, notations of clients' preferences, figure faults and assets, and even hair and eye color. The 1900 Amelia had apparently had a good eye for detail. The twentieth-century Amelia appreciated her care.

Before she could do more than glance at the neat writing in the book, she heard another knock out front. Amelia responded to an attractive redhead whose arms overflowed with clothes. More business, Amelia thought. At least she'd be able to pay Mrs. Smyser for her groceries come the end of the month—if she was here that long. Then she realized she'd have to ask the friendly grocer exactly when the month would end. Amelia only knew for sure that today was Tuesday. In the year 1900.

"I know, I know," said the redhead in a breezy tone. "You couldn't possibly have finished the costumes I brought you last week. And, yes, here I am with more work for you."

Amelia nodded. *Last week, huh?*

Her customer continued. "It's just that with the fast changes backstage, I tear seams out all the time."

At least Amelia understood that. "I know. There's nothing to prevent the wear and tear of costumes. Let's see what we have here."

Beautiful chiffon made up ethereal, fairy-like gowns, while bold cottons and linens added up to stylized ethnic outfits. Satins and velvets came together to form luxurious period garb. Amelia thought she'd died and gone to costume Heaven.

Remembering her "angels," she stifled a chuckle at her appropriate thought. "These won't take long," she said, bringing her attention back to business. "It's just repair work."

Then, to finesse the woman's name out of her, Amelia said, "It . . . it's been a rather difficult few days, and I'd appreciate if you'd remind me exactly what you brought last week . . ."

The look on the performer's face was priceless. "You don't remember? I was only here on Thursday. Are you quite all right, Amelia?"

Damn! That hadn't gone over as well as she'd hoped. Oh, well, time for the amnesia again. "I guess you didn't hear about my accident."

Briefly Amelia related the pertinent details of her circumstances. The actress responded sympathetically. "Why, how perfectly horrid for you, dear! And you probably haven't a clue who I am!"

At Amelia's sheepish nod, the woman placed a comforting hand on her shoulder and said, "You should have told me. I'm Myrtle Huntley. My husband and I travel with our vaudeville show. Anytime we're in Winona, I bring you what needs repair."

"Thank you, Mrs. Huntley—"

"Myrtle, dear. You've called me Myrtle for a while now."

Amelia nodded and smiled. "Thank you, Myrtle. I appreciate your kindness. When do you need the costumes?"

"We've changed our program for the next few days, so I won't need what you have right away. In about ten days we should be back in town, and after the performance here, we'll go on to Rochester."

Ten days. Two projects due in ten days. In the 1990s it

would have been no sweat. But with that treadle machine. . . .

Amelia took a deep breath. She'd make it work. "I don't foresee a problem. I'll see you in ten days, then."

Myrtle left. Amelia had to move Mrs. Stoltz's bolt of cloth and Myrtle Huntley's costumes out of her way before collapsing on the sofa. Between all this work and the wild things going on inside her head, her immediate future looked complicated indeed.

Then the banshee wailed again.

Amelia groaned. Poor child couldn't be blamed for her misery, but the noise she made could deafen. "I'm coming, Katie. Don't cry, Amelia's on her way."

Thinking she had the child-taming trick down to a T, Amelia cuddled Katie, and began to hum again. This time, her efforts had no effect on the unhappy girl.

Then Amelia felt tell-tale dampness on her lap. A toddler. Diapers.

Where were Pampers when she needed them?

She gingerly set Katie down on the floor, braced herself against the sharpened edge to the girl's crying, and began a haphazard search for something to use as a diaper.

A sheet came closest. Since it was miles too big for little Katie's behind, Amelia quickly made alterations with scissors and some large pins she found in yet another sewing cabinet drawer.

Her efforts didn't even earn her a pause in the noise. Remembering the women's magazines she occasionally read, she tried walking with Katie in her arms.

Her ears rang more.

What? What could possibly be wrong with the child? Aside from the fact that her mother had died, and her father was a raving lunatic who had left her with an inexperienced baby-sitter.

"That's it!" she exclaimed, rushing to the kitchen, Katie saddled on her hip.

With a plunk, Katie landed on a kitchen chair, and

Amelia found the leftover biscuits and ham. The little girl's blue eyes brightened. She fisted the tears from her eyes, and tried to smile. "Katie hung'y."

"It's not all *that* hard," Amelia murmured, scoffing at the terrible-twos tales she'd heard. Anticipating the child's thirst, she pumped water into a small tin cup at the kitchen sink.

No sooner did Amelia set the cup before her, than Katie grabbed it in one hand, a gnawed-on biscuit in her other. A grin curved her lips. "Tursty."

What a sweet little face she had! At least, she looked sweet now that she wasn't screaming. Amelia allowed herself to relax. She was doing fine with her charge, and the sewing, although it would be grueling to run that treadle, wouldn't be difficult.

Sitting across from Katie, Amelia cast a look around the small kitchen. A sense of well-being suddenly filled her. Maybe her fantasies had been on the mark. Now that she could take a breather in 1900, she did feel at ease in this house, even though everything remained as incredible as it had since she fell through the Opera House floor.

Then came more rapping at the door. "You stay right there, Katie. Finish eating, and I'll be right back."

Amelia waited till the golden-brown curls bounced in assent. At the door stood her "angel" Mildred. "Why, hello, there! What brings you by. . . ."

Her words faded as Mildred handed her an enormous canvas bag stuffed with worsted wool cloth the color of a damson plum. *More sewing.*

"Humph! You said I should come by today so we could discuss my new traveling suit. You know I'm going to St. Louis for Thanksgiving, and since I'm visiting my brother and his wife, I can't very well not wear the fabric they sent for my last birthday."

Yet another "forgotten" conversation. "Mildred, you should remember that I hit my head. I have no recollection of anything that happened before you and the others helped me up from under the stage floor."

"Humph! So you say."

Aaargh! Figures she'd get at least one skeptic. Eyeing Mildred's soft pink cheeks, white cottony hair, round brown eyes, and perky movements, Amelia had to admit that appearances were often deceiving. She suspected a Miss Marple mind hid behind the innocuous exterior.

"Anyway," she said, "why don't we take your measurements, and you can tell me again what you want made up."

Appearing appeased, Mildred submitted to Amelia's tape. Her mouth, however, never paused. "I need a very stylish suit, Amelia. We decided on a bolero-style jacket with the leg-o-mutton sleeves, lined with silk and trimmed in soutache braid. I want a very full skirt, lined with rustling taffeta and interlined with crinoline. Oh, yes, and don't forget the velvet binding for the skirt."

When Mildred paused for breath, Amelia slumped to the floor at the woman's feet. "How soon do you need this suit?" she asked, dread building.

Those sharp brown eyes narrowed. "You said we'd have the first fitting in about ten days, and that you'd be finished in a fortnight."

Ten days, again! Did the 1900 Amelia have only one stock answer for all her customers? "Could we make that a fortnight for the fitting, and ready a week after that?"

"Amelia! It's October. I fully intend to leave the week before Thanksgiving. Wouldn't that be pushing it a mite close? I do, after all, need time to pack my trunks."

Amelia sighed. "Ten days, then." She hadn't pulled an all-nighter since college, and the prospect didn't thrill her, but barring complications, she'd pull it all off. "Oh, what about the complementary fabrics and the trims?"

Mildred finished pulling cream kid gloves over her plump fingers. "They're there," she said, waving at the large bag she'd brought.

Amelia sighed in relief. Then it hit her. What if her idea

of what Mildred wanted was nothing like what the Victorian lady envisioned? "Tell you what, Mildred. I'll draw up a rough design for the suit, and you can stop by to make sure it's exactly what you want."

Pausing at the door, Mildred cracked a ghost of a smile. "I like that idea, Amelia. In fact, I like it very much. When do you want me to come?"

"How about tomorrow afternoon? I don't want to take too long before starting the work. I do need time to finish the pieces adequately."

"Splendid!" For a moment Amelia thought Mildred might start clapping, but instead, the older lady waved and stepped outdoors. "Tomorrow, then."

Leaning against the closed door, Amelia felt the tension seep from her body. How long was she going to be here? Although she enjoyed certain aspects of her adventure, there were parts she definitely could do without—not knowing what was what, wondering when she'd be zoomed back to the twentieth century, guessing, hinting, pretending she'd lost her memory.

Dammit, when would Michael Hayak pick up his daughter? Amelia had too much work to spend her days watching the girl.

Then she remembered what he'd said. What Mrs. Smyser had echoed. She'd promised the toddler's dying mother she'd watch Katie after Christina was gone. Or Amelia had promised. The *other* Amelia. The one whose curvy body, neat little house, and sewing career she'd taken over. The *new* Amelia—the *old* one . . .

Oh, damn! Even *she* couldn't keep it all straight. No wonder Katie's father always graced her with such contempt. She looked exactly the same as she'd looked when she cared for his dying wife. Although *Amelia* knew it hadn't been her at that bedside, *he* had no way of knowing that. And she had no way of proving it to him.

For him to believe her, he'd have to swallow, hook, line,

and sinker, the entire time-travel explanation. He didn't seem disposed to do so.

So here she was. Alone with her bewildering thoughts, in a strange house that somehow didn't *feel* strange, faced with more work than she could shake a stick at, wondering if she'd lost her mind, and charged with watching an unhappy two-year-old.

Speaking of that two-year-old . . . where was she?

Then Amelia remembered. She'd left her charge eating. She'd forgotten all about the child while she'd dealt with Mildred.

Not good.

Even *she* knew better than to leave a toddler alone for any length of time. "Katie," she called, crossing her fingers, hoping for the best.

Nothing.

"Katie," she repeated, louder.

"'M here!" she heard coming from the kitchen.

Phew! Looked like Katie had listened. But when Amelia reached the kitchen doorway, she froze. The chair Katie had occupied now stood next to the white enamel sink. Fat drops splashed from the pump spout and waves crested over the edge of the sink, forming an unnatural waterfall. The remains of Katie's meal had become a glutinous paste speckled with scraps of reddish ham, and she'd used it to create a Picasso-esque masterpiece on the tabletop. The pint-sized felon, however, had perpetrated her most heinous crime against Mrs. Stoltz's bolt of ice-blue satin. She'd dragged it from the sewing room, and now wore it draped over her three-foot frame.

Star-shaped handprints in the unmistakable shades of flour-glue and ham marched up one side and down the other of the tiny monster's borrowed finery.

As horror kept Amelia immobile, a door opened and closed nearby. Before she could react, she heard Pansy Pritchard call, "Yoo-hoo! Where are you, Amelia?"

Her knees gave way. She crumpled to the floor, tears

flooding her face, sobs ripping through her body. How much did a woman have to take?

She'd hit her head, and it still hurt. She stopped being herself and became a seamstress of nearly a hundred years ago. She couldn't defend herself from accusations leveled against her as a result of actions taken by the woman from the past, and there wasn't a soul who'd believe the truth if she dared tell it. As if that weren't enough, she'd been saddled with a kid who rivaled Dennis the Menace, and she'd promised to finish a mountain of sewing in ten short days. On top of all that, she kept having incidents of déjà vu . . . or hallucinations . . . or maybe incipient insanity.

Amelia was scared. Her entire existence had spun out of control, and there seemed to be nothing she could do to regain even a measure of that lost control.

Pansy's cannon-solid arm braced Amelia's quaking shoulders. Surprisingly, the older woman didn't say a word. She just held Amelia, letting her pour her battered emotions out in a stream of salty tears.

She wanted so badly to talk this out with someone, but Amelia was all alone. True, Pansy was there, holding her, but she didn't think Pansy could handle a discussion on time-travel, body transmigration, innocence, and guilt. Amelia wasn't even sure *she* could.

Again, she was as alone as she'd ever been at the orphanage, in the foster homes. She had no one to turn to, no one who could help. Even though she didn't know what kind of help she really needed.

Had she lost her mind? She'd already established that she hadn't died, nor was she sleeping. The disaster Katie had wrought was all too real.

But what would explain all this? Could wishing she lived in a different historical time than the one she'd originally been born into *really* bring the change about?

Was she sane?

"'Melia?" ventured Katie.

Opening her stinging eyes, Amelia answered, "Yes."

Katie dropped Mrs. Stoltz's ruined ballgown and approached. "Katie kiss? Make all wight?"

Something in the bell-like lisping voice reached Amelia's frightened heart. She took a good look at Katie, noticed the worry and fear in the child's features. It didn't take a rocket scientist to figure out what Katie suddenly thought. Tears were for tragedy, and she'd seen more than enough tragedy in her short life. She'd lost her mother. The old 'Melia had abandoned her, too. Now her father dumped her on a very different 'Melia than the one she'd always known. Yet another tragedy to a toddler.

"'Melia go wiz angels 'n Mama?" she asked.

Chapter 5

HOURS LATER, AMELIA jumped like a flea at every last creak the farmhouse uttered. And for good reason.

When her crying jag approached its natural end, Pansy had offered comfort and advice. Surprisingly good advice, as Amelia had first thought. Then she realized she didn't know the woman well enough to have formed an informed opinion, and although Pansy seemed a bit flighty, she quickly put Amelia, the kitchen, and Katie back to rights.

Neither woman had known what to do with the ice-blue satin.

Pansy also came up with what at the time seemed like an excellent idea. "Why don't you take the child home?" she suggested. "Watch her there, where things are familiar, where she has her bed, her toys. It should make it easier to keep her out of mischief in her own home."

That was how Amelia came to be at the Hayak farmhouse when the sun began to set. Now, however, her opinion of Pansy's idea plummeted at the same rate as the orange ball in the western sky. Mother Nature wasn't cutting her any slack, since she would soon force Michael

Hayak to return from the fields. Amelia had no idea how he'd respond to finding her on his turf.

A very sloppy turf, she might add. The kitchen abounded with dried out, unwashed dishes, cups, pots, and pans. Toys were strewn from one end of the house to the other. In what was obviously Katie's room, dirty dresses awaited attention, and in the sick room, medicine bottles, basins, towels, pillows, and blankets littered every surface.

A fine layer of dust had begun to accumulate, which told Amelia that the house had only been neglected in the most recent past. A tragedy had clearly disrupted the normal rhythms of its inhabitants. Although the house remained in disorder, Amelia's assessment changed. There was a reason for the mess.

While Amelia had itched to straighten up, she hadn't dared risk leaving Katie unsupervised again. With luck, the child in her arms would continue to sleep when Amelia set her down on the bed.

Amelia didn't think she had the fortitude to deal with both Hayaks at the same time. A confrontation with Michael was inevitable. He'd made abundantly clear what he thought of her, and Amelia was certain she had been his last resort in child care. So how would the man react when he found her in his home?

"I don't even want to think about it," Amelia muttered, then stood, Katie cradled close. Upstairs, she laid the child on the rumpled bed, covered her, then watched her sleep. Amazing how different she seemed from the tiny tornado who'd churned up Amelia's kitchen!

At that moment, Amelia had thought she wanted to throttle the little terrorist, but something about the child had tugged at her. She hadn't had the heart to yell. As she stood by Katie's bed now and watched the even rise and fall of her chest, Amelia realized that she could easily run into trouble here. This beautiful little child could steal a large chunk of her heart.

Then she heard heavy footsteps on the front porch. Amelia's stomach clenched. *Michael.*

Taking a deep breath for courage, she ran down the stairs, skidding to a stop before the opening front door.

Blue eyes met green.

The air grew thick.

Silence roared.

Amelia felt a current of electricity ripple through her, leaving her skin sensitized and very, very alive. She couldn't remember ever feeling this way, but she was reasonably sure it wasn't fear she felt. Not that the rage that returned to those sapphire eyes as soon as he saw her wasn't daunting.

"You!" he exploded.

Amelia swallowed and squared her shoulders, hoping to shake off the effect of the man. "Yes, me."

"What are you doing here? And where is my daughter?"

"I'm following your orders. And Katie's asleep in her bed."

The rugged features eased somewhat, although the turbulence in Michael's gaze remained unchanged. "Why are you here?"

"Because your daughter is Hell on wheels!"

Michael's nostrils flared, his jaw tightened, and a muscle flexed in his cheek. "What does that vulgar expression mean?" he asked, distaste in his voice. "And since when do you use such language, Miss Baldwin?"

Uh-oh, she'd better watch herself or more of those slips of the tongue would continue to set the man off. "That expression means that in less than ten minutes Katie caused more trouble than any one little person should be able to. It may be a vulgar expression, Mr. Hayak, but you dumped her on me, without so much as a warning about her . . . um, talents in the area of demolition."

"You know damn well what Katie's capable of. Are you still trying to persuade me that you're suffering from amnesia?"

"I'm not trying to persuade anyone of anything. You can form your own conclusions. I fell, injured my head—if you care to check, there's a gash under my hair—and know nothing that happened before I opened my eyes under the stage floor. That's the only truth"—as far as it went—"I know."

Again the muscle in the cheek worked. Again skepticism and something else burned in Michael's eyes. Again Amelia felt a strange response build inside her, a sensation unlike any other she'd ever experienced.

It was time to go. The last thing she needed was more disturbing fodder for her thoughts. And this man disturbed her on a variety of levels. For Pete's sake, she couldn't even string two thoughts together in his presence. "Your daughter is safe, although I can't say the same for Mrs. Stoltz's ballgown. You'll have to arrange to pay her for the damaged fabric. Now that you're back, I can go home."

As she headed toward the still-open door, Michael clasped her elbow. "Mrs. Stoltz's ball . . . gown . . . ?"

Amelia's breath caught. A tremor shook her as the heat from his hand seeped in at the point where they touched. She turned her gaze to the hand on her arm, then up to Michael's face. Her eyes widened as they caught the stunned look in his. So she wasn't the only one feeling the . . . *whatever* that was between them.

His eyes closed, veiling the response she'd seen. When he opened them again, nothing remained where so much had been revealed seconds before. Amelia knew a pang of loss.

How strange.

"What about tomorrow?" he asked, his voice rough.

"What about tomorrow?"

His jaw tightened again. "There is no need to mock me, Miss Baldwin. What do you mean to do with Katie tomorrow? I can't stay away from the fields any longer. Our livelihood depends on the farm—the farm I had to neglect while my wife died. I can't work with Katie at my side."

Remembering the chaos in her kitchen, Amelia smiled wryly. "I'll say."

Michael's narrowed gaze said he didn't like this comment any more than he'd liked her repeating what he'd said. She hurried to amend her words. "What I meant was, of course you can't take her along to work in the fields."

That was true enough, and everyone Amelia had spoken to said she'd promised to watch the little imp after her mother died. Christina was dead. The imp needed constant supervision. "I'll be back in the morning," she promised with reluctance.

"Make sure you're here at dawn."

Amelia swallowed her spontaneous refusal. She'd never been a morning person. "Dawn . . ."

At her response, Michael ran a rough hand over his face. Amelia took a closer look at the man. Exhaustion painted shadows under his eyes. His jaw remained clenched, and the muscle in his cheek stayed taut beneath his tanned, stubbled skin. His broad shoulders seemed bowed, as if the burden he carried were too great for even such a sturdy expanse of sinew and bone.

Unable to stop herself, Amelia again met his gaze. Where she expected to find some measure of relief, she found only more of those mixed emotions she'd noticed before. Yes, he was tired, but his eyes also displayed anger, frustration, pain, and . . . could that be guilt?

What did Michael Hayak have to be guilty about?

Amelia didn't know. She didn't even know if she dared try to uncover that guilt. She only knew that this man had had an unusual effect on her, even before they'd actually met.

Against her better judgment, she had just promised to return in the morning. For some clear-as-mud reason, she felt driven to keep the other Amelia Baldwin's promise. But that wasn't all. Something else prodded her.

She didn't want to let Michael Hayak down again.

Hours later, Michael lay on the sofa, the blanket half on, his aching hand cradled against his chest. There were times when he questioned his sanity.

How could he let the encounter with Amelia rattle him so? Why had he felt such an urge to hit something, to strike out in pain, in rage? And why had he chosen that thick beam in the barn? He had most likely broken a bone or two.

How could he let Amelia get under his skin each time they met?

Therein lay the truth. Amelia Baldwin affected him more than any other woman ever had. Even his wife. Even though he had no right to feel what he felt for her.

True, his marriage had been based on mutual friendship and similar goals. He'd never pretended a grand passion for Christina, and he was quite certain she hadn't felt one for him either. They'd married shortly after his father had died, leaving him the farm—just after Christina had arrived in Minnesota from Bohemia. She had come to help her recently widowed aunt raise the fatherless cousins. When her Aunt Sophie remarried unexpectedly, Christina hadn't wanted to return to Europe. By that time, Michael had come to realize the farm was too much for him alone. He needed help.

Soon they knew they'd struck an excellent bargain. When they learned that Christina was increasing, joy filled their days. They'd both adored their daughter.

But Christina's health failed to return after Katie's birth, and the doctors said the pregnancy had weakened a flawed heart. Despite the gravity of Christina's condition, neither of them regretted having the child. Especially not Christina.

Then Amelia Baldwin, who also befriended the lonely young woman from Bohemia, took over the running of the

Hayaks' home. Christina never got back on her feet, and to Michael's surprise, Amelia took to bringing sacks of sewing to work on while she nursed his wife, tended his daughter, and ran his house.

To Michael's horror and dismay, Amelia's presence affected him like a flame did a moth. He'd watched her every movement with a hunger he hadn't known before. But unlike a moth, he'd known the danger in the flame of desire.

Eternally willing to help, Amelia embodied all that was good in life—charity, loyalty, tenderness . . . a tenderness he'd watched her lavish on his daughter and dying wife. Michael had yearned to know such attention. He'd been jealous of Katie and Christina. He'd wanted Amelia's care for himself.

He'd also noticed her womanly form all too frequently. The generous curves on her petite body had aroused him, far more than Christina's willowy shape had ever moved him. He'd wanted Amelia with an intensity that shocked him.

He'd always been aware of the vows he'd taken. Before God and man he'd promised to want no woman but Christina.

What a weak fool he was! No sooner had his wife taken to what would eventually prove to be her deathbed, than his eyes and his lust had turned to her closest friend. His sinful desire seemed even more despicable since the two women had grown so close.

As if to prove what a wretch he was, last Friday morning, when Amelia ran from Christina's bedside, overcome with the grief that accompanied the certainty of imminent death, he'd followed her, knowing she wept for the friend she was about to lose. He'd found her in the kitchen, hands gripping the enameled sink, sobs wracking her small frame.

He'd only intended to comfort her. He'd placed his hands on her heaving shoulders to turn her around, then wrapped his arms about her. But he never counted on his own damning weakness. Instead of giving, he'd taken, stealing from Amelia what she hadn't been ready or willing to give.

He'd apologized. In his clumsy fashion. She'd nodded, waving his concern away, but as soon as he'd returned to Christina, she must have fled, because when his wife began to call for her friend, Michael found no trace of Amelia. At least he hadn't left the dying woman to chase after one who was very much alive.

He'd accused Amelia of playing them false, of pretending she couldn't remember what she'd promised. Amelia, he'd said, had betrayed Christina and Katie.

But if truth be told, Michael was responsible for the betrayal. He'd committed adultery in his heart while his wife lay dying. That deserved no forgiveness. A just God had to mete out chastisement. Michael suspected Amelia's rejection of her promise was part of it.

Now the woman he desired wanted nothing to do with his daughter, the innocent victim in her father's fall from grace. And that was by far the hardest punishment for him to bear.

By declaring Amelia false-hearted, he had launched his attack before she could point a finger his way. After all, she wanted nothing to do with her best friend's husband. She'd proven her innocence by running away from him. By pretending amnesia, for God's sake.

Michael silently accepted responsibility for his dishonorable actions, but he wasn't yet able to admit his guilt to the woman who'd inspired them. Not yet. He couldn't tell Amelia he was the one who'd betrayed his wife.

With another yawn, Amelia climbed the front steps to the Hayaks' home the next morning. "*Come at dawn, he says. Easy for him. He's used to keeping ungodly hours. But me, I have to reorganize my entire system!*"

It occurred to Amelia that she had to rearrange her system regardless of what Michael wanted. She no longer lived in the 1990s. This was a different time. Life had a very different pace than what she'd known.

Taking a deep breath, she rapped on the front door. When she heard no answer, she checked the horizon. The most perfect shade of apricot tinted the sky where the sun strove to peek over the edge of the world. She wasn't late, but precisely on time.

Amelia knocked again. When she still got no response, she gathered her courage and twisted the doorknob. It gave under the pressure of her hand. Feeling more timid than she ever remembered, she entered the house, wondering where Michael was. Had he overslept?

The sound of water splashing in the kitchen gave his presence away. Maybe he was making coffee. The thought immediately energized her. A cup of java might redeem the ornery creature. She was a desperate woman. A sleepy, caffeine-deprived, desperate woman.

"I hope you've started the first pot of the day—" Her throat up and dried on her mid-sentence. She'd never seen anything like this before.

Michael stood before the kitchen sink, a rough cotton towel in his hands, water dripping off his chin. He'd obviously just shaved, as his skin gleamed smoothly and with a farmer's golden tan. His shoulders, every bit as broad as she'd figured they were, sloped to muscular arms that hovered motionless beneath his face. His chest was banded with the same taut muscle as his arms, and his flat belly rippled to the waist of his unbuttoned jeans.

Damp, curly brown hair grew across his chest, then thinned to a fine line as far down as his belly button. Amelia followed the path of Michael's body hair right past his navel and the unbuttoned placket of his jeans, to where it thickened the lower her gaze strayed. From the hair and the open placket it was only a matter of inches till she arrived at the bulge that determined Michael's gender.

Amelia gulped. She'd never ogled a man before, maybe because she'd never come across a man who deserved ogling more than this one did. Who'd'a thunk Michael Hayak would fill the bill for a *Playgirl* centerfold?

Her examination of the masculine pulchritude before her disproved the claims of magazine articles in the late twentieth century. A woman could indeed become aroused by strictly visual stimuli.

Amelia was aroused.

Her nipples had tightened in response to the heat that swirled through her body, making it nearly impossible to end her scrutiny of Michael's body. Although Amelia had dated, she'd *never* felt the burn of desire for any of her companions. She'd been uncomfortably sure that she was the last twenty-eight-year-old virgin on the face of the earth.

Had Michael Hayak asked her out, and had they gotten along better than they did in this century . . . who knows what might have happened?

As she watched, the small brown disks on his pectorals puckered, and Amelia realized her interest had caused that physical change.

She blushed. Great! Not only did Michael think her the reincarnation of Benedict Arnold, but now she behaved like a desperate, lusty old maid. Oh, yeah, she was great at presenting her best side. If only she could read his thoughts. . . .

Damn her! How could she just stand there, devour him with those great green eyes of hers, then expect to prance around his home as if nothing had changed? As if Christina still lay on that bed in the upstairs room?

Michael had often wondered what Amelia thought of him. And he'd often thought he'd seen the light of interest in her gaze. But he'd never seen what he saw today. He had his answer now. He could almost feel her eyes caress him. On every inch of his skin. And he was only human.

He couldn't have prevented his physical response. The tautening of his flesh was surely visible, and he forced himself to turn away. Roughly he tugged his trousers closed, then casually held the towel navel-high. When he thought he could face her again, he donned a scornful expression.

All the while his every nerve ending was on fire. "I see you haven't forgotten the virtue of promptness," he said, his tone sharper than he'd intended.

She gasped. Then she closed her eyes, clasped her trembling hands, and straightened her shoulders. "You did say dawn."

"Yes, I did. And it's time I went to tend to the animals. I'll eat breakfast after I've milked the cows."

Michael took the opportunity and ran. He couldn't have stayed in that stuffy kitchen another second. Not while Amelia stood there. He'd be damned if he knew what to do when he returned to eat. Surely she'd still be there, cooking his meal, raising his daughter, acting very much as a man expects his woman to act.

But Amelia Baldwin wasn't Michael's woman. With his wife scarcely cold in the ground, he had no right to think along those lines.

He needed saving from his own baser instincts, and he'd grasp at anything right now. A farm always abounded with work. Michael would gladly work until he dropped. He'd work until he no longer had the strength to think of Amelia, until he exhausted the hunger he felt for his late wife's closest friend. Until he was too tired to remember the matching hunger he'd seen in those beautiful eyes.

His eyes, Amelia thought as Michael left the kitchen. He had the most disturbing blue eyes. They changed from moment to moment, at first displaying heat, then anger and rage.

A tug on her skirt announced Katie's arrival. "'Melia, Katie hung'y."

Amelia shuddered, as if waking from a particularly disturbing dream. "Well, munchkin, it seems the only thing you know how to say is that you're hungry."

"Uh-uh," Katie replied, her curls shaking with her denial. "I thusty, too."

Amelia grinned. "Okay, kiddo, you win. You're hungry and thirsty, and I'm the only one around who can do anything about it. Boy, are you out of luck! I can't cook worth beans."

"Beans? Don' wan' beans."

With a chuckle, Amelia turned to the row of cabinets on the left kitchen wall. "Don't worry, I couldn't make them even if you did. Let's see what we can find. Maybe a box of corn flakes. I seem to remember reading somewhere they were invented way back when."

Opening a door, Amelia exclaimed, "Look at all this!"

In one cabinet she found two packages of Arbucles Ariosa Roasted Coffee, a five-pound can of Wilbur's Breakfast Cocoa, a package of Queen Mary Scotch Ground Oatmeal, two pounds of Cerealine Flakes—nothing like good old Kellogg's®—a two-pound box of Best White Hominy, and a one-pound package of Granula—not granola, mind you.

But nary a corn flake could be found. Nothing Amelia might make edible.

Another tug at her skirt. "'Melia, Katie hung'y!"

"I know, munchkin, but 'Melia can't cook."

Katie's puzzled expression was adorable, unfortunately it got them nowhere. "Let's try this," Amelia suggested. "What do you want to eat for breakfast?"

A smile broadened Katie's lips. "Ham 'n biskits."

"Oh, no you don't, young lady! That was yesterday. I'm onto your tricks today. Nope, I think today's an oatmeal kind of day."

After scrubbing one of the many food-encrusted pans clean, Amelia followed the brief—*extremely* brief—directions on the package of oatmeal. Water, salt and oats were all she needed to turn those flat flakes into a porridge fit for a queen. Amelia just hoped it was reasonably acceptable to a hungry little girl.

With considerable respect, Amelia approached the black metal monster she knew was the stove. It proudly displayed the name Othello across the oven door, and another sign, just beneath the six-hole cooktop said it had been manufactured by Orr Painter & Co. of Reading, Pennsylvania.

How in the world did she get this thing to cook Katie's porridge?

She placed the pan on one of the circular burner hole covers, and heard the droplets of water clinging to the pan sizzle from heat. "Holy cow! It's hot. Your papa must have started the fire so he could shave."

Katie nodded. "Papa's wid cows. 'Melia's cookin'."

"We hope." With a wary eye, Amelia watched the oat flakes and water start to bubble. "Katie, could you please find a spoon for Amelia?"

"Um-hm." Little feet trotted to the table, then a chair scraped against the floor.

"Better yet," she hurried to amend, visions of trashed kitchens dancing in her head, "show me where *Amelia* can find a spoon."

By the time she got back to the stove, the stuff bubbling in the pan no longer looked like what she'd mixed together. Unfortunately, it didn't resemble what came from her microwave when she nuked a bowl of instant oatmeal, either.

This stuff had formed clumps between which fat bubbles burst, reminding Amelia of the geysers in Yellowstone Park. The shots of steam looked dangerous. "It's done," she said to Katie, pitying the poor child who'd become the taste-tester to Amelia's first endeavor in the 1900 kitchen.

As she placed a steaming bowl of blobs before Katie, she caught the unmistakable sound of steamed male.

"Damn it all to Hell!" Michael blasted just outside the kitchen door. "Females! Nothing but a curse to mankind. Blasted bovines are as irritating and disagreeable as the two-legged ones—"

"Excuse me!" Amelia called before Michael's tirade taught Katie too many new words. "There's a child here. You might want to vent your feelings elsewhere."

By the end of her suggestion, Michael had entered the kitchen, bringing with him a burst of crisp autumn air. "Yes, well, that child will go hungry if her father can't finish milking his cows. We need the money from the cream."

"So why are you here instead of with the female bovines you were maligning?"

Ruddy color spread over Michael's cheeks. "Contrary beasts won't let me milk them with one hand."

"Is that some secret country method?" Amelia asked, puzzled. "I'd always thought you needed both hands to milk a cow." *When you lacked an electric milking machine.*

Michael's eyes narrowed. "Are you being purposely difficult? Of course I use two hands. Normally. It's just that I . . . uh, had a . . . an accident last night and can't get my left hand to work right."

"You're hurt?"

"Some."

"Have you seen a doctor?"

Michael looked at her as if she'd lost her marbles. "Of course not. My knuckles are just bruised."

"Here, let me take a look."

An eyebrow shot up. "You're pretending to be a doctor now?"

"Don't be obnoxious. Let me see what you did to your hand."

"Damn my hand! It's the cows that need milking. Luther's due to arrive shortly to take the milk to the collective."

"Well, then, if you don't want me to see your hand, what *do* you want from me, Michael Hayak?"

"Use your head, woman! You have to help me milk the cows."

Amelia's jaw dropped. Her eyes opened impossibly wide. "You . . . want me to do . . . what?"

"You heard me. Come help me milk the cows!"

In one fell swoop the last of Amelia's daydreams of an easier, more genteel lifestyle in Victorian times shattered as she followed Michael Hayak and came face to face with her first cow.

Chapter 6

ALTHOUGH AMELIA FOUND no evidence of the source, the overwhelming smell of manure filled the close confines of the barn stall. Sitting on a three-legged stool in the vicinity of the cow's distended udder put her up close and personal to the producer of that source. Too damn close for Amelia's comfort.

Being reasonably intelligent, however, she maintained a respectful distance from the frustrated, irritated male hovering over her shoulder. "Harder," Michael insisted.

"I can't squeeze any harder than I already am!"

"Yes, you can, Amelia. It isn't the first time you've milked a cow. Now stop this amnesia foolishness and take pity on poor old Hazel."

"Hazel, huh? How about me? Why won't you take pity on me, you stubborn male? I don't know the first thing about cows, much less milking. I've never milked a cow!"

There they went again, she thought. Not even the proverbial snowball's chance that he'd buy the theory of time-travel, and she still couldn't milk this poor beast!

Well, it wouldn't hurt to try again. "Look, for the sake of expedience, why don't you pretend to accept my memory loss? Teach me to milk, and all three of us will be much happier than if you continue to accuse me of lying."

Just then Hazel piped in, letting loose a mournful moo in which even Amelia could hear the animal's discomfort. "Oh, you poor thing," she murmured, commiserating with her gender mate. "See, Michael? She agrees. Teach me to milk, and we'll solve the problem."

As she spoke, Amelia turned and met Michael's gaze. For a moment, she thought he was about to blast her again, but then he set his jaw, tightened his lips, and stepped closer to where she sat.

"For the sake of the cows," came through gritted teeth.

"Cows?" she asked, dismayed. "As in more than one?"

"As in six."

Amelia groaned. "Get with the program, Michael. If I'm supposed to milk six cows, we'd better get a move on."

He shook his head, a puzzled look overtaking his previous anger. "Can't say I've ever heard you talk so strangely, Amelia. But you are right. The cows need milking."

Before she knew what was happening, Michael wrapped his large frame around her, his arms bracketing hers, his hands covering her fingers. "It's best if I show you how to start."

Now he'd gone and done it. Not only had he earlier given her a glimpse of the most delicious male body she'd ever seen, but now he'd enfolded her in its strength and heat.

She could feel the firmness of his chest at her back, and the length of his fingers as they guided hers in what should have been an impersonal lesson. No matter what he'd meant it to be, it turned personal, intimate, arousing.

Close as they were, Amelia felt the moist warmth of his breath against the curve of her ear, the rough texture of his chin on her neck. She scented the rich fragrance of clean male. On her either side, hard thighs aligned with hers, while her bottom pressed up against Michael's groin.

"Curve your fingers around the cow's teats," he murmured, his voice sounding suddenly very deep.

Good grief! Did he really have to say what he'd said? As if in response to his no-nonsense term, Amelia's nipples sprang to attention, putting her on notice that this man was far more dangerous than even her suspicions had suggested. Mellow heat curled through her body, pooling in her belly, seeping lower until she felt it between her legs. Moment by moment, she grew more aware of their intimate position.

"Pull," he rasped.

She was supposed to think of the cow at a time like this? *Sorry, Hazel, old girl,* Amelia thought, while wondering where her common sense had fled to.

Reaching for sanity, Michael dragged in a lungful of air, but with Amelia cradled against him, sanity seemed long gone. She was warm, so very warm and sweet. The scent of honeysuckle teased his senses, and the softness of the knot of her dark hair caressed his face. If he curled his arms under hers and laced his hands across her middle, he'd finally embrace the woman he had for so long desired. In that position, the fullness of her breasts would rest on his forearms.

That thought sent a shock of heat straight to his groin, awakening flesh that had no right to rise. But rise it did, as did his hunger for Amelia Baldwin.

Then she sealed her fate. She turned her head just far enough around that their gazes met, their lips separated by only a breath of cool autumn air. Michael prayed for forgiveness, but obeyed the clamor of his desire.

Her lips were soft and damp, and slightly parted. Michael's need urged him to press them farther apart. The moist silk of her lower lip beckoned, and his tongue yielded to temptation. Amelia tasted sweet, and so arousing,

Michael felt he'd surely explode from wanting her. God in Heaven, he was drowning.

Flooded with unfamiliar sensations, Amelia could have avoided the kiss, but then she would never have known the delicious touch of Michael's lips, his rich masculine taste. Now that she'd experienced his desire, she couldn't fault herself for allowing the caress. The rough silk of his tongue again swept her mouth, leaving a hunger for more in its wake.

Although Amelia had never been kissed like this, had never felt like this before, she recognized the sensations for what they were—pure, distilled passion.

Michael kissed her as if he needed to do so in order to live. He kissed her as if she were the only woman who could give him what he needed. As if he'd perish if he didn't caress her mouth one more time.

Michael Hayak kissed as if he meant business, and that business wasn't about to end with just a kiss. As soon as Amelia realized where the hot lashes of his tongue were leading, she began to pull away. His hand captured the back of her head, holding her for yet another searing sweep of her mouth.

Then Hazel lowed, still miserable, still unmilked. Michael stopped his determined plundering of Amelia's mouth, but didn't release her soft lips, instead pressing a chaste, gentle kiss where he'd moments before revealed the power of his passion. When he fully realized what he was doing, he was forced to question his actions.

But before he could answer his questions, Amelia lunged at him, throwing him flat on his rear. She landed pressed up inch to inch along his painfully aroused body. He hissed at the contact of their pelvises, stunned by her voracious attack.

She gasped, eyes open wide. Her face drained of color. She opened her mouth, again tried to breathe. Suddenly Michael realized she wasn't taking over this seduction. Something was very wrong. "Amelia! What is it?"

She shook her head. Her eyes filled with panic. Her chest heaved. She fought for air. Finally he heard a tiny sibilance, indicating she'd drawn breath. "What happened?"

Tears spilled from her eyes, falling on his face. Michael rolled gently out from beneath her, then cradled her in his lap. "What's wrong?" he asked again, worry eating at him.

As she inhaled, Amelia shuddered, then coughed. "H-Hazel," she wheezed.

"Never mind Hazel! What's wrong?"

She shook her head, the tears no longer gathering in her eyes. In fact, it looked like she was trying to smile, or laugh.

"It was Hazel!" she exclaimed after taking a few deep breaths. "She got impatient . . . tried to get my attention . . . kicked me off the stool!"

Relief made him giddy, and he found himself laughing for the first time in at least a year. The woman in his lap joined her laughter to his, her emerald eyes gazing openly into his.

"Papa, why's 'Melia on yer lap?"

At the sound of Katie's question, Michael dumped Amelia on the pile of hay strewn over the floor of the stall, and turned his back to his curious daughter. The last thing he needed was for Katie to point out his state of arousal.

From the rustling of hay behind him, Michael assumed Amelia was busy putting herself to rights as well. But she didn't say a word. And his daughter had directed her question at him.

"Papa!" called Katie, growing impatient. "Why?"

"Er . . . Hazel knocked Amelia over, and I wanted to make sure she was all right." Dammit! Even to him his voice sounded rough, and his words rang hollow. Just his luck that his daughter had caught him with his hands full.

But what *had* he been doing with his hands on Amelia Baldwin in the first place? The woman who had made it abundantly clear she wanted nothing to do with her friend's widower. The woman who had fabricated the biggest pile of lies Michael had ever heard just to avoid him. The woman who had set aside a promise made to a dying friend rather than risk his sinful, unwanted attentions.

"Yes, well," he said, trying to ease away. "I think you know now what you must do to milk the cows. The fields are waiting for me."

When he could no longer keep his back to the two females in the barn, Michael turned. What he saw pushed whatever else he'd been about to say right out of his head. "Katie! What have you done?"

Her small forehead wrinkled, her blue eyes stared. "Huh?"

Michael waved in the direction of the mess on his daughter's face, her nightdress, even clumping up her curls. "What did you get all over yourself?"

"Breskfat."

Amelia cried, "Oh, no!"

Michael cried, "Oh, no!"

"Uh-hu-uh!" the little darling sang out.

"I suppose the kitchen looks just like you do," muttered Amelia as she hurried to take Katie's sticky hand in hers.

Katie nodded, grinning.

Certain that his daughter would be well supervised—although not at all sure how his cows would fare—Michael pounced on the opportunity to escape Amelia's allure. For more than ever, although he knew how wrong it was, and despite his efforts to convince himself of her false-heartedness, Michael still wanted Amelia Baldwin, his late wife's closest friend.

The kitchen looked every bit as awful as Amelia expected. Lumps of congealed oats lay around the chair where she'd left Katie and on the table where the child had apparently tried to repeat yesterday's artistic accomplishments. Everywhere else, random dibs and dabs told the tale of Katie's adventures in the kitchen. "I can't turn my back on you for even one minute, can I?"

Katie shrugged, submitting to yet another swipe of the wet towel Amelia brandished. That removed the worst of the mess on her face and arms. The hair needed washing, and the nightie a thorough scrubbing. Only then could Amelia tackle the kitchen.

"I'm going to have to clean up the dirty dishes your papa's been collecting, too, won't I?"

Perfectly agreeable, Katie nodded.

Judging her charge as clean as she could get without the benefit of a good soaking, Amelia set off to find the bathroom, Katie's pudgy fingers clasped in hers. "Show 'Melia where you take your baths."

"Yuck!"

"Yuck, nothing. You're sticky, and I can't let that stuff turn to concrete on your nightie. You need a bath, Katie, my dear."

Golden brown curls bounced violently from side to side.

"Oh, yes, a bath is just what you need." Amelia wasn't willing to lose this battle with the precocious two-year-old.

Katie slammed on the brakes, effectively shackling Amelia, since she wasn't about to free the child's arm. Shrewd blue eyes took her measure. Then, resigned to her fate, Katie conceded with a dramatic sigh. "Katie bath."

After much splashing, which left Amelia wondering just who'd been bathed, Katie was once again clean and fragrant in a blue gingham dress. "You look like an angel," Amelia said, still awed by the child's ability to wreak havoc despite her heavenly appearance.

"Papa's angel," supplied Katie with a smug smile.

"I'll bet!"

"Wha's bet?"

"Oh, no, you don't! I refuse to be blamed for expanding your vocabulary. Your papa made too clear what he thinks of mine."

A dainty shoulder rose. Then, at a trot, Katie exited the kitchen through the unlatched back door, followed closely by a jogging Amelia. Outside, Katie chortled when she reached a bright red ball floating in a mudhole. "'Melia play ball?"

"Nope," Amelia answered, snatching the filthy toy from the clean child. "We have to help our sisters in gender. Somehow, I'm going to have to milk six cows, and Heaven help the poor beasts, since I haven't a clue how to go about it."

Entering the barn again, Amelia sensed the animals' discomfort. Restless snuffling came from every stall. Hooves trampled hay, making a muted shuffling sound. Straightening her shoulders, she approached Hazel's cubicle. The large tin pail Michael had provided was where she'd last seen it under the cow near the overturned stool.

"Let's see if we can get it right this time," she said in what she hoped was a soothing, reassuring voice. Holding the pail between her feet as Michael had shown her, Amelia again sat on the stool and grasped the cow's teats.

Uninvited, the memory of the moments spent in Michael's arms came rushing to her once again. She blushed, feeling warmth on her neck, her cheeks, her ears. Michael's kiss had been a revelation. Now she understood why she hadn't allowed any of her relationships to progress past a few innocuous dates. She'd instinctively sought the richness of passion, the urgency of desire, but failed to find it with any of those men.

"I sure found it now," she muttered, shaking her head, "when I'm least prepared to do anything about it." She had to set Michael Hayak on a mental back burner. "After all, poor Hazel can't be left like this any longer." And Amelia didn't know how much time she had left in 1900.

So she tugged. She squeezed. *Hard,* as Michael had said. And she tugged again. For all her efforts, only a few drops *ping*ed into the pail.

Hazel mooed.

Katie laughed.

Amelia squeezed. All to no avail.

"Shore do look like you need some help, Miz Baldwin," said a male voice from behind her.

Amelia leaped up, turning, and felt instant relief at the sight of the kind-faced older man who stood outside Hazel's stall. "Ol' Hazel's been givin' ya what fer?" he asked.

"Not really. I just don't know what I'm supposed to do."

"Ah, Miz Baldwin, so them tales is right! Ya did lose yer mind."

Damn and double damn! She was tired of the amnesia excuse, but she doubted this man would take to the idea of time-travel any better than Michael Hayak would. "Looks that way," she answered, surrendering to her fate.

"An' ya don' know ol' Luther Schwartz?"

"Can't recall meeting you, but I'm honored to make your acquaintance now."

"Ah, Miz Baldwin, yer always so nice! Here, let me give ya a han' with Michael's testy crones."

Amelia smiled and offered a prayer of thanks. "Actually, Luther, I'd rather you teach me how. It seems Michael had an accident last night and hurt his hand. He can't do the milking, and since I'm already here to watch Katie, I'd like to help him."

"Won' take long ta teach ya. Oncet one larns how ta milk a cow, one cain't never ferget. Ya useta be right good at it, too. You'll fall back to it straightaway."

Amelia had a few more doubts than Luther, but she hoped milking a cow was an easy lesson to learn. And although she didn't credit prior knowledge with the results, by the time Luther left to continue his rounds—the milk from Michael's small herd in tall cans on his wagon— Amelia was proudly milking the last cow for the farm's allotment of milk. Like a pro—even if she did say so herself.

She counted as another victory Katie's presence at her side.

Nary a disaster to correct.

Until they returned to the scene of Katie's last stand.

"Uh-oh," said the little person at Amelia's side.

"You got that right," Amelia answered. "Let me figure out what I'm supposed to do with this milk so it won't spoil, and then we can get down to business."

"Biznuz?"

"Um-hmm."

"Figewator," Katie offered.

"Refrigerator? You have one of those?"

Katie pointed to a tall, upright wooden cupboard near the stove. "Yeth."

Opening the latched door, Amelia exclaimed in delight. "An Acme icebox! Do you have any idea what this is worth?"

Then she remembered. She was no longer in the 1990s. A household appliance, although pricey by Victorian standards, probably cost no more than twelve to fifteen dollars. She had traveled back in time.

"Won't keep me from enjoying it," she murmured, running a finger over the well-finished oak exterior. If not the best way to prevent food spoilage, it was the most beautiful.

Moments later, she covered the pail of milk with a clean cloth she'd found in a chest stuffed with linens. Careful not to slosh, she slipped it into the icebox. Then Amelia armed herself with more cloths and the large bar of yellow soap she'd found on the sink. She ladled steaming water from the reservoir on the side of the stove and added just enough cold so she could get to work.

"Here, munchkin," she said to Katie, handing her a small, wet washcloth. "We're going to clean the mess you made."

"Um-hmm, Katie clean!"

"Yup, Amelia and Katie will make the kitchen shine."

Hours later, as the sun made its way down the sky again, Amelia maintained a gentle pace on the maple rocker in the parlor. In her arms, she held an exhausted child who hadn't thrown a tantrum or bellowed all day. In fact, Katie had been a model child from the moment Amelia took her firmly in hand.

"You're not that scary after all, munchkin," Amelia whispered, then dropped a gentle kiss on the child's forehead. "I could get used to this mothering thing."

Yes, it seemed Katie had stolen straight through Amelia's decidedly weak defenses. With her big blue eyes and her tendency toward trouble, the lonely little girl had touched an empty spot in the lonely woman's heart.

Although as a child she'd yearned for parents, by the time she reached adulthood, Amelia had known what she really wanted. A child of her own. She'd hoped the child would come after she found a mate, but fate seemed to have intervened. By thrusting Amelia back in time, the universe had found a child as needy as she herself was. Somehow, holding Katie, scolding, teasing, mothering the little imp felt exactly right.

And Amelia was scared.

What would she do the day her time in 1900 was up? When fate ripped her away from the child? How would she ever piece her life back together again when she left her heart in a time before hers?

Tears filled Amelia's eyes, and she choked on the knot in her throat. What would she do when she no longer had Katie to fill her day, her arms, her heart?

Weary, hungry, and cross as a wounded bear, Michael trudged up the porch steps and into his home. Immediately he realized something had changed. Back to what he'd been accustomed to. Before Christina's death.

The scent of soap sweetened the air, and he found not even one toy to trip on. The taint of scorched food was a new addition, but he figured Katie must have distracted Amelia, who had probably allowed something to burn.

Pity. As hungry as he was, having ignored his stomach's

grumbling at noon rather than face Amelia again, Michael lamented the waste of even a scrap of food.

Heading toward the kitchen, he came up short when he spotted the object of his distraction rocking his daughter in the sturdy maple chair. As his eyes adjusted to what light came from the kitchen, Michael saw more than he was ready to absorb.

Amelia held Katie close to her heart, and with her free hand she smoothed the curls from the child's face. Peace radiated from his daughter's features, a calm he hadn't seen there since before Amelia disappeared.

Amelia's eyes were turned toward his daughter, a sweet, maternal smile curving her lips. As he watched, she lowered her face and kissed Katie's forehead in a gesture filled with love.

He caught his breath. How could he fight his yearning for Amelia when she lavished such care on his child? A child who by circumstance was as much Amelia's as Christina's own.

A woman's love for a man's child did something powerful to his emotions, built a bridge between them, regardless of how wrong it was.

Again Michael realized how deeply his feelings for Amelia ran. Had he only felt lust, he would surely have been able to control it. Lust was easily tamed by a physical act. But this longing, this need for her presence in his home, at his side, was what created chaos in his conscience.

He could have explained away wanting a woman's body as a result of two years' abstinence due to Christina's failing health. Although he couldn't deny his desire for Amelia's body, his feelings ran much deeper than that. As they had for a very long time. Since well before Christina died.

There lay the essence of Michael's guilt. When he should have focused his entire life on caring for his sickly wife, he'd only gone through the motions, letting his heart stray closer and closer to an adulterous love.

He had betrayed his marriage vows, if in nothing else than thought . . . and one clumsy, ill-timed deed. Because of that reckless, unguarded moment Amelia fled his home when Christina had needed her most.

As if sensing his presence, Amelia glanced up. "Oh," she whispered, "I didn't hear you arrive."

Despite the lack of light, Michael caught the gleam of tears on her cheeks. What had made her cry? Was it grief for her dead friend? Or was it guilt for what had happened between them moments before Christina drew her final breath?

Could it be the kiss in the barn?

With pain, he set those questions aside. He couldn't very well ask them without confessing. "I just got here," he answered.

"It's time I head home." She rose with Katie snuggled close. "I'll put her in bed. Won't take but a minute."

Silently he nodded, admitting that despite his longing for her presence, it was best indeed if she went home. He strode to the kitchen, seeking sustenance of a physical sort, since he had to deny the tenderness his heart so craved.

Moments later, she stood in the kitchen doorway. "I'm afraid I scorched the chicken I found in the icebox."

"Watching Katie is consuming," he said with a knowing smile.

"Can't blame her for this one. She was an angel for the rest of the day. I'm the one who can't cook."

Not again! "Dammit, Amelia! Can't you go for even a moment's chat without calling out that false amnesia to excuse everything that happens?"

She flinched. Then she squared her shoulders, unfortunately drawing his attention to her generous breasts. The inevitable heat began roiling in his gut, but before it grew to its usual searing strength, she threw him a scathing glare and whirled around. She stomped into the parlor, where he heard her open the door.

"Aren't you even going to say goodnight?" he asked.

"Why? So you can call me a liar again?"

"What's wrong? You can't stand to have your fabrications called by their rightful name?"

"I'm too tired from watching your daughter, cleaning your house, milking your cows, and cooking your food to argue with you. I'm leaving. I'll be back in the morning— not for you, but for Katie's sake. It's not her fault her father's blinder than a bat."

"Blind! I see perfectly well. And I see a woman who ran away from a defenseless child when things got tough."

Another glare raked over him. "Somehow, Michael, I don't think your lousy temper is due to what I've done or haven't done. You protest too much. Could it be that you're hiding regrets? Guilt you refuse to face?"

Out on the moonlit porch, Amelia drew a shaky breath. She couldn't believe she'd just hurled those questions at Michael. But she'd had enough of his accusations. She wasn't a liar, and she wasn't stupid either. Telling him the truth wouldn't help. And she had seen the shame of guilt in his gaze before. Something seemed to be eating at the widower.

Could it be the desire they'd experienced in the barn?

That possibility scared her. Amelia was too honest with herself to try to deny the attraction Michael posed. She was also too smart to think passion that strong sprang from the mundane act of milking a cow. Raging lust didn't usually spring from doing farm chores.

She'd felt Michael Hayak's pull on her senses from the moment she laid eyes on his portrait. Seems Mr. Hayak may have been hiding a secret yen for his dying wife's friend.

The feelings she'd experienced in the barn were frightening in their potency. That killer kiss of Michael's was enough to turn a woman into mush. But Amelia couldn't afford to let him do that to her. She couldn't let her heart bond with yet another person in this time. She had no idea how long her adventure in 1900 would last.

Michael and Katie belonged to the past. Amelia didn't. And she didn't know when her time here would be up.

Chapter 7

AFTER AN UNUSUALLY restless night, one where her dreams were veiled so that she couldn't identify the faces she saw, Amelia rose well before the sun. Anticipation and reluctance duked it out inside her.

She couldn't wait to see Katie again. Or Michael, to tell the truth. But after last night's confrontation, she had no idea what she would say or do when she next saw the man.

It wasn't her fault she wasn't who he thought she was. Well, she was . . . but she wasn't, too. Damn, it was confusing!

Once awake, Amelia was forced to examine at least one of the many questions that had haunted her sleep. When Michael kissed her, had he been kissing the other Amelia, or had he kissed *her,* the new and improved Amelia Baldwin? The one who'd come from the future to find what was missing from that other life.

Amelia's thoughts were so snarled she had to ask herself if *she* knew who she really was. Even though her memories belonged in the future, the life she now lived belonged in the past. Amelia couldn't deny she now inhabited a body from the past, but that past was her present, too. And although the new physical version of herself felt unfamiliar, it somehow embodied all she'd ever thought would make her comfortable with her looks.

So how much did the exterior affect the internal same-as-always Amelia?

She couldn't be sure. In fact, this Amelia had no idea what the old Amelia had thought of Katie, Michael, her life. Since it looked like she'd taken over that life, the new and improved Amelia had no choice but to wonder what else she'd taken over—and didn't yet know.

Had the original, 1900 Amelia been attracted to Michael Hayak as she now was and had been since first seeing his portrait? Had there been more between them than the desire to care for a dying loved one?

What made Amelia Baldwin run from her friend's deathbed?

There was no way for Amelia to learn these intimate things about a woman she didn't know. A woman who could very well be costuming a vaudeville revival at a theater on the outskirts of Chicago.

Did that woman exist? What did she think of Amelia's work-filled existence? How did she deal with the loneliness in her days?

"If I feel lonely now," Amelia muttered, "it's only because I'm wasting time wondering and worrying. Katie and Michael are waiting at the farm."

Tucking the knowledge of their need in a warm corner of her heart, Amelia set off toward the Nevius Brothers' Livery for her ancient wagon and broken-down nag—poor thing should have been put out to pasture long ago. But she had no other means of transportation, and Michael had said dawn.

As she approached the Hayak farm, she noticed a number of wagons trundling down the road in the same direction. Others were pulling out of dirt drives that led to other farmhouses. What was going on?

She had no idea, and none of the other travelers bothered to illuminate her, even if each one she passed—or those who passed her—took the time to call out a polite greeting.

Rounding the bend in the road just yards away from her destination, she realized that the informal caravan was headed to the Hayak farm, too. Her curiosity perked up a notch.

When she pulled up outside the Hayak barn, she noticed some men setting up a number of tables. Chattering women swarmed around them, covering the tables with colorful cloths. Still curious, Amelia spied other ladies bearing large black pots that they then *thunk*ed on the tables.

Could this gathering be a party of some sort? At dawn?

Catching sight of Michael talking with five other men, Amelia overcame her natural reserve when in crowds, and approached. As she reached Michael's side, she heard him say, "You really didn't have to do this."

"We know," responded a denim-overalled, middle-aged man.

The others in the circle nodded enthusiastically. "We wanted to help," said a tall, balding fellow.

"After all," called a woman passing by, "you're now all alone with that little girl of yours. You haven't the time or the opportunity to bring in the wheat. It would be a sin to let the crop go to waste."

"Pshaw, Lucretia Ziegler!" countered a bearded giant with steel-gray eyes. "All you want is to gossip with the other womenfolk!"

The men laughed heartily. The women at the tables glowered in response. The accused gossip chuckled good-naturedly, but didn't deny the charge.

A commotion from the road caught Amelia's attention, and she watched an odd piece of farm machinery come up the drive.

"The combine's here!" she heard from someone close.

The men surrounded the contraption, then headed down

the pathway to the golden field behind the house. Amelia stood watching, uncertain what to do next.

"'Melia!"

She sighed in relief. "Morning, munchkin," she called, spreading her arms wide. With the ease of familiarity, Katie homed in on the embrace. Amelia smiled, savoring the warmth of the little body.

"'Melia, Katie hung'y!"

"Predictably," she answered.

"Huh?"

"Never mind," Amelia murmured as two women approached. A bit uncertainly, she added, "Hello."

From off to Amelia's right, and drowning out the women's greetings, Pansy Pritchard waved and hollered, "Yoo-hoo, Amelia!"

To her relief, Amelia counted her entire contingent of "angels" on the approach. At least she'd learn who the strangers were without having to go into further recitals of the amnesia explanation. Pansy would have the feminine army marching to her orders in no time, and, keeping a sharp ear, Amelia could learn the names of those troops she didn't yet know.

Before Amelia knew quite what was happening, the women split into two groups. One went in through the front of the house, armed with pails, brooms, cloths, and feather dusters. The other company made a beeline for the kitchen, and in no time the scent of well-seasoned food mingled with that of lemon oil and yellow soap.

Following Pansy's orders, Amelia fluttered between groups, ferrying messages and supplies as needed.

Hours later, exhausted in the very best of ways—satisfied in a job well done—Amelia stole a private moment on the back porch. In silent admiration, she watched the men wield the combine to gather the grain. She didn't notice Pansy's arrival until the drill sergeant sat next to her on the top porch step and announced, "We came to help."

"I can tell! Thank you, Pansy. It's very kind of everyone."

With a chiding glare, Pansy lightly slapped Amelia's hand. "Well, what do you expect, child? We're neighbors."

Not knowing what to say, Amelia nodded and made an assenting sound.

Pansy needed no more encouragement. "Poor boy's been working himself to an early grave these past two years. Why, with his determination to find a cure for Christina's ills, he worked night and day. You know that."

No, I don't, Amelia thought, *but I'm glad you told me.*

"And you, too," Pansy added. "You've managed to sew more than ever while mothering that baby of his."

Amelia's gaze flew straight to where Katie played with two other, slightly older little girls. "She's a joy, Pansy."

"When she's not making mischief," the older woman countered, a twinkle in her eyes.

Amelia chuckled. "True."

Then the expression on Pansy's face changed. The light in her eyes went from humorous to piercing, as if trying to discern Amelia's most intimate thoughts. Meeting that sharp stare, she began to tense. She didn't know exactly why or how she knew, but she was certain Pansy's chat had a point to it. And it wasn't one Amelia was going to appreciate.

With a pat to Amelia's shoulder, Pansy continued, clearly determined to have her say. "You've given up two of the best years of your life, child. For what? Why, to live another woman's life."

Amelia gasped. *If you only knew the half of it!*

"And what did you get out of it?"

At a loss, Amelia shrugged.

Pansy wriggled her ample rear, settling more comfortably on the porch step. "I'll tell you what. Nothing! Nothing but a lot of coming heartbreak, child. You love that little girl. And she loves you. But what's going to happen when Michael marries himself a new wife?"

Sudden discomfort shot through Amelia's heart. She found she couldn't take another breath. Was the thought of someone else raising Katie the source of her anxiety? Or was it the thought of Michael remarried that she didn't like?

Amelia refused to examine her feelings too closely.

Pansy nodded with satisfaction. "Think on that a bit," she urged Amelia, coming into the fullness of her role. "What'll you do when another woman has the right to hug that child, to scold her, to teach her, on account that her papa can't keep house and farm all alone?"

Amelia remembered the words of the tour guide. Wendy had said that Michael raised his daughter while running the farm alone. She clung to that memory, seeking comfort in it, trying not to think of the possibility Pansy described. "Oh, that might not happen."

"Horsefeathers, child! Michael's a young, healthy man. If not because of the amount of work, sooner or later he's going to want himself a woman. Why shouldn't he get one who'll do for both him *and* Katie?"

Amelia sighed. Pansy had arrived at her point, and Amelia didn't want to hear any more. "That's none of my business—"

Pansy flung her arms up in frustration. She snorted. "That's what I'm trying to tell you, child! *Make* it your business. Why shouldn't you be the one he marries? Why shouldn't you continue to raise Katie? After all, Michael's not homely to look at, and he's a fine provider. Sober, too."

Homely? Not likely, Amelia thought as the image of a naked, well-muscled male chest rushed into her thoughts. "Good Lord, Pansy Pritchard!" she exclaimed, dismayed when her companion narrowed her eyes, gauging the flush that heated Amelia's cheeks. "Where did you come up with this? Michael's wife isn't yet cold in the ground, and you're marrying him off! And to me, at that."

"Why not?" Pansy retorted, as persistent as a telemarketer. "He needs a mother for Katie, and he needs her straightaway," she continued, counting off the particulars on a sturdy thumb and index finger. "He needs a body to clean and cook and do around the house, and he needs her straightaway, too." Up went the middle and ring fingers. Taking a shoulder-lifting breath and snapping her pinkie to attention, Pansy launched her final round. "As for Michael, after two years when his wife couldn't be his wife—if you get my meaning"—*Oh, did she ever!*—"I'd wager anything he needs a woman straightaway!"

Amelia's jaw dropped. Her skin grew hotter than she figured Hades could be, and despite her efforts to avoid them, the moments in the barn returned to her memory, as strong, arousing, and exquisite as they'd been to live through.

Pansy had Michael's number, all right!

But had that been what prompted his caresses? Had it only happened as a result of two years of repressed physical need? Would any other woman have been held, touched, kissed the same?

Amelia didn't like that possibility one bit. So before she got herself into further trouble, she frowned at her companion. "*That's* even less my business than who Michael marries."

Pansy waggled a finger under Amelia's nose. "Amelia Baldwin, how many times am I going to have to tell you this? You must make it your business. Or you're going to lose that heart of yours real soon."

Amelia couldn't refute that sentiment. "Oh, I can always love Katie, even after Michael remarries."

Pansy stood and smacked solid palms on Gibraltar-like hips. "I never reckoned you to be so dense. I don't know the woman who spends two whole years caring for a man, his child, and his home without feeling something more than Christian charity." This last was offered with a furtive glance in all directions. "Wouldn't want anyone else to hear what I'm telling you, you know."

Horror pushed Amelia to her feet, hoping to bring the uncomfortable tête-à-tête to an immediate end. "Good grief, no!"

But Pansy wouldn't be put off. "Grief? You both can

grieve Christina together. While raising that baby, and however many more the good Lord gives you."

Amelia couldn't bear a second longer of such talk. "Hush, Pansy," she hissed, standing. "You shouldn't talk like that. Besides, I have to . . . ah . . . oh, yes! I left Katie's nightgown from yesterday soaking. I'd better get it washed. She's going to need it soon."

With that Amelia hurried off, trying to escape the images Pansy's well-meaning, thought-provoking conversation had set loose in her head.

"Sometimes," Pansy murmured as she watched the younger woman scurry away, "a body's got to do it all herself." With a decisive nod, she turned. Catching sight of the very person who could best help her campaign, she marched off in hot pursuit. "Oh, Herbert! Herbert Weidel, come here this very instant! I have something for you to do."

As the sun began to set, Michael knew no words to express his gratitude to all the neighbors who'd so generously given up a day on their own farms to come and make sure his was taken care of. Such generosity of spirit humbled him, made him proud to be part of the community that took such good care of its members.

After shaking many hands, and repeating what he felt were inadequate thanks, he counted only two more rigs waiting by the barn. One was Amelia's buckboard. The other looked like Herbert Weidel's buggy. Michael wondered where the old busy-body was, and what he was up to.

He didn't have long to wonder. "Michael!"

"What are you doing in the barn, Herbert?"

"Why, I'm a-waitin' on ya, boy! Come on over, there's some man-ta-man you an' me gotta do."

Michael crossed the distance with slow, wary steps. What could Herbert want to talk to him about?

Entering the darkened interior of the barn, Michael paused momentarily to let his eyes adjust. Then he saw

Herbert making himself at home on a hay bale nearby. He joined the older man, and watched him chew on a piece of straw. When Herbert didn't proceed with the chat he'd suggested, Michael asked, "What's this all about?"

"'Bout you, boy. You an' that purty liddle Baldwin gal."

Icy dread fisted into Michael's gut. *God in Heaven, did everyone know of his shame?*

After a breath for courage, he asked, "What do you mean, me and Miss Baldwin?"

"Why, son," answered Herbert, gesturing expansively, "she's been more wife to ya than that there sickly wife o' yourn ever wuz."

Was that what the gossip-mill in town was saying about Amelia? Michael's anger began to simmer. "I don't think so," he said in a deadly, unshakable voice.

Herbert's eyes widened. He gulped and brought his hands defensively close to his face. "That's just it, boy! Yore not gittin' the best part!"

Michael's stomach plunged toe-ward and his anger reached a boil. "Herbert . . ." he said with menace.

Herbert's hands stayed put, but his words continued to march down the same path. "See here, boy! She's cleanin' an' cookin' an' washin'. She's raisin' yore youngun, an' doin' it right, too. But it ain't natcheral! Y'ain't had a woman fer two years or more!"

Embarrassment joined his steaming rage. "Whose business is that but mine?"

"None, boy! But everyone'z worried 'bout ya now. Christina's gone, an' she ain't comin' back, ya know?"

"Better than anyone," he bit off.

Herbert nudged Michael's tense shoulder with his own bony one. "Yore a *man,* ain't ya?"

Michael chuckled grimly. "Last time I checked."

"See? A man needs a woman. Fer his private needs. *You* know."

Michael set his jaw. "It's too soon to think on that, Herbert. Christina's only been dead a few days."

"But y'ain't dead, an' yore Katie ain't neither, an' some fast-talkin', smooth-movin' sharpie could snap up that purty liddle Baldwin girl what's been doin' fer ya."

That had occurred to Michael, and he'd hoped it would come to pass, effectively eliminating temptation. But now that Herbert put the notion into words, a sick feeling filled Michael's middle, and the thought of another man's lips where his had been just yesterday curdled his innards. Keeping his feelings from betraying him to Herbert's sharp eyes was one of the hardest things Michael had ever been called to do.

"She's unmarried," he offered. Then he waited until Herbert met his gaze. "And uncompromised."

"I know that! But there's allus some what's not got much upstairs, if ya follow me."

"None who know me or Miss Baldwin."

"Mebbe. Mebbe not." Herbert crossed his arms across his chest, a bullheaded look on his homely face. "Whilst Christina wuz livin', boy, it were all right fer Miz Baldwin to come and do fer ya. But now, there ain't no Christina. An' Miz Baldwin's still comin' and doin'. There's some what's askin' what all she's *really* doin' fer ya." This last was said with what Michael knew was supposed to be Herbert's man-of-the-world look, but what looked more to him like a gossip fishing for a juicy new catch.

His anger blew its lid. "That's ridiculous! I'd be very careful if I were one of those who are wondering. I won't stand for them maligning Ame—Miss Baldwin."

A triumphant gleam blazed in Herbert's eyes. "So what ya gonna do 'bout it, boy?"

"Why—I . . . well . . . ah—"

"'Zacktly!" exclaimed the older man with a sharp jab to Michael's chest. "Only one thing ta do, boy. Marry 'er up! That way there won't be no gossip, an' yore bed will be nice and hot nights."

The image Herbert's words brought to Michael's mind got his body reacting. Tightening. Readying itself. *Amelia in his bed.* God knew how many times the very thought had destroyed his every chance of sleep.

"I'm not ready to marry," he said, trying to diffuse his longing. "I'm mourning my wife."

"Seems ta me, boy, ye've been mournin' fer more'n two years. When you gonna allow as Christina wuz no wife fer a long time?"

But that's just it, his conscience pointed out, *Christina was your wife, and you had no right to covet her friend. You had no right to touch—*

"In God's and man's eyes," he ground out, trying to silence that accusatory voice, trying perhaps too late to honor his vows, "Christina was my wife until that morning—"

"But she ain't here no more," cut in Herbert, pigheaded. "An' you an' Katie an' Miz Baldwin are."

"It's too soon to think like that."

"You gonna wait till some smarter fella gets 'er ta his bed?"

The thought again did something foul to his insides. Michael stood, paced, refusing to hear any more that would encourage his most secret desires. "It's too soon."

"Tell me this, boy. Duz Katie need a mama?"

A quiet "Yes" slipped from his lips.

"Kin ya run this farm all by yerself?"

Silence. Then honestly, reluctantly, "No."

"An' you, boy, don'cha need yerself a woman? A mate?" Herbert waited for Michael's answer. When he realized it wasn't coming, he tried again. "A lover in yer bed?"

Michael whirled around and growled, "That's my business, and mine alone, Herbert. I appreciate your concern, but you needn't worry. Katie and I will be fine. And so will Ame—Miss Baldwin, so long as everyone in town has the decency to remember she's a good, moral woman. She's done absolutely nothing wrong. And you can tell them that."

Except maybe miss her best friend's funeral.

But that was more your fault than hers, countered his damning conscience. He spat out a curse.

Herbert flinched, frowned, then stood.

Michael paused and, spotting resignation on Herbert's homely features, forced his shoulders to relax. "Now, Herbert, it's time for me to see to my daughter. If you'd be so kind as to excuse me, I shall go relieve Miss Baldwin in her charitable efforts."

Without waiting for a response, Michael turned and headed toward the house. When he reached the porch, he heard Herbert's horse clop down the drive. A second's relief was welcome. But then he heard Amelia laugh. Katie joined her giggle to the richer, womanly sound.

Something stirred in Michael's heart. God in Heaven, they sounded so good. It felt so natural to come home to them.

Could Herbert possibly be right? Could something that had been so wrong only a short while ago be right today?

Michael didn't dare search his heart for the reply.

"Katie's already fed and tucked into bed," Amelia called when he entered the house after an hour of fortitude-bolstering.

He closed the front door and ambled back toward the kitchen. With a sniff, he again caught the acrid stench of scorched food. He frowned. "What did you feed her?"

"There was so much left from the noonday meal that I just warmed up a pot of stew. There's plenty for your supper."

Coming to a stop in the doorway, Michael absorbed the sight of the woman at the sink. She looked exactly right where she stood. "Smells like you did more than just warm it up!"

With a ferocious whirl, Amelia aimed a glare his way. "I told you I can't cook, didn't I?"

"But you've been cooking here for two years now," he

argued, feeling the now-familiar irritation he experienced each time she brought up her unlikely amnesia.

She closed her eyes, clenched her fists, bit down hard on her bottom jaw. Then he heard her count under her breath. When she reached ten, she opened those glorious emerald eyes of hers and sent reproach his way. "I'm not going to argue this again." Quickly, she untied the strings of the apron she wore, slipped it off over her head, and dropped it onto the ladder-back of one of the kitchen chairs.

"I'll be leaving now," she said, opening the back door. "Oh, before I forget. Katie gathered some wildflowers for me while she played with two little friends. I filled a beautiful crystal vase with water and put them in it, not knowing where you might keep something less valuable to hold what are mostly weeds. Please don't throw them away."

Michael glanced toward the table. In the center of the scarred wooden top she'd spread a cut-work napkin his grandmother had embroidered when his mother was a child. On top of the delicate piece, she'd placed the vase his grandfather had given his bride on their wedding day. By contrast, the droopy blossoms were even more unsightly than they would have seemed outdoors.

Michael smiled, touched by her thoughtfulness. "That's very kind of you, Amelia."

She lifted a shoulder. Her cheeks colored. "Katie picked them for me. They mean a lot."

He nodded. "I understand." Approaching the table, he picked up the vase. "You see this?"

"Of course," she answered, leaning back against the partially opened door. "Who could fail to notice something so perfect?"

"It is, isn't it?"

When she nodded, her black hair caught the golden lamplight, making the silky strands seem fluid and sleek. Michael felt an urge to touch and see if it felt as soft as it looked.

"Magnificent," she said, echoing his thoughts, albeit not

about the same thing at all. "It sparkles and shines, and rainbows dance over each cut."

Michael nodded with satisfaction and a large measure of pride. "My grandfather made it."

Amelia's eyes widened. "Really? What a rare talent he had."

"Indeed. But do you know what meant the most to my grandmother?"

A quizzical look crossed her face. "No, what?"

He came to stand at her side. Once there, he caught a whiff of honeysuckle, the fragrance he associated with Amelia. Breathing deeper, filling his senses with her essence, he leaned close to show her the inscription at the bottom of the vase. "See the date there?"

"Mm-hmm."

"He cut it in on their wedding day. This was his gift to his bride."

Amelia's green gaze met his, her eyes holding a wealth of warmth, a bounty of tenderness. "What a fortunate woman she was," she whispered, never letting her eyes stray from his.

For a moment, Michael couldn't speak. It was all he could do to keep from reaching out for her warmth, her tenderness—for the woman who understood.

"They both were," he answered in a hushed tone.

Silence descended. It grew thick and charged, and Michael swore he was drowning in a pool of his own longing. But he wasn't alone, he realized. For shining in the green light of Amelia's eyes was the same sort of want, the same sort of need he felt deep inside. With his free hand he reached out and caught a curling wisp of the black hair he'd wanted to test only moments ago. Soft as a whisper and warm as Amelia's gaze, the thin strand enticed him to reach for the wealth she'd tied into a knot at the back of her head.

Hairpins slipped out, aided by his curious fingers. Michael caught his breath when the rich waves unraveled in his palm. The mass was warm and fragrant, releasing even more of her special, honeysuckle scent.

Closing her eyes, she caught her bottom lip between her teeth. Although he knew he shouldn't, he was about to do what he'd wanted to do again since that heated moment in the barn. He realized it was what she wanted the moment her teeth released her plump lower lip. He'd soothe the marks they'd left, just as he longed to soothe the need raging within. He brought his mouth closer.

"Papa?"

Michael leaped back. His heart raced, spurred by being caught again in a compromising position. Amelia blinked owlishly, looking completely at a loss, disoriented.

Michael knew a moment of satisfaction. If nothing else, he'd learned that he affected her as much as she affected him.

"Papa, Katie wan' nigh-night kiss."

Answering the sleepy mumble, Michael said, "Coming, angel." He took two steps back, never taking his gaze from Amelia's. Neither did she break that tenuous touch. When the back of his legs hit the kitchen table, he set the vase back down. "It's late," he said. "You'd better be on your way."

Her cheeks pinkened, and her eyes closed. She murmured what sounded like agreement. Then with a kiss and a wave toward Katie, she opened the door and slipped out into the night.

Suddenly Michael felt as if the fire had died in the stove. As if the flame had blown out in the lamp. As if life had left his home.

Amelia was gone.

Loneliness arrived. Michael wondered how he would make it through yet another empty night.

Chapter 8

ON THE PORCH steps at the farm, Amelia paused, amazed by how quickly she'd risen, dressed, and set off for the Hayak home. Anticipation had fueled her actions in spite of her allergy to mornings. As much as she liked the house the "angels" had deemed hers, she preferred the warmth of Katie's company and the possibility of stealing glimpses of Michael as he worked the farm.

She refused to examine her reasons for wanting to keep Michael within eyeball range.

As she let herself in the front door, Amelia heard the bell-like ring of Katie's laughter mingling with the rich rumble of Michael's own. Something deep inside, disturbingly close to her heart, glowed warm, setting off an urge to run to their side, to take part in their joy. She dropped the bundle of sewing she had brought next to the parlor sofa, and hurried to find father and daughter.

At the kitchen doorway, Amelia caught her breath. Before her stood the embodiment of her most treasured dreams. Michael, naked to the waist, held Katie in his arms and rubbed his stubbled cheeks against hers. "Fuddy,

fuddy, fuddy," she cried, patting his face, his chest, his head.

"Papa's a fuzzy bear, you say?"

More chortles. "Yeth!"

Michael buried his face in Katie's neck, growing silent, tightly embracing his daughter. Amelia heard him whisper, "Papa's a lucky man to have you."

"Lub you, Papa."

"Oh, Katie," he answered, "I love you, too."

Amelia's eyes filled with tears. She would have given anything for the right to join them, to put her arms around Katie and link fingers with a man like Michael. A man who showed his love, who confessed it freely. More than ever she felt alone, unloved, unwanted, the outsider. She hadn't needed to travel back in time to feel that way.

Was she unlovable? Was she cursed by some inborn, fatal flaw? A sob shuddered through her, and a tear ran down her cheek. It wasn't too much to ask, was it? A family of her own? Someone to love? Someone to love her?

Despite Christina's wasting illness and precipitated death, Amelia considered her a very lucky woman. Michael had obviously loved her. He'd cared for her, sought the best medical attention, and he mourned her—had probably done so for the better part of her illness.

Then there was Katie. The child had clearly loved her mother. In fact, the few times Amelia had managed to wheedle her into taking a nap, she had cried out in her slumber for her mama. Each time, Amelia had run to her side, held her in her arms, offered comfort. But she'd known that wasn't what the little girl really needed. Katie needed a mother.

Amelia would give anything to be Katie's mother.

A sob escaped her lips, and Michael turned around. Their eyes met over Katie's rumpled hair. Remembering the day before yesterday—the best moments she'd ever lived—Amelia's cheeks warmed. That kiss in the barn had seared an indelible memory into her heart.

But it wasn't just the kiss she remembered. There was his family pride, his respect for the love between his grandparents, the way Michael treasured the unique gift his grandfather had given his bride. Amelia suspected that when Michael loved, he loved like that other man—totally, respecting his mate, cherishing her forever. Christina Hayak had been a very, very lucky woman.

Amelia would prefer a shortened life if, during that time, she could know Michael's kind of love.

Katie squirmed in her father's hold. "'Melia!" she cried, then, turning to Michael, she urged, "Down! Katie want down!"

When Michael closed his eyes, Amelia felt strangely cold, empty once again. She recognized then the danger Michael Hayak posed. It wasn't just to his daughter that Amelia could lose her heart; the man was likely to walk off with what Katie left of that lonely, yearning part of her.

He turned, offering her another excellent view of his powerful build. Amelia could easily see why Katie called him a fuzzy bear. His waving dark hair, his unshaven face, and his chest, covered with a liberal smattering of dark, curly hair, all worked to give him a very earthy look. Amelia gulped, knowing she'd lost the ability to speak.

He hadn't. "Good morning, Amelia," he said in his rumbly voice. "I'm glad you're here, since I must take the wheat to the mill this morning. I can't take Katie with me and I can't very well leave her alone, either."

Amelia took a deep breath, even though her eyes refused to quit admiring that chest, those shoulders, those muscular arms. It seemed that the peaceful, intimate moments of last night were bearing fruit. Michael looked at ease, more so than he had appeared when they'd first met. Just now, he hadn't addressed her with his usual anger, and his gaze was friendly, not the outraged glare she'd begun to think was all he could muster.

Despite the mental meltdown caused by her shameless

ogling, she managed to string some words together. "Have
you eaten yet?" she asked, her voice low.

Michael shook his head. "Can you put something together quickly? I could do with breakfast."

For a moment, Amelia wished she could offer him the
sort of meal a working man needed. But considering her
lack of culinary talents, oatmeal was likely to be Michael's
morning fare. "Let's see what I can find," she said, not
ready to bring up contentious topics like her alleged amnesia. "Would you like some coffee or tea?"

"Coffee, and plenty of it," he answered, donning a heavy
flannel shirt.

Half of Amelia bemoaned the covering of that outstand-
ing chest and shoulders; her other half breathed a sigh of
relief. She hadn't known how long she could remain ex-
posed to his blatant masculinity without reaching out,
maybe even touching him accidentally-on-purpose.

Hoping he hadn't noticed her sensual scrutiny, she
pasted on a bright smile. "Coffee it is," she said, then took
off to make the one thing she excelled at.

The back door slapped into place as Michael went out to
the barn. He'd be tending to the animals, and with his years
of experience, Amelia knew he'd be back before long. She
had to get moving if she wanted to have food ready for his
return. "Would you like to help me, Katie? We need to
make breakfast for your papa."

Bright blue eyes sparkled. "Yeth! Katie holp."

From the linen chest, Amelia withdrew napkins and
passed them to her helper. "Put one where your papa sits
and another one where you do."

"And you?"

Intent on exploring the contents of the icebox, Amelia
glanced back at the child and smiled. "Thank you. You can
put one out for me, too." She returned to her rummaging.

Yesterday's bounty yielded a thick slice of ham and half
a jar of peach preserves. With the bread she'd saved, it

would make a fine meal. Coffee was the only other necessity.

Moments later, she had the ham warming in a cast-iron skillet. After slicing thick slabs of bread from the leftover loaf, she placed them around the jar of spiced peaches in a small basket she set on the table.

"All done," chimed the child.

Amelia scrambled to find another "task" for her helper before Katie took advantage of her distraction to find more intriguing exploits. "Spoons!" she exclaimed, and offered her three.

Carefully measuring the coffee grounds and water into the coffeepot, Amelia put it on a hot burner and waited for the beverage to brew. Before long, the fragrance of morning filled the air.

Heavy footsteps climbed the back stairs, then Michael entered the kitchen, bringing with him the fresh autumn air. "Smells good," he said, heading for the enameled sink.

Joy fizzed up inside her. Unnecessarily, since she'd hardly done more than warm the ham, slice the bread, and set a pot of coffee to boil. But it wasn't the actual achievement that pleased her, it was the approval in Michael's deep voice that warmed her insides, made her proud of her efforts.

"It's ready," she said, sliding the warm meat onto a platter. "We had plenty of ham left from yesterday, and Pansy insisted on leaving these peach preserves for you. I think they'll be perfect with the bread."

She cursed *herself* for a fool and *him* for being such a brain-scrambling distraction. She sounded like an idiot, babbling about food. Michael didn't need her to point out every detail of the meal—he could see it, smell it, eat it for himself. And it wasn't as if she'd really prepared it.

But he sent her a smile as he washed his hands, a genuine expression of pleasure. Amelia saved its memory for a grouchy day. Who knew when—if ever—she'd see another grin on his face. This was, after all, only their second amiable exchange.

When he'd dried his hands and Amelia had settled Katie on her chair, Michael offered thanks for their food. The feelings roused by the simple action of sharing a meal caught Amelia by surprise. At the foster homes where she'd grown up, mealtimes were often rushed, the various members of the family running to their individual activities. More often than not, Amelia had found herself eating alone.

Today she experienced her first family meal, and the yearning inside her expanded, growing so strong that the lump in her throat threatened to choke her. She set down her fork and watched her companions enjoy their food.

"You're not hungry?" Michael asked after a bit.

"Not really. Besides, watching Katie is a full-time job."

Michael chuckled as she wiped a dribble of peach juice from the toddler's chin, but never slowed his consumption of food.

"'S good," the imp murmured, tilting her head as she tried to dodge the swabbing of Amelia's napkin.

Draining his coffee cup, Michael dropped his napkin by his empty plate, then pushed his chair back. "*Very* good, Katie. But I'd best be on my way. The mill won't wait for me."

"Will you be back at noon?" Amelia asked.

"Can't be sure. I will be back for supper, though."

"I'll have it waiting."

Another friendly smile accompanied by a look that lingered came Amelia's way, but she didn't dare believe the message she thought she saw in his brilliant blue gaze.

With reluctance, or so it seemed to her, Michael left the kitchen, heading for the front of the house. "I'll be hungry," he called back.

Amelia followed him without comment. He'd said he'd be hungry. She had offered him another meal. Did she have enough leftovers to satisfy him? She knew she couldn't get away with heating up the bounty of their neighbors' much longer—they'd eventually run out. But, since she never wanted to see anger and accusation in his gaze again, she had to find a way to make that promised meal.

Placing his hat on his waving brown hair, he opened the door. Katie's footsteps came charging from behind Amelia. "Papa!" she cried. "Kiss Katie bye-bye!"

Michael bent a knee and opened his arms wide. Katie burrowed into the broad chest, smacking kisses everywhere she reached. Michael nuzzled her neck. The child giggled. Then he hugged her tight and kissed her cheek. As he held her close, he glanced at Amelia.

Tears had formed again, and she knew he saw them when his gaze turned quizzical. She waved his concern away. "Just being silly," she murmured.

He shrugged, then set Katie aside. "I'll be no later than sunset."

Amelia nodded.

Katie offered, "Yeth!"

Then he was gone.

Amelia had only part of a day to figure out how she was going to feed the man, especially since she didn't cook today any better than she had yesterday or the day before. And she still had Katie to keep out of trouble, and the impossible mountain of sewing still loomed over her. Beyond all that, she didn't want to make a fool of herself again. In his eyes.

Michael had the devil of a time that day. His distraction was such that he only listened halfheartedly to the others waiting for their grain to be processed at the mill in town, all friends, all bent on conversation. His mind seemed fixed on only one thing—Amelia Baldwin, and how natural it felt to have her running his home again.

After he milked the cows that morning, he'd been greeted in the kitchen by the scents of sizzling ham and

percolating coffee. Amelia had then served the food with
no more of her lame excuses about forgotten abilities.

He had to admit she'd been adamant about not knowing
anything whatsoever. Between her earnest expression and
her fierce defense of her actions, one might think Amelia
did suffer from amnesia.

Suddenly it occurred to Michael that he hadn't considered that possibility. Could the knock on her head really
make her forget *everything?* Christina, Katie, himself . . .
and the kiss?

No. Of course not. That was absolutely preposterous.

Her recent response to his touch showed a distinct improvement in her attitude toward him. Had she gotten over
her revulsion to his touch? That agitation he figured she
must have felt when he'd overstepped the bounds of decency shortly before Christina died.

He hoped so. After all, she hadn't run away in horror
after his unplanned caresses just two days ago. It was
difficult enough for him to bear the guilt of his adulterous desires during his wife's final moments, and the
knowledge that his sinfulness had deprived Christina of
the presence of her friend at the end. A heavy burden indeed.

He certainly didn't want his lust to deprive Katie of
Amelia's company. The child seemed to thrive in the
woman's care.

Once done transacting business and headed home,
Michael wondered what would greet him there. It didn't
take long to find out.

As he approached the house after seeing to his horses'
comfort, Michael heard two feminine voices raised in
song. Katie would yell out a word, and Amelia would
respond, singing a definition of the word his daughter
had yelled. It was a cheerful song, sprightly. Something about a doe being a female deer, and a ray a drop
of golden sun.

The joy in their voices beckoned, leading him closer. He

took the back steps two at a time and opened the door quietly, wanting to watch them unobserved, at least for a moment.

Katie stood at one end of the rectangular kitchen table, a long-handled wooden spoon in each hand, gleefully conducting Amelia's song. When the sprite yelled out "Far!" she punctuated the word with a rousing slap to the tabletop. Amelia's response, "A long, long way to run," was greeted by giggles and more grandiose gestures.

"Sew!" sang Katie.

Amelia turned, grinned at the child, then responded, "A needle pulling thread . . ."

As she turned, Michael forgot the presence of his daughter in the cozy kitchen. He only saw Amelia, her smile. He only heard her sweet voice carrying the happy tune. He leaned back against the door, crossed arms and ankles, and allowed himself the freedom to admire the object of his interest.

Amelia wore her black hair pulled into a fat knot atop her head, but by now tendrils had escaped the bounds of her hairpins. Wisps curled at the nape of her neck, soft and feminine. When she turned sideways to look at Katie, Michael saw more of the curly locks at her temples and around the delicate shell of an ear. Unbidden, the thought of slipping a finger through the ringlets made him take a step forward.

Reason made him step back again. He hoped his movement hadn't alerted her to his presence. He enjoyed the picture they made too much.

When Amelia took a ladle from its hook in the wall near the stove, he watched her stretch, the motion emphasizing her lack of height. Although her stature was meager, little else about her figure could be labeled that. As she stirred something in a large kettle, her hips swayed from side to side with her efforts. Her slender waist contrasted perfectly with the roundness of those hips.

Michael nearly groaned out loud as his body responded.

Although he managed to swallow the sound, Amelia must have sensed his presence, since she spun toward him, her eyes wide with surprise.

"Oh! I didn't realize you were back."

Pushing away from the door, he went to the table, ruffled Katie's curls, and dropped into one of the chairs. "Just—" He stopped himself, coughed to clear the thickness in his throat, then tried again. "I just got here. Don't mind me, go on as you were. The two of you sound mighty fine."

Amelia's cheeks reddened, then she giggled—something he'd never before heard her do. She sounded nervous. "It's nothing more than a silly children's song," she said.

"Katie liked it," he countered. "Even though I don't recognize the tune."

Emerald eyes opened wider, and Michael thought he saw a glimmer of fear. That was certainly odd. "Ah . . . it's . . . a song from when I was little," she stammered out, surprising Michael again, since Amelia Baldwin was rarely at a loss for words. He decided, however, not to comment on the apparent return of a single memory.

Wanting a dry change of clothes, Michael stood. "You have a nice singing voice," he said. "I'm going upstairs to change. It's been raining all day."

"Bring me your wet things and— Michael Hayak! You stop right there this very instant. Just look at those boots! Where do you think you're tracking all that mud and muck?"

Sheepishly, Michael glanced floorward. She was right. His boots were a disgrace. "Sorry."

"Hmph!"

Amelia's sniff carried more reproof than most women's diatribes. Michael sat and unlaced his right boot. The smart flip of her plum-colored skirt caught his eye as he undid the left. He followed the graceful line of the garment all the way up and came to a full, pulse-stopping halt.

Bending at the waist, Amelia checked something in the oven. Her rich-colored skirt poured from her curvy, heart-shaped posterior, over surprisingly long legs considering her height, and down to only inches above shapely ankles. Realizing she was barefoot, Michael noted how delicate her feet were. He could palm one dainty heel, sole, and five toes in each hand.

Although he knew he shouldn't, he indulged in an appraisal of her outthrust bottom. "Mmmm," he murmured appreciatively. His body responded accordingly.

Amelia's behind was generous enough to fill his hands. Michael didn't have to actually do the measuring to know that, but what a pleasure it would be! Those womanly curves would give a man plenty to hold on to in the dark—

She whirled and caught him staring.

He flushed and dropped a boot on his unshod toes. He leaped up, yowling in pain.

She narrowed her gaze, questioning his behavior.

"I'm going," he said, holding his hands out defensively.

"Hmph!"

Such eloquence in a mere sniff, he thought, trying but failing to hold back a very masculine grin. His body still thrummed with arousal. He'd enjoyed his study of Amelia's figure. She'd caught him in the act, and clearly knew he'd relished every second of it. What's more, that sniff had been followed by the *clunk* of her ladle on the floor, telling him his perusal had affected her, too.

Michael left the kitchen for his room and dry clothes, and found himself whistling snippets of the song Amelia and Katie had sung.

A short while later, when they were well into yesterday's roast chicken, boiled potatoes, and buttered carrots, Michael drank the last of the water in his glass.

Immediately Amelia jumped up. "Let me fill the pitcher again. I'm thirsty, too."

She scurried to the sink, worked the pump handle, and filled the container to the brim. Dodging Michael's bewildered gaze, she hurried back to the table but in her rush spilled some of the water down her white cotton blouse. "Oh, no!" she cried out, clearly flustered.

Michael followed the path of the water and groaned. The vision before him killed what was left of his earlier hunger.

For food.

The liquid drenched Amelia's garment, rendering it sheer, virtually transparent. And it clung. Like a lover, the fabric molded Amelia's breasts, accentuating their fullness. Round and firm, her flesh filled her undergarment and blouse, revealing rose-toned shadows at the tips. Michael's desire for Amelia grew, and his body hardened with pent-up need.

She was a beautiful woman, with a woman's warmth and a woman's softness. Michael had gone a long time without both. He feared his need had grown so that he wouldn't be able to bear it much longer, that he would no longer succeed at dousing his desire with the memory of his wife. Not even the memory of his betrayal of their marriage vows could stop his need.

He wanted Amelia so badly his teeth ached from clenching his jaws as he fought to silence his inappropriate passion.

She uttered another sound of distress. Spinning, she plopped the pitcher back on the table and said, "It's late. I have to go." Then she fled the kitchen as if a detachment of demons were nipping at her heels.

Guilt swamped Michael, effectively cooling his overheated flesh. He'd done it again. With his uncontrolled desire, he had chased Amelia from his side. And while he had no right to want her there, the reality was that he did.

"Where'd 'Melia go?" asked Katie.

Michael shuddered, shaking off the last of his sensual distraction, ashamed that his lust had scared Katie's source of tenderness away. Precisely what he'd feared would happen. His child was an innocent victim of her father's lack of discipline.

Again.

Hours later, after he'd put Katie in her bed, Michael sat on the parlor sofa, unable to sleep. Each time he closed his eyes, the image of Amelia, her breasts displayed by the clinging cloth, returned to his mind. His body invariably hardened, erotic visions playing in his thoughts.

Yes, he was a healthy man with all the physical needs a healthy man had. But his desire for his late wife's best friend was wrong, had been wrong from the start. Toward the end of Christina's life, he'd spent more time thinking of Amelia—trying to keep from thinking of her—than he'd spent with Christina. True, he'd done all he could for his wife—he'd enticed every doctor he found into coming to Winona. In the end, when there'd been nothing more to do but wait, he'd tried endlessly to make her final moments of life tolerable.

But Michael hadn't loved Christina, not in an all-encompassing way, not with hunger, desperation, passion. He'd loved her like a sister, and like he would a sister, he mourned her passing.

Still, Christina hadn't been his sister. She'd been his wife. He'd vowed before God and man to set aside all thought of other women, cleaving only to Christina, his wife. He'd been weak. When Christina hadn't risen after childbirth, hadn't recovered and returned to her previous vitality, Michael had again known loneliness, the very feeling he'd tried to escape by marrying his agreeable, congenial spouse at the outset.

It was then that he noticed Amelia Baldwin. How could he not? She'd taken to coming every morning to his house, cleaning, cooking, nursing Christina, loving

Katie, filling the void his wife's absence had created in
the normal running of the home. The comfort she'd
brought to their lives had allowed him to see her in a different light.

Amelia wasn't just the perhaps censurable seamstress to
the vaudevillians who passed through town. She was a
warm, caring woman, her energy, compassion, and desire
to help those in need eclipsing even her sewing and cooking talents, her ease at making his house a home again. Her
smile had brought a measure of sunshine into a place that
would soon know only the dark of impending death.

Michael had longed for that smile, the nearly palpable
touch of those shining green eyes, that lushly curved figure,
the mysterious richness of her glossy black hair.

He wanted her more now than he ever had.

A fiendish spirit perched on his shoulder and began to
feed dangerous thoughts to his hungering heart. Some he
couldn't even refute. It was fact that Amelia was unspo-
ken for. It was true, too, that he was newly widowed, in
effect, as unattached as Amelia herself. Although society
prescribed a period of mourning, Michael had in essence
been mourning the death of the Christina he'd married
from the moment ill health forced her into total bedrest.

Truth was—as Herbert had pointed out—Michael needed
a woman as much as Katie needed a mother. One look at
his lap confirmed that fact.

Amelia would eminently satisfy all their needs.

"Damn!" Why could he no longer stifle his physical
needs? Why couldn't he turn a deaf ear to the tempting sug-
gestions of the devil on his shoulder? Why could he no
longer ignore the hunger in his heart?

Because Amelia was free.

He was now free, too. Nothing tangible stood between
him and the woman he wanted.

Only his guilt.

And her refusal to disclose where she'd been those two
hellish days when he'd needed her.

Then, too, he couldn't forget her fictitious amnesia.

And he had to consider the impropriety of a scandalously stunted period of mourning.

This was turning into one Hell of a long, sleepless night.

Chapter 9

IT WAS A sin what a woman could do to a man's life.

Upon opening his scratchy eyes, Michael had nothing but curses for the one whose image had haunted his night. As he forced his frame to creak out of bed, urging each limb to come alive, his irritation with Amelia—she was, after all, the source of his perturbing dreams—grew to where he knew today would be a rotten day. He was cross, sore as a bear with a bee in its hide, tired and sleepy from his disturbed rest, and if truth be told, as hard as he'd instantly gone when he first spotted the dark tips of Amelia's breasts beneath her transparent blouse.

At that moment, it had taken every ounce of his strength to keep from reaching out, testing the firmness of her flesh, learning how responsive she might be to his touch. But Amelia had done nothing to encourage him—in fact, she left immediately after he began ogling. Just as she'd chosen to flee after his earliest, unexpected surrender to temptation. Now Michael was pretty damn near certain that her unusual jumpiness last night had come from her awareness of his sensual interest.

Again she'd fled.

He had to wonder if she would come back today. Would Amelia again desert Katie because of her father's unruly lust?

Amelia had never been the indecisive sort. She'd always known what she wanted and had gone for it, but this morning she ping-ponged back and forth between staying home and returning to the Hayak farm.

Yesterday had been a revelation. Not only had she realized the depth of her attraction to Michael, but she'd also caught an equal measure of interest in his blue eyes. She had no idea what to do about that passion looking for an excuse to happen.

She'd never indulged in free-wheeling romantic affairs. Heck, she'd probably been the last living adult virgin back in the 1990s! It hadn't been difficult to retain that distinction. She'd never felt the need to join her body to another's, to share the completion of emotion, desire, pleasure, with anyone else. At least, not with anyone she'd known then.

Now, however, her nerve endings, her thoughts, even the breaths she took seemed to propel her closer to Michael Hayak, the need to know him completely overtaking reason and logic.

She'd never considered herself a sensualist, but she couldn't deny the hunger she felt for Michael. She longed to touch him, hold him, feel his arms around her, to hear his heart beat when she pressed her cheek against his chest.

If it had only been a physical urge she felt, she might have been able to discount it. Her need to help him, to comfort him, to bring about more of those rare, dazzling smiles of his, bothered Amelia the most. She wanted to be at his side more than she wanted anything else.

There lay her problem. How long would she be able to do just that? To stay at his side, to know him as a partner, a friend, a lover? How much more time could she count on spending in 1900?

The irony of it all didn't escape her notice. Her other life had been filled with nothing but work and loneliness, yet she'd had all the time in the world, or so she'd thought. Then, the miracle. She'd woken up in 1900 and found a man she could all too easily fall in love with and a child she'd lost her heart to from the very start. Now, when she knew what she wanted, and it seemed attainable, she needed that precious time that had weighed so heavily upon her in her other life. She wanted forever with Michael and Katie.

How long would she have?

Should she pursue the goal of a family of her own even if at any given moment she could be ripped away from her loved ones? Could she stand to return to the future knowing she left everything that mattered in the past? Could she bear the knowledge of Katie's renewed misery and grief? Could she bear the thought of Michael damned to more mourning at her disappearance?

Choking back a sob, Amelia gave a shaky little laugh. How ridiculous! Here she was worrying about Michael's broken heart when she didn't even know if that heart was interested in her. Katie would indeed miss 'Melia, but did her father want more than just a baby-sitter and house-keeper? A convenient romp in a bed to scratch a physical itch?

In the end, that uncertainty made her mind up for her. She needed to know exactly what her time in 1900 held. She needed to know if she'd found the love she so desperately craved.

She had to know if Michael Hayak could ever love her.

Lost in her difficult thoughts, Amelia traveled the distance between town and the Hayak farm without noticing a thing but the cold. The morning chill made her huddle deeper into the coat she'd found in that other Amelia's wardrobe, and she was grateful for the warm wool fabric, the fur-trimmed hood, the generous cut that covered her to her boots.

That was all she noticed. Her mind refused to relinquish its grip on the possibilities before her. Her heart—senseless muscle—beat faster the closer she came to her destination. Much though she wanted to see Katie again, the child didn't make her pulse race. Michael did. Every time she thought of him, even his name, her heart pounded louder, harder.

Once at the farm, she unhitched her geriatric horse from her rickety wagon and led her into the barn, where Michael had prepared a stall for the deserving beast. The moment old Bess began to munch from the feed tray before her, Amelia flew from the barn, up the porch steps, and burst inside.

After removing the coat and hanging it on a brass hook by the door, she hurried to the kitchen, where she could hear Katie's sweet chatter. At the doorway, Amelia paused. As he had those other mornings, Michael stood at the kitchen sink, finishing his morning shave. The planes of his cheeks gleamed cleanly, and the cut of his jaw looked firm and square. As before, he'd dispensed with his shirt, and as before, Amelia's senses responded enthusiastically to all that male flesh displayed before her.

The man had a perfect body, large and muscular where it should be, lean and tight where it counted. He had no qualms about displaying it. At least, he seemed impervious to her scrutiny.

As she stood and stared, her pulse rose to an alarming rate, sending fire straight through her body. Her skin tingled, her breasts felt heavy, her nipples hardened. She felt the heat between her legs, she grew damp, and her sudden rush of need stunned her. This had never happened to her back in the sexually revolutionized 1990s.

She was so absorbed in admiring Michael's body and contemplating the sensations her body was experiencing, that she didn't notice Katie's approach until the child clasped her chubby arms around Amelia's navy-flannel-clad knees. " 'Melia. Katie hung'y!"

At the child's words, she blinked. Then she shivered. With a shaky grin, she picked up the little girl. "Why am I not surprised?" she murmured, her voice low and husky.

Michael started. Amelia glanced his way. She saw what looked like anger cloud his features. Uh-oh. Were they back at square one? What had changed since last night?

Then Katie patted Amelia's shoulders. Shrugging tiny shoulders, she held her hands out. "Dunno."

Amelia forced her attention from the father to the child. "You're *always* hungry, munchkin," she responded, sitting Katie in a chair. "Stay there while I make your break—"

"What did you just call her?" asked Michael, suspicion threading the words.

Heading for the stove, Amelia answered, "You know, munchkin, like in *The Wizard of Oz* . . ." Her words died off.

"No, Amelia, I do not know. What *is* a munchie . . . a munchkat . . . whatever!"

She'd done it again. She'd slipped a twentieth-century–ism into her conversation. Michael had no way of knowing what a munchkin was. If she remembered correctly, Dorothy and Toto's story was published right about now. Without turning around, and pretending great interest in the hot water in the stove reservoir, she tried to explain. "Ah . . . a munchkin is a character in a story I once read. They're tiny and cheerful and full of life."

"A munchkin, you say?"

"Yep. Munchkin."

"And Katie's one?"

"Absolutely."

"Yeth!" piped the munchkin in question. "Katie's a munkchin!"

Risking a glance over her shoulder, Amelia noted an easing of his features. Perhaps that had been enough. She really had to watch what she said. Many more slips like that and Michael's suspicions would give rise to more unanswerable questions.

He ran a hand through his tumbled hair, then waved vaguely. "Well . . . I need to finish here and see to the animals."

"I'll milk the cows," Amelia offered, hoping for a smile.

She got a sarcastic scoff. "You will?"

Amelia faced him. "Now that I know how to do it, I have no problem with milking the cows. Luther showed me."

Michael's blue glare narrowed. "Luther showed you how to milk the cows." At Amelia's nod, skepticism again twisted his features. "And he didn't think it absurd to teach you something you've been doing for years?"

So they were back to the amnesia thing. "No, Michael Hayak," she snapped back. "He found it perfectly understandable that a person who'd suffered a significant head wound would also suffer memory loss."

Jabbing her chin higher, Amelia returned to the stove where she plunked down a pan she'd filled with water. She grabbed the box of rolled oats in the cupboard and dumped a pile of cereal flakes into the pan. Still fuming at Michael's doubts, she gave the mess a careless stir.

Would she have to tell him the truth?

Would he believe her?

A snort and sharp footsteps leading away from the kitchen told Amelia that no matter what she decided, Michael Hayak was nobody's fool. Persuading him would be an uphill battle, and time-travel, in her opinion, rivaled Mt. Everest.

Aside from the oatmeal being lumpy, breakfast for Katie went without a hitch. Then Michael stomped back into the kitchen, cradling his injured hand, and muttering imprecations under his breath. Amelia coughed discreetly, and Michael's eyes flew to his daughter, who stared back at him, intent on his every word.

"I'm ready for my breakfast," he growled.

"I guess it's good I made oatmeal," she said, placing a bowl of porridge before him. "You're grouchy as a bear."

Michael's good hand stopped in midair as he graced Amelia with one of his patented glowers. "You would be, too, if you'd lost the use of one hand, had work enough for a crew of three, and got no sleep the night before."

Amelia's irritation vanished. Sympathy took its place. "Is there some way I could help?"

"Since you offered, there's plenty you can do. Hilda and Fred Smyser are due here any minute now. They'll help me butcher a hog and prepare the meat for the winter."

Amelia frowned. "Sounds like you have enough help coming. What could I do?"

As surprise spread on his features and his jaw clenched, Michael dropped his spoon. It clinked against his bowl. "Sausage, Amelia," he ground out. "Just as you've done the last two years."

Amelia's eyes widened. "Are you telling me that *I'm* supposed to make sausage?"

Michael's gaze grew sharper, damning. "Just like you did the last two years," he repeated in that same, grating voice.

Sausage? She was supposed to make sausage? "But . . . but I don't know how to make sausage! I'm not even sure I know how to cook it once it's made."

Michael slammed his hands on the tabletop, cursed ripely, shook his sore hand, then scraped his chair back. "I don't want to hear that word again, do you understand?"

"What word would that be, oh, mighty master?"

"Amnes—"

"Do you have a better one for the loss of memory?"

"No."

"Then stuff it, you dense mule! You're the one who always brings it up. I just admit I don't know how to do something and ask for help. I sure as He—" Amelia caught herself when she saw Katie grin. "I have no idea how to

make sausage. If you want me to make it, someone's going
to have to teach me."

He ran rough fingers through his hair, ruffling it even
more. If it weren't for the disgust on Michael's features,
Amelia would probably have been mesmerized by his
good looks. As it was, however, her temper rose apace
his.

Then he turned his back to her. "Bah!" he spat. "I've had
enough of this. Just make sure you fill every kettle with
boiling water. And don't let the stove reservoir boil
empty." As if for good measure, he gave her a final pointed
stare.

Amelia tapped two fingers against her temple. "Aye, aye,
Cap'n!"

Her pert salute only earned her another snort and
Michael's immediate departure, punctuated by the slam of
the kitchen door.

Mercifully the rumble of buggy wheels rolling up the
drive didn't give Amelia time to dwell on her situation. The
Smysers had arrived. She had water to boil. At least that
was something she could handle, since it looked like she'd
never learn how to handle Mr. Hayak himself.

As Amelia went toward the kitchen door, she saw Mrs.
Smyser through the upper glass half. "It's so good to see
you," she said, ushering her visitor inside.

Mrs. Smyser wrapped her arms around Amelia. At first
the gesture surprised her, then she relished its warmth.

"Well, my dear," said the older woman when she let go,
"I've been wondering how you were making out."

Amelia rolled her eyes. "I think you can guess."

"Michael's being difficult."

"And how!"

Mrs. Smyser donned a crisp white apron that covered her
from throat to hem, and went to wash her hands at the sink.
"What is it?"

"He wants me to make sausage!"

"And . . . ?"

Amelia groaned. "Don't tell me you expect me to know how to make it, too?"

Mrs. Smyser narrowed her eyes, then shrugged. "It's something you do quite well. But I suppose you've forgotten that."

Amelia bit her tongue to keep from blurting out the truth. "Mm-hmm."

"There's no help for it, then. Let's go outside and get started. There's a world of work to be done."

"Come with us, Katie," Amelia said, taking with her the apron she'd appropriated the first time she came to the Hayak farm. Holding Katie's hand, she followed Mrs. Smyser outside.

They found Michael and a rotund gentleman Amelia assumed was Fred Smyser near a kettle hung from a metal hook over a blazing fire. More boiling water. Why on earth did they need so much?

She was sure she'd find out soon enough, since Michael and Mr. Smyser then headed for the pig-pen. Suddenly a cacophony of snorts, grunts, and panicked squeals ripped through the peace of the chilly morning. Katie clung to Amelia's leg, burying her face in the soft flannel of her skirt.

Amelia didn't blame the child. That was one scared pig, and his fear was contagious.

Mrs. Smyser held her hand out to Katie. "Come on, sweet, we can go feed the chickens."

Working in smooth synchronicity—this was obviously something they'd perfected over time—Michael and Mr. Smyser held the boar as close to immobile as one could expect the beast to be. A blade caught the frosty sunlight, sparkled, and the next thing Amelia saw was an ocean of blood spewing from the pig's neck.

"Oh!" she cried, then bit her lip. They were slaughtering the animal, after all. She couldn't be squeamish about it. She had to think pork chops . . . at the grocer's . . . on a pink Styrofoam tray . . . covered with clear, shrink-wrapped plastic.

Calling "I wasn't ready!" Hilda Smyser ran up with a large tin pail which she angled directly in the path of the spurting blood.

Amelia watched for a second, her stomach twisting. She took a step toward her friend, averted her face, and managed to choke out, "Why?"

"The pail?" asked Mrs. Smyser.

"Yes," moaned Amelia, overwhelmed by the animal's stench.

"Why, to make blood sausage, of course."

Amelia's knees wobbled. "Blood . . . *sausage?*"

"That's right. Blutwurst."

Michael had said she was to make sausage. Although she kept her gaze averted, Amelia still saw the slashed jugular, the rushing blood, and the gleaming tin pail in her mind's eyes. Suddenly her breakfast rebelled, and she groaned, "Never—"

She sprinted for the outhouse, barely making it to the plain wooden structure in time.

When she felt steady enough to leave the privy, she slipped away, making a beeline for the kitchen door. Although she urged herself not to look, Amelia couldn't resist a final glance at the cauldron. The by-now hairless pig hung near the kettle, stretched out on sticks, slit down the middle.

"Pork chops, spareribs, bacon," she chanted, mantra-like. Right then and there, Amelia swore off pork. She didn't think she'd ever be able to eat another sausage, a slice of ham, a hot dog.

Reaching the relative safety of the back stairs, she came to a decision. From here on in, she'd defend pigs' rights to life. Her theme song would be, "Oh, I wish I were an Oscar Mayer wiener—"

"Amelia Baldwin, what *are* you singing?" asked Mrs. Smyser when Amelia opened the back door. "Is that one of those bawdy vaudeville songs? Well, I never . . . singing about that poor Mr. Mayer's . . ." Mrs. Smyser glanced surreptitiously around, ". . . privates."

Amelia stifled a laugh, realizing she'd goofed again. "No, no, Mrs. Smyser. Nothing like that at all. It's just a silly little jingle about the frankfurters Mr. Mayer's company makes."

Mrs. Smyser gave her a suspicious stare. "Never heard of the man or his frankfurters."

"Oh, you will," Amelia added, hoping the lady lived that long.

After the episode with the twentieth-century Madison Avenue advertising bit, Amelia spent the rest of her day following Mrs. Smyser's instructions. Fortunately the woman had a kind heart. At no time did Amelia so much as catch a glimpse of the bucket of blood.

Each time she remembered the gory scene, Amelia shuddered. But to continue helping, she had to disassociate herself from the animal whose death she'd witnessed. It was only meat. She was preparing meat for the winter.

Despite Amelia's unsettled frame of mind, the two women spent hours scraping, washing, salting, and chopping hunks of meat. They prepared the sausage casings, then boiled them. They cut meat for drying and salted hams for smoking. Then, when a mishmash of odd pieces of pork was all that remained, Mrs. Smyser said, "We're ready to make sausage."

Amelia gasped.

Mrs. Smyser shook her head. "No, we won't be making blutwurst. We will only make medwurst."

"Medwurst?"

Mrs. Smyser sighed. "The meat sausage, Amelia."

Just then Michael entered the kitchen. "Butchering is thirsty work," he said, pumping water into a large tin mug.

"It's steamy work in here, too," Mrs. Smyser answered

as she opened and closed cupboards, obviously not finding what she needed.

"What are you looking for?" asked Amelia, tearing her gaze away from Michael's work-sheened face, his throat as he swallowed the refreshing drink, a drop of water as it coursed down his chin.

Mrs. Smyser's voice broke into Amelia's diversion. "Why, the meat chopper, of course. Where is it?"

Amelia cleared her throat. "I'll get it," she said, and hurried to the pantry to escape Michael's appeal. After dragging a chair into the small space, she scrambled up and stretched an arm to grope along the shelf. "Here it is. I stored it in the pantry last year since the kitchen cupboards are always . . . so full. . . ."

As Amelia realized what she'd just said, what she'd just done, her voice faded. She began to tremble. Icy fingers of fear crept up her back, chilling her middle, her hands. She glanced at the metal instrument, noting absently the Enterprise Meat Cutter logo cast on its side.

How had she known where that chopper was stored? And since last year? Could she have seen the implement during one of her forays through the kitchen?

Or was she getting some of Amelia's—the 1900 one— memories just as she'd gotten the woman's body, her life?

How had she known?

The trembling mushroomed into shudders. A sob welled in her middle, rushed up, choked her, then burst the moment she dropped the meat chopper as if it had turned into hot coals from the stove.

With a blunt thud the meat grinder hit the floor. It gouged the oak floorboard. As she slid down into the chair, Mrs. Smyser bustled to her side.

"Amelia! How wonderful. You've begun to remember. Perhaps your amnesia will be as temporary as Dr. Wilhite told Pansy it might be."

Since the woman stood before her, expecting Amelia's

exuberant celebration, she did her best. She stretched her lips out toward her ears. "Just ducky."

It was fine for Mrs. Smyser to rejoice about this latest development in Amelia's adventures in the 1900 wonderland. *She* wasn't the one ready to beg to be committed to a lunatic asylum. Amelia couldn't explain how she'd known where that . . . that thing had been stored. She remembered searching through the cupboards, the linen chest, the more accessible shelves in the pantry. She had *not,* however, dragged a chair into the pantry to scrounge around the uppermost shelf.

So how had she known?

"Yes, Amelia," she heard Michael say in a tight, strained tone. "How absolutely wonderful that you're beginning to remember. Perhaps we can soon get back to some form of normalcy without having to cater to your . . . amnesia."

Amelia saw red. "Cater? What the He—" She cut herself off, catching Mrs. Smyser's upward flying eyebrows. "What do you mean, cater?"

With deliberate control, Michael returned his tin cup to the hook on the wall over the sink. Then he aimed those blazing eyes at her.

Rage, Amelia thought.

"I never would have figured you for such a manipulative woman. What you intend to gain escapes me." He opened the back door. "I mean the time and effort everyone is putting in to teach you any number of things you've been doing since you were practically Katie's age. And incidentally, where *is* my daughter?"

"Sleeping," Amelia bit back. She'd had a bellyful of his attitude.

She'd never been the recipient of such strong, negative emotion. Why now? And why from this man, who could at times make her sizzle with desire from nothing more than a glance? This man, whose love for his daughter moved her to tenderness, whose family pride and respect revealed his honorable nature.

Amelia knew it wasn't the thought of amnesia that bothered Michael, it was his disbelief in her explanation. Hell, disbelief nothing. Michael believed, all right. He believed she was lying, using him, Katie, Mrs. Smyser for . . . for what? What would be the purpose?

As she went to question him, he spun on his heel. "So long as you continue to watch Katie and she's not hurt, I'll try to overlook your 'amnesia.' "

His insinuation hurt. More than Amelia would have imagined. How could Michael think she'd let anything happen to Katie? What kind of monster did he think she was?

Hours later, after Amelia and Mrs. Smyser had ground, stuffed, and boiled miles of sausage, Amelia finished up the scrubbing she'd insisted on doing alone rather than delay the Smysers' return home. She had sliced some of the fresh sausage, fried it in a cast-iron skillet as Mrs. Smyser had said, fed Katie, and prepared a heaping plate of potatoes, sausage, and boiled beets for Michael.

Who had yet to return to the house.

Amelia had bathed her charge, both of them giggling as Katie tried to burst soap bubbles. She'd dressed Katie in her nightgown—the one Amelia had scrubbed the oatmeal from—and tucked the child into bed. Sitting at the foot of the bed, she'd told fairy tales, carefully relating those she knew had been popular around the turn of the century.

Wringing out the washcloth she used to sop up the last of Katie's bath, she wondered if Michael intended to stay away until she left. Amelia refused to leave Katie alone. No matter how much the girl's father wanted to avoid seeing her, and how little he thought of her childcare abilities.

Turning off the lights in the kitchen, Amelia picked up some of her neglected sewing, and went for the rocker in the parlor. Setting up a soothing motion, she began to repair one of Myrtle Huntley's costumes.

After a while, she heard Michael at the back door. He opened and shut cupboard doors while cursing profusely. She debated going to see what might be bothering him now.

"Amelia!" he called sharply. "I need help."

Something in his voice alerted her to the urgency of his call. When she stepped into the kitchen, she gasped and stared at his bloody hand. "What happened?"

"Cut myself with a butchering knife I was cleaning. You're going to have to help me. I need the wound sewn shut."

"What?"

As he used his teeth to twist off the cap to what looked like a bottle of whiskey, he flinched in obvious pain. "Not now," he objected after downing an alarming amount of alcohol. "This isn't the time to play amnesia."

Amelia bit off her protest in view of the seriousness of his injury. Since he'd already hurt his other hand days ago, this new wound would probably pose a problem to a farmer in the fall. "I wasn't asking for that reason. I've never sewn human flesh before."

"I know, I know, but you certainly have enough experience with needle and thread to take care of this. Just do it before I bleed to death."

"Can the sarcasm, buster, or I won't even try," she spit back, knowing her threat was in vain. Her every fiber propelled her to the parlor to gather needle, thread, scissors, and a swath of trimmed-off white cotton cloth, but Amelia didn't think she could get through this at the same time she countered his insults. Heck, she'd never even taken a first-aid course!

By the time she returned to the kitchen, Michael was applying pressure on the wrist above his bleeding palm, and the level of booze in the bottle had decreased substantially. Since she didn't have anything resembling anesthesia, and she was sure Michael didn't either, she didn't comment, but knew that before they were done, Michael would probably pass out in a drunken stupor. Although it was best for him to be bombed during her first surgical procedure, she didn't think she could perform it without someone to guide her along. Michael was her only candidate for mentor.

"What do you want me to do?" she asked.

He released his wrist to down another inch of whiskey, and Amelia saw the bleeding intensify again. The cut was deep and bled profusely, so she had to hurry.

"Clean it up, then sew it shut."

"What should I clean it with?"

Michael gave her a disbelieving look. "Soap and water work wonders against dirt. I can't spare the whiskey."

Amelia glanced at the bottle, then winced. He still had half the bottle to go. Hell of a hangover he'd have tomorrow.

"Did you get dirt in the cut?" she asked, opting for discretion. "I thought you said you'd done this with a butchering knife."

With an impatient snort, Michael poked his chin in the direction of the sink. "Don't ask so many ques-shions. Just do it."

While they'd been wasting time, the whiskey had obviously been doing its job. Amelia ran to the sink, soaked a clean washcloth, then lathered it up. She rushed to Michael, and after offering a prayer for help, began swabbing the deep cut. Although she refused to look at his face to see the pain she was causing him, she couldn't help hearing his guttural moan.

"Drink some more," she begged, checking for any flecks of dirt in the two sides of the gash. Finding nothing obvious, she ran to the stove, dunked the thread into the boiling water, then stole a bit of whiskey for the needle. Threading with shaking hands was a new experience, but her need was so great that somehow Amelia managed it.

As she returned to his side, Michael closed his eyes, his breath uneven, raspy. When she leaned close, she smelled the sweat of the day, the stench of the pig, the tang of the liquor. She still had no idea how she would manage, but she clearly had no alternative.

"Ready?" she asked.

"As I'll ever be . . ."

Then Amelia drew the sides of the cut together, and pierced Michael's flesh. With another groan, he went limp.

Chapter 10

THE FOLLOWING DAYS ran into each other, one blurring into the next. Michael had lost a lot of blood. And, as she'd expected, he developed a raging fever. He spent much of that time unconscious or in restless sleep.

Amelia opted to stay at the farmhouse, since she couldn't very well leave a seriously sick man to watch a rascally two-year-old. So she cared for the Hayaks. She soon established a smooth routine with Katie, interspersed with hours of watching Michael, checking his temperature and bandages, trying to feed him, and get him to drink—not to mention all the sewing.

Finally the fever broke. Days filled with disagreements with a lousy patient followed. Finally, after a rousing argument about who would milk the cows and feed the chickens and pigs, Amelia realized Michael was on the mend.

Before leaving for the barnyard, she informed him that a man as ornery as he was could watch Katie long enough for Amelia to go home and get herself a few changes of clothes and more of her sewing.

On her way home the next morning, she admitted to herself that she was no longer falling in love with Michael Hayak. She'd already fallen.

These past few days she'd felt his pain. She watched him during the long, dark hours he spent unconscious. Then when the fever hit, and he twisted and turned in misery, she'd wanted more than anything to lie beside him, to press herself alongside this man she loved but didn't understand.

Something about her detonated a hidden trigger in Michael, and Amelia was no longer sure it was just his belief that she'd lied about the amnesia. Anger was one thing, but this push and pull he used to such advantage pointed to something deeper that dragged him away every time he seemed to grow closer to her. She had no idea what it was, only that it was something about her, Amelia—maybe both Amelias. Since she didn't know the other one, she couldn't begin to figure out what it might be.

That left her not knowing how to act around him. She never knew what to expect. That uncertainty, that backward and forward movement, had her feeling emotionally seasick, out of balance.

Letting herself in her front door, Amelia sighed. She didn't know what to do. At least, not about her feelings. For the moment, she was going to wash up, gather more sewing and clean clothing, then return to the Hayak farm.

The cut on Michael's hand had begun to heal. The pain from the severed nerves that were now mending, however, made it impossible for him to sleep. All they'd had in the house to ease his pain was yet more whiskey.

When he awoke this morning with the predicted hangover, Amelia had worried about leaving Katie with him. But in spite of his obvious discomfort, Michael had insisted he was well enough to watch his daughter. As disturbed as she'd been by the feelings that had overpowered her in the last few days, Amelia had let herself be talked into going home. At least for a short while.

So here she was, already preparing to return to Michael's side. Still questioning the wisdom of her actions.

Amelia was closing the box where she'd packed her work and her extra clothes when a sudden knock at the door had her hurrying to respond. On her front stoop stood Mildred, her one-time "angel" and dressmaking customer. "Mildred!" she exclaimed in dismay. "Your suit . . ."

"My traveling suit indeed, missy!" Mildred sailed into the parlor without waiting for an invitation. "I have come every day since we last spoke to see those drawings you agreed to make, and what do you think I found each time I came?"

Amelia winced. "I haven't been here. I'm so sorry. How can I—"

Sharp black eyes peered at Amelia. "And where *have* you been, missy? Under the stage again?"

"No, of course not. I was at the Hayak farm, helping Michael with Katie and the housework."

The dark lasers narrowed, deepening their study to dissection. "At the Hayak farm? Just you, Michael, and Katie?"

"Well . . . yes. His wife is dead, and I went to help. Everyone said I'd promised to do just that before Christina died." That unwavering, piercing stare was getting to Amelia. "Besides, I'd been doing it for two years, or so I was told. I figured I should continue what I'd been doing."

"And just what *have* you been doing, missy?"

Growing impatient with the inquest, Amelia blew loose wisps of hair from her forehead. "What I did all along. Clean, cook, watch Katie." With a shudder, she added, "Make sausage."

"And is that where you were when I came calling, even as late as half-past eight last night?"

"Well, yes. Michael hurt himself very badly a few days ago with a butchering knife. I had to sew the wound together, and then couldn't leave them alone. He couldn't have cared for Katie in his condition. Even after his fever broke, he drank whiskey to kill the pain."

Amelia noted the shock on Mildred's face when she

mentioned the whiskey, but when she admitted to staying nights at the farm, Mildred turned apoplectic. "You mean to say you slept in that house with that man drinking? And no one to ensure propriety?"

Amelia frowned. "What do you mean, ensure propriety?"

"Why . . . just the suspicion of an unwed couple spending the night alone together is enough to ruin the woman's reputation, never mind going ahead and just . . . doing it."

Doing it, huh? Clearly Mildred meant something very different than what Amelia's more liberated, twentieth-century imagination called up. Chuckling, she turned back to her box. "Oh, don't worry about my reputation," she said with a careless wave. "We're no couple, and no one's going to think twice about those nights. Michael was hurt—very badly—and for the most part, drunk stupid. Nothing happened."

"But no one *knows* that nothing happened."

"Oh, yes, they do," Amelia countered. "They know nothing happened because I say nothing happened."

Mildred sniffed, then pursed her face as if she'd bitten a sour lemon. "We're supposed to accept your word for it, missy? Remember, there's an innocent child in the midst of all this."

Mildred had become a serious irritant. "Katie is fine, and she will continue to be fine. And, yes, Mildred, you must accept my word for it. I don't lie."

The ebony stare sharpened again. "I'm not so sure the entire town is as benevolent and willing to believe you as I am. After all, you do consort with the shady element of the vaudeville troupes."

Amelia had heard enough. "I don't have your designs ready, but I'll make a point to have them tomorrow evening. If you return then, I'll be happy to discuss your traveling suit." Mildred's eyebrows met her hairline. "As to my reputation, I don't give a da—er . . . fig what anyone thinks about me staying at the Hayak farm to care for Katie and an injured man. I answer to my conscience, and I did what I had to do. If anyone is offended, that's their problem, not mine."

Mildred rose, then sniffed again. "We'll see about that, missy! The ethical fiber of our community, our very society, is at stake here. It concerns all moral-minded citizens."

"Stuff it, Mildred! A bunch of gossips will have a field day with this today, then they'll go on to the next scandal. By tomorrow it'll be yesterday's news."

The "stuff it" caught Mildred off guard. Jawing like a mammoth carp, she seemed unable to string words together. Then she snapped her jaws shut, took a deep breath, and Amelia knew to get ready for another spit of sanctimony.

"Not in our proper, upright city it won't," said the self-appointed arbiter of decency. "With such an abominable lack of ethics, you just might be run out of town. We don't cotton to fallen women, you know."

At that, Amelia let out the laughter she'd been fighting. The image of herself as a fallen woman—through the stage floor and on to her ruined reputation—was too funny not to laugh. "But I *am* a fallen woman. Through the stage floor, you know."

Mildred's face blotched up red. She'd obviously missed the humor in Amelia's words. "This is no laughing matter, missy! And I will see to it that it's taken seriously. Why . . . yes, I do believe you *should* be run out of town."

The martinet turned and stalked to the door, letting herself out with a smart click of the lock.

Amelia chuckled grimly. Who knew? Maybe Mildred would get her way, after all. Amelia had no idea when her time in 1900 would be up. She might get yanked back to the 1990s as early as later today.

All she knew was that she didn't want to go back. She wanted to stay here, with Michael and Katie, at the farm.

*   *   *

All day long, Amelia fetched, carried, bandaged, and otherwise saw to Michael's comfort. Although better, he remained a lousy patient.

At the same time, she chased, retrieved, disciplined, diapered, fed, bathed, and tucked in his very active toddler.

Now that evening approached, Amelia looked forward to some moments of peace in the parlor while she worked on Mildred's designs and stitched some of Myrtle's costumes.

After Mildred's visit earlier that day, Amelia had been even more determined to follow her original plans. What right did Mildred or any of her "moral-minded" pals have to decide whether she should help someone in need? Just because the someone was an attractive widower and she a single woman, it didn't automatically follow that something questionable had to happen when they were alone. Besides, even if something personal were to occur, it was none of the "moral-minded" crew's business.

Conscious of her uncertain tenure in this time, however, Amelia felt driven to set aside her wants in favor of the greater good. Since she had no way of knowing how long this . . . adventure would last, she had no right to allow a relationship with Michael to grow. And, if truth be told, with Katie, either.

In view of the emotional risks to Michael and Katie, Amelia decided she would continue to watch the child while her father's hand grew strong enough for him to take over. Loving her more each day, and letting Katie's feelings for her deepen as time went by would only cause an innocent greater pain. It would be easier on the little one if Amelia withdrew from her life slowly rather than suddenly not show up one day.

For the same reason, Amelia swore to keep her feelings for Michael from eclipsing her common sense. She couldn't let him get close enough again to scramble her brain as he'd done with his caresses. The man was hazardous to her mental health, and coincidentally, to his own emotional future. Amelia couldn't expose him to another heartbreaking loss.

So she would take care of the Hayaks only until Michael's hand healed. And it would be a cool, professional sort of caring. She would pretend to be a visiting nurse or a housekeeper, someone uninvolved with father and daughter.

It wasn't an easy course to follow. Each time Katie did something charming, funny, outrageous, Amelia's arms ached to hold the child close to her heart and never let her go.

Each time Michael needed something, fought to get out of bed, grumbled out of frustration, Amelia wished she could join him on that bed, to hold him and kiss his pain away. The power of her need stunned her. She wanted more than anything the right to love him back to health.

But she couldn't do that any more than she could deliberately lead him along. The only way she saw to gain that right, even temporarily, was if she told him the truth. What had really happened to her. Once he understood the complexities of time-travel, body-switching, and the mystery her future posed, only then could she consider letting their relationship deepen. Only after Michael knew that at any given moment fate might take her from his side forever.

It would be bad enough for her when she was forced to leave Michael and Katie. Life had been, and would again be, bleak without them. The loneliness she'd known in the 1990s inspired nothing but dread. She would give anything to stay with the Hayaks. If she knew she would stay for the rest of her life, then maybe she could encourage Michael's attraction to her; maybe they could fall in love and marry, just as Pansy had said.

But—and there was always that but—what if she was forced to leave?

Amelia couldn't stand the thought of Michael and Katie suffering the same misery she'd face once she was taken from them. She loved them too much to expose them to such pain. It would be kinder to begin the separation immediately.

But nothing said she couldn't enjoy them privately while she remained here. With determination, she stuck her needle in a prominent corner of the gown she was mending, and set the cloud of silk chiffon down on the seat of the rocker. She stood, stretched, and smiled.

She would love the Hayaks secretly, holding that love close to her heart.

Standing in the doorway to Katie's room, Amelia saw a moonbeam spill silver light over the curve of the child's cheeks. The brown fringe of lashes seemed darker in contrast to the brilliance of the moon. The even rise and fall of the covers over the sturdy little body gave evidence of the child's peaceful slumber, a great improvement over those nightmares Amelia had been called on to ease her through.

She approached silently, careful not to startle Katie. The closer she came, the more her heart swelled with her love for the beautiful little girl. How she longed to lie down beside her, to hold her in her arms the whole night through, to be there when the bad dreams came to haunt her and to greet her when the sun called her from her sleep. Had Katie been born to her, she couldn't have loved her more than she already did.

And because she loved the child, she couldn't let the depth of her feelings show. It wouldn't be fair to Katie.

Bending, Amelia pressed a kiss to the girl's temple and realized that a tear went with it. She swallowed the lump in her throat, dabbed away the moisture on the soft cheek, then dashed away the drops on her own face.

She approached the door to Michael's room. Actually, it had been his and Christina's room, and Amelia realized he hadn't occupied it for a very long time. Probably since shortly after Christina became bedridden. As soon as he came to, she'd insisted on helping him upstairs. He'd argued, blustered, cursed, and fought—much to Katie's chortling enjoyment—the idea of recovering in that bed.

Amelia had pointed out that she'd changed all the linens, aired out the hint of antiseptic that had clung to the air, that she'd boxed Christina's things and stored them in the attic. Her assurances had shut him up long enough to get him in the bed. She'd handed him the bottle of whiskey, and he'd fallen asleep.

Earlier today, he'd tried to move downstairs again, but Amelia stood firm. Then, with his supper, she'd given him a pain remedy Dr. Whilhite had supplied when she stopped by his office on her way to the farm that morning. Michael had finally fallen asleep.

Since he'd taken the envelope of medicine, Amelia knew it still had to be in full force, otherwise she'd never have risked opening the door to his room. At least, not to just look at him and etch in her heart the image of his face, his strong arms spread wide across the bed, one of his legs, naked and slightly bent at the knee as it extended beyond the edge of his blanket.

Despite his bandaged hand and bruised knuckles, there was latent power in the man. Even while in bed, sleeping, at rest. It came from his well-developed muscles, from his sense of pride, his self-confidence. As he slept, he remained powerful, capable; sleep didn't diminish Michael Hayak's presence.

Growing bolder, Amelia opened the door a fraction more. She slipped in and went close enough to hear his deep breathing. Quite a difference between the response she felt when watching first the child and now the father.

Again, Amelia felt the stirrings of desire. How could she not? She'd fallen for the man despite his bad moods, especially since she knew they were caused partly by his recent loss, and partly by something about her. She discounted whatever it was about her that bothered him. He could get used to it soon enough.

Besides, since she'd decided to keep their relationship from growing any deeper, she didn't need to worry. She could just watch him, care for him, help him whenever possible.

She could love him in silence.

As she stood at his bedside, the longing in her heart grew to need, and a wave of tenderness swept through her at the same time. When she'd first seen the blood pouring from his hand, her heart had nearly stopped. The wound had struck her as hideous as the stream of blood he'd drawn from the boar. Her mind connected the two incidents, and she'd feared for Michael's life. She didn't know how she'd managed to sew that gaping gash.

Then while she'd sewn, Michael had uttered strangled moans, guttural utterings that had deepened her anguish. She'd wanted to ease his suffering. She'd known the need to hold him close, to love him.

She'd held back. Wisely.

But tonight wisdom took a trip on a moonbeam, that silvery puddle of light centered on Michael's prone body. Amelia leaned over and, with the faintest touch, kissed his lips. When he didn't react, she repeated the caress.

The warmth of his mouth affected her like a magnet, pulling her back a third time. Suddenly his lips returned the kiss, and a steely arm wrapped itself around the back of her neck, effectively pinning her to him as he stole control of the kiss.

And what a kiss it was! Long, slow, rocking from side to side, pressing her lips open, seeking more of her. Which she didn't hold back. She couldn't. Amelia wanted this as much as Michael seemed to.

The hot, rich taste of Michael's mouth became accessible, just for her, if she dared take it. His lips pressed hungrily against her, his tongue took daring dives into the privacy of her mouth, tempting her, luring her to follow when it withdrew.

Then she was kissing him. Deeply, with the same need he'd shown her, with the same passion that had driven his kisses. A foreign sound, dark, private, welled up from inside him, revealing how much he liked her kiss.

His response gave Amelia the confidence to bring her hands to his cheeks. She touched him. As she'd wanted to from the moment she saw his portrait at the Opera House. Rubbing her palms against the rough stubble of his evening beard, she relished the contrasts between them. Releasing his lips for a gasp of air, she glanced at his eyes, only to find them turned to pools of darkness. The flush on his cheekbones revealed his arousal, as did the roughness of his breathing.

As they stared at each other, Michael took the arm he'd wrapped around Amelia and used his bruised knuckles to follow the line of her cheek, her jaw, her neck, then back to her jaw. Cupping his fingers over her cheek, he drew her down for another of his devastating kisses.

As Amelia thought she might die from the sensations swirling through her, she felt Michael's touch again at her neck, but this time he didn't stop. That large, warm palm caressed the swell of her breast, pressing into the fullness of her flesh, molding itself to the generous mound. It felt so good to have him touch her there that she arched into the caress, wanting more, everything he was willing to give her.

Michael made another of those private sounds in his throat, and Amelia felt her heart soar. He clearly enjoyed the intimate touch as much as she did. Encouraged, she angled herself more fully over his sprawled frame, bracing her hands on his shoulders. He moved to accommodate her.

A tug of his teeth on her bottom lip sent a shaft of heat through her body, enervating her skin, swelling her flesh, stoking her desire. "Michael."

"Amelia . . ."

It was wrong to continue this, and she knew it. Although passion burned hot enough to incinerate both of them, there were other considerations. What about their eventual separation? Wouldn't knowing what she was missing make matters worse when she no longer had him close enough to touch, kiss, to hold through the night? What about his feelings? His loss?

What if she let the moment pass them by? Wouldn't the regrets be just as bad to live with?

Suddenly Amelia had her answer. She found it in her heart, in the need displayed in his gaze. She would take what fate was willing to give her, and she would give Michael all she had to give. If their time together was to be short, at least they would have the memories to ease them through the empty times ahead.

And no regrets.

With the instinct of a temptress, Amelia pressed every inch of her body to Michael's, relishing the hard masculine planes as much as he obviously enjoyed the contours of hers.

"Yes . . ." he hissed, then returned to her lips for another endless kiss.

The hand that had held her breast proceeded with its exploration, running down the curve of her spine, cupping a buttock. He squeezed and again made that sound in his throat. Her thoughts when she'd inspected her new body in the mirror that first morning had been right. A man liked finding enough to fill his hands. At least, this man did.

Little by little, as they continued to kiss, nip, taste, he tugged the length of her skirt up until it bunched at her waist. Then his hand clasped her bare thigh above her lace-trimmed garter. His fingers were hot, nearly as hot as his lips, his chest, the crux of his legs.

Amelia squirmed, feeling her intimate folds grow warm, moist, swollen. His work-rough hand rubbed up and down her thigh, then curved around and palmed her bottom again. Amelia pressed deeper against Michael and knew she would take all he was ready to give. She would make love with him and treasure their passion, the beauty of his touch.

Leveling herself off him, she noticed his erection tenting the thin blanket that still covered essential parts of the man.

His eyes burned with desire as he watched her. With deliberate motions, she slipped button after button through the holes on her blouse, then eased the soft cotton off her shoulders.

Michael continued to stare.

Amelia went to work on the closure at the waist of her skirt, her fingers turning clumsy as the occasional rational thought began to register. What would he think of her? Would he agree with Mildred that she was a shameless fallen woman?

Then, before fear and doubts stilled her hands, she slid her skirt down her legs. Standing in only her chemise, drawers, stockings, and garters, Amelia trembled. Michael must have read her indecision, because he held out his hand.

She shook her head.

Slowly again, she continued disrobing. Shrugging the chemise straps off her shoulders, Amelia unfastened the row of pearly buttons down the front of the lace-trimmed garment.

Michael drew a rough breath.

Next, she untied the laces that held her drawers on and released them. With another lift of her shoulders, she allowed the camisole to fall to the floor with the rest of her clothes.

Finally she stood before Michael, bare but for frilly green garters and light-colored stockings.

"Amelia . . ."

She placed her hand in his. He brought her down on himself, his flesh hot against hers. Amelia closed her eyes and absorbed the sensations. The length of Michael's legs bracketed hers. His chest, rough with dark hair, rubbed against her breasts, heavy and aching for his touch.

Which he gave. With his less damaged hand, Michael covered one breast, chafing its taut tip with his thumb. Amelia felt the tug of passion all the way to her core, burning, heightening her need even more.

"I've wanted this for so long . . ." he whispered as he kissed the upper swell of her breast.

"Seems like forever," she responded, lifting her shoulders to give him better access.

She glanced down, wondering what he thought of her admission, but saw only the need in his gaze. As his lips approached an aching tip, his eyes held hers, but only until the pleasure of his kiss on her flesh forced them both to close their eyes again.

As he lavished attention to her breasts, Amelia wondered if she was doing this right. She had no prior experience, and obviously Michael did. Did she seem awkward? Demanding?

When he began to wiggle under her she grew alarmed. "What's wrong?"

"Damn blanket!" he sputtered, pulling and tugging on the offending fabric. "It's taken damn near a lifetime to get this close to you, and there it is, keeping me just that much farther away!"

Stunned by what he'd said, Amelia slid to his side, then helped him with his bedding problem. What she found far exceeded her admittedly inexperienced imaginings. Michael's flesh stood erect, proclaiming his need.

Amelia stared, fascinated by his male beauty. The play of muscle over bone, the shadows cast by the defining cover of hair, his shaft ready for her. There was no woman alive who wouldn't find this sight arousing, more pleasing because of what it meant. It meant Michael needed her as much as she needed him.

He gave another twist, seemingly uncomfortable again. "Ah . . ."

In the moonlight, Amelia saw red steal over his cheeks. "What's wrong?" she asked, fearing the worst, that his head had decided to overrule the demands of his sex.

"Well . . . it's my . . . hand."

"Your hand?"

"Yes, er . . . well, I can't hold myself up . . ."

Amelia cast a glance between his legs. "Doesn't look to me as if you're having any trouble."

"Not *that*. I mean, I can't take the lead, I can't make love *to* you."

Amelia sighed in relief and gave an embarrassed chuckle. "Well, maybe that puts us on some kind of even ground. You see, I have no experience at this . . ."

"Didn't think you had. And that leads to an indiscreet request on my part. Will it bother you to . . . would you . . . I mean, would you be willing to . . ."

His hand gestured over his body, not at all clarifying his request, but Amelia took a guess. "You want to know if I'm willing to . . . er . . . go on top?"

His breath rushed out in a gust of relief. *"Yessss . . ."*

Amelia smiled. "If you're willing to give me instructions."

"You were doing just fine before."

"I was?"

"Any more fine and I'd be dead by now."

"Oh, no! Not before we get to the good part!" Then she winked.

He chuckled, and the humor dispelled the discomfort they'd felt. In a feline gesture, Amelia flowed back over Michael, aware of every inch of male she touched.

Michael nipped Amelia's neck, tasting the sweetness of her flesh. He had no idea how this had come about, but a dying man didn't refuse final gifts. And he felt as if he'd been dying for a long time. He'd held his body under the strictest control and denied the clamor of his flesh. Now, Amelia's lips had roused him from what felt like an endless sleep . . . a two-year slumber.

Not at all the sleep she'd thought he slept, since he'd only pretended to take the latest dose of medication, refusing to feel out of control ever again.

With his bruised hand, he pressed Amelia closer, as if two could become one. And that struck him as exactly what he wanted. To become one with Amelia. In every possible way.

He didn't care how this had happened, all he cared about was that Amelia Baldwin, the woman who'd consumed his every thought and desire for the past two years, seemed to want him as much as he wanted her. She kissed him with a need so great, he felt he touched her soul each time their lips met. When she first pressed her soft, warm body onto his, he'd wondered if he'd imagined the pleasure in her eyes. Finally, when she began to unfasten her buttons, totally of her own choice, no coercion or seduction on his part, he'd known.

Amelia Baldwin wanted him.

And, determined woman that she was, she was going to have him.

Chapter 11

A VELVET-ROUGH PURR washed over him, telling Michael how much Amelia enjoyed his touch. He pressed his pelvis upward, imprinting his rigid flesh against her softer, tender skin. She wriggled, as if to come closer still.

Pride filled Michael, and a smile broadened his lips. He could accommodate her wishes. And if he didn't do it soon, he'd likely die of denied desire.

He kissed his way to her ear, nipped the lobe and relished her indrawn breath, the shimmer of pleasure that ran through her body. There was nowhere he couldn't feel her, nowhere but where he most needed to right now.

"Lift up," he asked.

She did, arching her spine, displaying her breasts for his pleasure. His eyes drank her in, the rounded softness, the tightened tips proclaiming her desire. When she sat astride him, he groaned; he was so aroused, and she presented a better vision than those in his most elaborate fantasies.

With his bruised knuckles, Michael caressed milky-white curves, a pouting tip, her belly, and down to the curls meshing with his own. "Here, too," he requested.

Her eyes grew wide. But not with fear. It seemed Miss
Amelia Baldwin was ready. His thumb burrowed through
the silky hair of her mound and found what he'd been seeking. Her flesh was hot, lushly swollen, damp and ready for
him. When his thumb drew a slow circle around the heart
of her need, Amelia dropped her head back, caught her
breath, then let it out with an earthy moan.

That did it. Michael had waited as long as he was going
to wait. Careful to protect his wound, he placed both hands
on her hips and urged, "Up."

She straightened her head, looked into his eyes, and
smiled. Hadn't she said she had no experience? If that was
true—and Michael had no reason to doubt her—then she
was surely the most naturally sensual creature alive. Placing her hands on his shoulders, Amelia rose to her knees
and rubbed herself against the tip of his sex. It was
Michael's turn to moan.

She was hot, and he was ready. Slowly he helped her
down, inch by exquisite inch. She gasped. Her eyes
widened once again. Her mouth opened on a silent cry as
she took him in. Then her eyelids floated shut, and another
smile curved her mouth.

It was the sign Michael had been waiting for. Flexing the
muscles of his pelvis, he rose deeper and deeper into her.
She countered his every lift, tightening around him, taking
him as far as he could go.

The rhythm rose, steady, stronger, until it flew out of
control and instinct took over. Harder and harder they came
together, their bodies striving to reach a peak that lay just
beyond the edge of sanity. Madness overtook them, and
their lusty pounding shook the bed.

Michael clasped Amelia's hips as spasms clutched at
him, indicating her impending climax. With renewed vigor,
he stroked her deeply, feeling every tug on his ready flesh.

She cried out and threw her head back again. Pleasure
filled her face, her lips parted in a primal cry, her eyes shut
against everything but what he gave her. She trembled, and

her breasts quivered before his eyes. Her thighs clutched him as if she'd never let go.

Then he, too, cried out, echoing her sounds of completion, shuddering, pouring the very essence of himself within her. He soared, higher than he'd known a man could fly, on pleasure so overwhelming that he lost all sense of time, of place, of everything but the clasp of Amelia's body on his.

It took what felt like forever to float back down to earth, and when he did, he realized Amelia slept atop him, her arms holding him, her lips kissing his neck with her every breath. Making sure he lay his abused hand—it ached after participating in Amelia's seduction—at a safe distance from their bodies, Michael drew in a long, sweet breath, feeling its freshness renew him, giving birth to hope.

He joined her in her sleep.

He was alone when he awoke. Amelia was gone. As were her clothes. He in turn had the blanket tucked up around his neck, something he never did. He smiled, her tender gesture warming him. It felt good to have someone see to his well-being, especially after years of looking after everyone else.

Michael stood and, needing to relieve himself, decided to take advantage of his keeper's absence and skip another bout with the bedpan. He couldn't even hear her in the kitchen. After dressing quickly, he tiptoed down the stairs.

He briefly wondered where Amelia and Katie had gone, then shrugged. They had to be somewhere, and right now nature called.

When he stepped outside, he grimaced. It had suddenly turned cold. Very cold. And it was starting to snow.

Moments later, he returned to the house, tiny snowflakes melting on his cheeks, absently buttoning the placket of his trousers. He opened the door, then paused to fasten his waistband.

He heard a gasp. A familiar one. One he'd heard last night as he breached Amelia's body. Images of moonlit

madness flew before his eyes, making it difficult to keep
them open, to spot her across the kitchen, standing by the
stove. As he gazed at Amelia, she could just as easily have
been bare. His mind replayed visions of every luscious
curve, every secret spot he'd found.

She avoided his eyes. The moment grew awkward, yet it
stirred him. He doubted she harbored regrets; studying her
pose, her twisting fingers, her flush, he suspected she had
shocked herself with her lusty appreciation of their exploits
during the night of loving. One he would make damn sure
was only the first of many.

Studying Amelia, tenderness filled him at her discomfort. Michael held out his hand to draw her close. Hesitantly she reached for him.

"Yoo-hoo! Amelia!" Pansy's cry sent Amelia's hand
back to her side. "Where are you?"

"Oh, no!" Amelia cried. She patted her hair, straightened
her apron, rubbed her cheeks.

"Oh, no!" Michael groaned, running a hand through his
hair.

Heavy footsteps sounded out back. "I came to see how
you were making out, child," said Amelia's "angel" as she
came in through the back door.

Amelia spun to face the stove. Her blush and sudden
shyness around Michael would give Pansy plenty to think
about—not that the woman's imagination needed any help.

"That's nice," she murmured, stirring blobs of oatmeal.
She wondered how long Pansy was likely to stay, especially since she'd barged in just as Michael had reached out
to her. Amelia wanted to get back to that outstretched hand
and those glowing blue eyes.

A chair scraped along the floor, and Pansy huffed and
puffed as she sat down. Amelia swallowed a groan. Looked
like the "angel" planned to stay a while.

"Actually," announced the cherub, "I come bearing an
invitation. Everyone is so certain the snow that's coming
will be a storm that some of the neighbors are planning a

sleigh-riding party followed by a hot dish supper for next Saturday night. We thought it would do you both good to come."

" 'Bout me?" asked Katie from the kitchen doorway. Amelia stole a peek at the three behind her.

"Especially you," stressed Pansy with a sage nod.

Amelia didn't know what to say. Particularly in view of all that had happened. Mildred's accusations, Michael's lovemak—

"It'd be unseemly for me to go," said Michael, his tone somber. "My wife just died."

With a backward glance, Amelia saw Pansy waggle a finger at him. "That's precisely why you should come. You and Katie and Amelia have been living with death for too blasted long. Christina's resting in peace—praise the Lord—and you three should get back to living again."

Michael seemed taken aback by Pansy's blunt words, but to her surprise, Amelia agreed. "I think it would be very good for Katie," she said, turning. "She needs to see other children, to laugh and play and be a part of the community."

Michael glanced her way. She failed to decipher what she found in his gaze.

After a lengthy silence, he said, "You're both quite right about Katie, but it's not proper for a recent widower to take part in any sort of festivities. Amelia can take Katie."

Pansy was having none of it. "Michael Hayak! You mean to tell me you'd let these two girls come and go to the schoolhouse all alone at night? In this cold? Shame on you! You have better manners and more common sense than that. They need a man to protect them."

Michael snorted. "Who do they need protection from? They know everyone who is likely to go—certainly the Bieseckers. I would think Arnold will use his large bob-sleigh. Katie and Amelia can ride along." He leaned against the icebox and crossed his arms over his chest. "Besides, shouldn't you be on your way? You wouldn't want to get caught in the storm."

Pansy came to her feet. "I'm leaving. As soon as you say yes."

"I gave you my answer."

"But, Michael—"

"Papa? Please come," Katie asked, turning her blue eyes on her father.

They'd go, Amelia thought, they'd *all* go. There wasn't a soul alive who could say no to those eyes. She knew. She'd done all sorts of wild, intimate things last night when Katie's father turned a similar look on her.

To hide her smile, she faced the stove again. From behind she heard, "Aw . . . Katie! That's hardly fair."

Pacing came from where Michael had stood. He muttered under his breath. He blustered, voicing arguments, none of which was seriously received. The three females remained silent.

"Oh, very well!" he roared, still powerful in defeat. "We'll be there."

Amelia couldn't contain her excitement. They were going on a sleigh ride. She'd never gone on one, and anticipation had kept her humming through the past few days. Snowy days, at that. Although she'd initially planned to return to her house after Pansy left, the sky had blown down sheets of snow, piling it up in stark white mountains wherever she looked. Michael had been adamant about her staying at the farm, at least until the snow stopped.

It hadn't. Until today.

Although late October was early for such heavy snow, it wasn't unheard of, and remembering 1990s' weathermen forecasting snow in Minnesota, Amelia accepted her fate, concentrated on Katie, finished drawing Mildred's traveling suit, sewed, and avoided Michael.

Each time he entered the kitchen, it was all Amelia could do to keep from melting in mortification. Each time she clapped eyes on the man she remembered how he'd looked, sprawled on the bed, naked, male, aroused, and she suspected he experienced a similar reaction when he saw her. She couldn't make herself meet his gaze.

One would think that avoiding one of three people living in the same house would be difficult, but with two of them determined to stay out of the other's way, there was no difficulty, just awkwardness and sparse, impersonal talk.

But today the snow had stopped. The sun was out, its efforts weak, since it did nothing to take the bite out of the bitter cold. Amelia was grateful for the comfort of the Hayak farm, Katie's presence, and yes, even though he disturbed her in the most intimate ways, Amelia was glad to see Michael each time he appeared. Time and space between them had served to lessen her embarrassment.

Every once in a while she even chuckled when she thought of Pansy's visit. Katie had manipulated her papa like a pro. Now Amelia had a special event to look forward to.

She had memories, too. While Katie slept and Michael worked in the barn, she allowed herself to remember details of their passionate night. Her memories had the power to warm her—heck, they had the power to *scorch*—and she wondered what the sleigh ride would be like. Michael and her, snuggled under a blanket, moonlight above, snowflakes below.

But that was silly. They were going to a party. There would be other neighbors present. And, as always, Katie would be there, too. Not good indicators for snuggling of any sort.

Humming again, Amelia went to the oven to check on the savory dish she was baking. Before Pansy left that other morning, Amelia begged the older woman to write down a number of easy, basic recipes. Even Katie had begun to turn up her nose at the ever-present oatmeal. This morning they'd enjoyed fluffy pancakes, and Amelia had achieved edible bacon rather than her usual chunks of carbon. Father and daughter appreciated her efforts.

She, however, had yet to cross her lips with a bite of that poor, slaughtered pig.

The cheese she'd layered on the pan of potatoes, cabbage, meat sausage—not the infamous blutwurst—and a rich gravy, had begun to turn brown. With a folded towel, she grasped the pan and quickly set it down on another towel spread out on the table. The fragrant steam reminded her they'd eaten their midday meal some hours ago.

As she returned to the sink, the back door slammed open, and Katie flew in, followed by her father. "Ummm . . ." murmured the little girl, sniffing.

Michael glanced at Amelia, caught her gaze with his, smiled wickedly, and offered, "Um-*hmmmm!*"

Her eyes widened. Her already flushed face grew hotter. Her cheeks prickled with her blush. What happened to the man who for days had refused to say more than "Yes," "No," "Please," and "Thank you," while staring at his food? What caused the change? And why on earth was he bringing *that* up *now,* with Katie in the room?

Pretending she hadn't heard him, she said, "I'm glad to see you both. Are you ready to go?"

"Yeth!" Katie yelled.

Another grin brightened Michael's handsome face. "Always," he murmured in a husky voice.

"Michael!"

He approached and leaned forward to take his tin cup from the hook on the wall, trapping her between his chest and the sink. "Yes?"

"Michael!" she repeated, mortified by the sight they presented to the little girl.

With his bruised hand he began pumping water into his cup, the motion rubbing his body against hers. "Is something wrong, Miss Baldwin?"

"Katie's right there," she whispered.

"I know," he murmured, then louder he asked Katie, "What's Papa doing, Katie-angel?"

"Papa's thusty."

With a kiss to the tip of Amelia's nose, he backed off, innocence smeared across his smug face. He held his hand out to Katie, then sauntered toward the front of the house, taking his time, clearly aware that Amelia stared at him the whole way.

She stood frozen, jaw gaping wide.

After Pansy left that morning, Michael had grown silent, but not particularly angry. He'd seemed thoughtful, distracted. Amelia had assumed his conscience was doing a number on him.

But nothing like *this* had happened before. Amelia glanced down at herself, and noticed her nipples poking through the soft fabric of her blouse. Damn! He knew exactly what he'd done to her. Then he had the gall to kiss her, grin, turn away, and strut off. How . . . male!

She wondered what he'd do next.

It didn't take long to find out.

While the two Hayaks made various scuffing sounds upstairs, Amelia donned the pair of ladies' long wool underdrawers, two pairs of socks, gauntlet-type quilted gloves, a head scarf, her hat, and a plum-and-cream shoulder shawl that Michael insisted she needed. He'd predicted dire consequences—frostbite, for one—if she didn't put it all on. She'd grudgingly agreed.

Now, as she goose-stepped around, trying to forget she wore a dead woman's clothes, Amelia felt like the skins she and Mrs. Smyser had stuffed with sausage meat. She questioned the need for so much wrapping and wondered if she'd ever move again.

Before she could do anything about her woolen shackles, the ringing of sleigh bells announced the arrival of their fellow sleighers. Squeals of anticipation came from upstairs. Loud pounding raced down the stairs. A scarlet flame rolled by Amelia, and she guessed that somewhere in the layers of wool she would find Katie.

" 'Melia, come wiz Katie!" the girl cried, her voice muffled, eyes sparkling with joy.

Michael followed his daughter to the back door.

"Michael!" Amelia called, "Do I really need all this—"

"Yes, Amelia, you really need all that. And I don't need another reminder of your occasional amnesia. Let's not make everyone wait, shall we?"

Amelia's temper soared. She'd gone a few blissful days without mention of the sore subject. She'd liked them just fine. She couldn't believe that at this precise moment Michael had snapped the snide comment at her.

Unconvinced of the need for such extreme measures, she tugged her coat on and struggled to fasten the buttons down the front. Poor coat didn't want to cover so much padding.

Muttering imprecations against the male of the species, Amelia followed said male outside. The evening was clear, the air crisp with frost, the sunset a rainbow of roses, mauves, and blues. In the barnyard, Amelia saw the sleigh and Michael's horses hitched to it. At the animals' slightest move, the bells on the leather harnesses sang out into the icy evening.

The open sleigh was fairly small, of a graceful, elegant design, with sweeping body lines and curved runners. As Amelia approached, she noticed an upholstered seat wide enough to hold the two Hayaks and herself.

Michael called her name. Turning, she saw him run toward her, a steaming metal box held away from his body with towel-covered, mittened hands. "Move aside! You could get burned."

Scurrying, Amelia complied, curiosity keeping her by the sleigh. Moments later, she saw Michael reach into the conveyance and lift the seat to reveal a storage area where he dropped the hot case he'd carried.

"What's that for?" she asked.

Michael gave her a not-again glance, then rolled his

eyes. "It's to keep your dainty feet from freezing off. Get in. We shouldn't keep the others waiting. It's much too cold, and we have several more farms to go yet."

Amelia decided to squelch the jab of irritation she felt at Michael's resumed skepticism, and, holding onto his proffered hand, she climbed in the sleigh. On the floor she found a mountain of woolen blankets, fur rugs, and a pitiful amount of foot space. Before she could ask Michael what she should do, he pulled himself in and sat on the leather-covered seat, patting the other half with his hand. "Sit. It's time to go."

Amelia frowned. "Where's Katie?"

"She went with the Beiseckers."

"Oh." So they *would* be alone. She wondered what he'd do, especially since he had brought up the troublesome subject of her memory. She sat, thinking.

A silent Michael dropped layer upon layer of heavy blankets and fur carriage robes on her, carefully tucking the edges in. When satisfied, he wriggled into the cocoon he'd formed. His thigh nudged hers. Amelia tingled at the contact. He drew in a sharp breath.

He still said not a word.

Then they were off. For the most part, Michael concentrated on the business of driving the sleigh. Burning with curiosity, Amelia began asking questions. At first he glared at her, looking as if he were on the verge of calling her a liar, but her persistence must have gotten to him, because after ignoring her first two queries, he patiently explained what she wanted to know.

"Yes," he said, "that is a bear skin covering us. And that other one with the rougher hair is a buffalo skin."

Every so often, he stood and looked ahead, keeping a reasonable distance between them and the sleigh in front. Moonlight sluiced over him, emphasizing his solid strength, his self-confidence. Admiring the picture he presented, Amelia realized she'd never love another man, now or ever. Even if this one had the infuriating habit of irritating her on a regular basis.

When he sat back at her side, she noticed he came closer still. She welcomed not only his warmth, but also his nearness, the indication that although at times he grew angry with her, he wanted her close by.

As the purpley-red in the west gave way to rich indigo, Amelia noticed how the moonlight captured individual snowflakes in the air and on the ground, giving them life—a sparkle all their own. Magic filled the world around her, the magic of a perfect night in the company of a special man. It seemed as if nothing else existed. Just the sleigh, Michael, and her.

Without warning, he dropped his arm around her back, drawing her closer still. Amelia held her breath. Then slowly, as he kept her cuddled at his side, she breathed again and snuggled up against him.

Not another word was said. Not when the caravan of sleighs stopped at two more farms. Not when the sleighs again resumed their trip. The only thing Michael did the rest of the way was to discreetly lift his arm from around Amelia when the sleighs slowed to allow newcomers to join them. Once they were on their way again, the arm returned to keep her at his side.

Amelia felt treasured. Protected. And if she allowed her imagination the freedom, she might even believe herself loved as well. Despite her reservations, the feelings she experienced during the sleigh ride were so new, so special, she couldn't bring herself to return to logic.

Yes, she'd someday be gone from Michael's side. Yes, it was likely that another woman would take her place. Although that thought held the power to wring her heart and bring tears to her eyes, Amelia refused to dwell on her uncertain future.

Her present was too wonderful to miss.

As the sleigh slowed down once again, Amelia regretted

that the ride was coming to an end. But, she remembered, there was always the ride home.

Catching her totally by surprise, Michael dipped his head and with the tenderness of a lover, the wile of a rogue, stole a kiss from her lips. Her composure shattered. Her emotions soared high.

When they reached the Sugar Loaf School building, as Michael had called it, she found a number of sleighs already there, the horses housed in a nearby barn.

Amelia entered the school and took the dish she'd made to a table where other covered containers sat. She stepped to a side, not knowing what to do next. Under her layers of insulation, she began to perspire. A quick glance around offered no solution to her overheating problem.

Even though the building teemed with bodies, she saw no one she knew to ask what she should do with her winter clothing. Strangers bustled by, some voicing greetings, others merely smiling as they passed her on their way to the table or back outside.

Then Amelia heard a familiar voice. ". . . I *told* you they'd come," crowed Pansy. Amelia turned to find her friend.

Pansy held court in a crowd of women, some of whom averted their faces, clearly embarrassed to be caught gossiping. Not Pansy. With a pat to the pewter-colored knob on her crown, she hissed, "Hush!" to the others, who responded with affronted glares.

"How dare you hush *us!*" whined a stick-thin woman with a pince-nez perched on the tip of her long nose.

Arms outstretched, Pansy donned a Moseslike demeanor and parted the crowd before her. "Amelia!" she called.

"I'm so glad to see you, Pansy."

"I should say so! What *are* you doing in all those cold things? Come, come. Let's go to the coat room."

Amelia allowed herself to be led away, only glancing back in the hope of seeing either Hayak among those present. She had no luck. In a daze, she followed Pansy from group to group, mentally thanking the woman for helping her bridge the awkwardness of her amnesia.

"And did you hear," Pansy went on, furnishing Amelia with pertinent details, "that Cecily Mann's apple butter won this year's Harvest Festival fruit conserve competition? I've always felt her recipe is the best." Turning to a blushing, birdlike woman, she went on. "Now, Cecily, you know it's nigh torture to keep us all in the dark. What *is* that secret ingredient you swear by?"

Mrs. Mann fluttered hands in the air, and Amelia wondered if she would soon take flight. "Just promise you won't tell Mr. Mann," urged the sparrow.

With deadpan expression, Pansy crossed her heart. Amelia wondered if she could keep Mrs. Mann from divulging her secret, since before the night was done it would likely travel the room twice thanks to Pansy. "Oh, don't bother!" she exclaimed. "It's too late to make apple butter now. Besides, I always have too much sewing in the fall to even consider it."

"That's certainly true," commented Pansy. "But don't you think your circumstances might change by next fall?" The question was punctuated with a giant, knowing wink.

The gesture jolted Amelia right back to earth. She felt the blood drain from her face. Her hands grew cold. Fear squeezed her heart. It had happened again. She'd spoken details of a life she could know nothing about, and she had no idea what had prompted this latest bout of insight.

Was she losing her mind?

She'd already accepted the reality of her voyage through time. But this was different. This was part of that occasional, eerie ability to know things she had no reason or opportunity to know of her own accord.

Then Pansy waved her sturdy paw before Amelia's eyes. "Amelia," she said, clearly losing her patience. "Are you feeling well, child?"

Amelia fought the trembling, then stiffened her shoulders. "Ah . . . yes, Pansy, I'm . . . quite all right."

"Do you think you're fully recovered from that nasty gash on the head?"

The one that started it all? No. Amelia didn't think she'd ever recover from that transcendental experience. Slapping on a smile for her companions, Amelia nodded. "Of course. I'm just . . . hungry. Yes! It's been hours since I ate."

"Well, child, the youngsters are supping. Soon enough someone will start the games for them, and the rest of us can enjoy our meal in adult company."

Amelia nodded tightly, still shaky, still unnerved.

Pansy began scouring the room, clearly looking for someone. She rose on tiptoe and began waving in earnest. Amelia craned her neck to see who Pansy was so intent on greeting. As her gaze scanned the people present, a pair of dazzling blue eyes captured her attention. A smile of greeting curved Michael's lips.

"Here, son," said Pansy, wrapping her arm around Amelia and propelling her through the crowd into Michael's approaching chest. "She's not feeling rightly, and she says she's hungry. Why don't you see to feeding her before the children eat everything."

Michael's arms swept around Amelia, holding her tight for a second. Then, mindful of the room filled with curious eyes, he set her aside and studied her face. She was pale and averted her gaze. As they'd both been doing since their one night of glory.

But in the subsequent days, he'd come to terms with what had happened. His decision hadn't been difficult to make.

He curved a finger under her chin and made her meet his gaze. "Is it true you're not feeling well?"

She pressed her lips into a straight, pale slash, then shook her head. "I'm just hungry, Michael. You know Pansy. She has a constant need to give orders and a vivid imagination."

He allowed himself a wry grin. "Yes, Pansy is something special. Come on, I think we can get us a plate. Some of the children have finished eating. The games will start up again soon."

Tucking her hand into the crook of his elbow, he led her toward the tables laden with food. Suddenly he felt her shoulder shaking against his. "What's wrong?"

Her eyes sparkled. Her cheeks blossomed with their normal color. She laughed merrily. "How could Pansy suggest that all this food could disappear so fast? There's enough here to feed an army."

Michael grinned. "You know Pansy," he responded, repeating her earlier words. Relief at seeing her acting more herself filled Michael. Tonight was a very important night. After much thinking, he'd arrived at a practical, sound decision. He needed Amelia cheerful, thinking happy thoughts. A good disposition on her part would only help. Anticipation made his heart beat faster.

They piled potatoes, pot-roasted beef, carrots, and corn on large plates, collected utensils and cups of warm spiced cider, then went in search of a quiet place to sit.

A place to sit could be found. The quiet . . . well, Michael would have to make do with a corner far from the food and where the children had gathered to play charades.

With his back to the room at large, Michael did his best to shelter Amelia from the boisterous merrymaking. His anticipation grew with every bite of food he took, and soon he set his partly filled plate aside. He wanted to get on with what he'd decided to do.

"Amelia?"

"Mm-hmmm."

"Ah . . ." He didn't know how to begin, and, focused on a biscuit drizzled with honey, Amelia wasn't making matters any easier.

He tried again. "Amelia?"

She glanced up, just a flash of emerald. "Yes?" She returned to the food.

"Dammit, Amelia, would you stop devouring that biscuit and look at me, please?"

Startled, she turned her beautiful eyes toward him. "What is it, Michael? Are you all right?"

"Yes . . . No!" He ran a hand through his hair. It would be now or never. "I mean . . ." He took a deep breath. "Will you marry me?"

Chapter 12

WILL YOU MARRY me?

Michael's proposal echoed through Amelia's mind, bringing tears to her eyes, joy to her heart. Reality, however, came as a sinking feeling in her gut. Although her fondest dream lay just beyond her grasp, she had no right to reach out and make it come true.

"Oh, Michael . . ." she said, laying her hand on his arm. "You don't know how much your proposal means to me."

He narrowed his gaze. "But . . . ?"

"Yes, there is a but."

"What is it?"

I don't know how long I'll be here. "Uhm . . . ah, well . . . it just wouldn't be right. Not so soon after Christina died."

His eyebrows rose. "A long engagement, then? We can wait out the year."

Everything in Amelia pushed her to answer "Yes," but she couldn't. It wouldn't be fair to either him or Katie. They'd both suffered enough during Christina's lengthy illness and her recent death. Since Amelia had no way of knowing whether her presence here was permanent or not, she couldn't see her way clear to further involvement with the Hayaks. Not while she didn't know what her future held.

Tears filled her eyes. "I could say yes to the long engagement, just to put you off, but I won't do that. I can't accept, and I won't give you false hope for a distant future. If you still feel that way a year from now"—*and I'm still around*—"ask me then."

Michael frowned, the muscle in his cheek working as he clenched his jaw. "What about Katie? She needs a mother, and she needs her now."

Amelia felt as if he'd reached in and twisted her heart. "I can continue to watch her. I don't have to become her mother to do that." *Regardless how much I want to.*

Not ready to be put off, Michael countered, "What about this winter when I must work at the mill in town?"

"You're going to work in town during the winter? Where will you live? What will happen to the animals and the farm? What will you do with Katie?"

He sent her an unpleasant smile. "Amnesia again, I suppose."

Amelia closed her eyes for a moment. "Don't bring that up again," she spit through gritted teeth. "Pretend I'm new in town. We're just getting to know each other. Tell me what you would tell someone you've just met."

Anger began to burn in his gaze. "To what purpose?"

"To provide me with the information I need."

He ran his bruised fingers through his hair, causing a lock to tumble over his forehead. Despite his growing rage, he looked more appealing than ever.

"Why are you doing this, Amelia? Why the pretense? Does the guilt of abandoning Christina and Katie at the end make you lie?"

Things were difficult enough not knowing what she should have known, but for him to accuse her of lying was another matter altogether. "Think, Michael," she urged, fighting to stay calm, to find more patience. "What purpose would lying serve?"

He rubbed his forehead, then shook his head. "That is what I fail to understand. Why, Amelia? Why would you go so far as to invent this absurd story about losing your memory as a result of the accident?"

"Why won't you believe me? I'm not lying. I *really* don't know what happened before the accident." True enough, she thought. "And there's no reason for me to make it up. I don't know what happened that Friday when your wife died. All I know is that I came to under the Opera House stage. Nothing else."

Michael's brow sported furrows as he thought. Then he briefly met her gaze, uncertainty in his eyes. "I would like to believe you, but . . . there are some things you *should* know . . . things I can't imagine you'd forget."

"This isn't a selective process. I don't remember *anything* before waking up. Nothing, Michael. Not the good, much less the bad."

Suspicion again spread over his face. "What about the meat grinder? How do you explain knowing where that was?"

Amelia gulped. "Ah . . . I must have seen it one of the other times I looked through the pantry. That's not hard to believe, is it?"

His eyes seemed to pierce right through her, as if he could read the answers to his questions in the deepest corners of her soul. Amelia wished she could tell him what really happened, but she would probably alienate him even more if she did.

Then Michael looked away. "You have no idea how much I want to believe you. I . . . just can't." He waved his bandaged hand. "But that doesn't matter right now. What matters is that I've asked you to marry me, and you've refused. Please reconsider. Katie needs you."

It became Amelia's turn to frown. "I wouldn't be marrying Katie in any event."

Michael's cheeks colored. "True. I need you, too."

Amelia's heart began to soar. Common sense forced a crash landing. "Why—"

"I can't run the farm alone, much less watch Katie while I work at the mill. I need a wife, a partner."

What about that other night? her memory cried. Had that been about a mother for Katie? A co-worker at the farm? A *partner*? She refused to believe it, but she couldn't make herself bring it up. "You don't need to marry me for that. I've already agreed to continue as we've been. I'll watch Katie, help you at the farm. I'll keep running the house, too."

Her promise didn't appease him. "What about your reputation?" he asked. "You can't continue to live in my home without being shunned by decent folk. And I can't allow that sort of scandal to affect Katie."

Amelia sniffed. "I don't give a da—*hoot* what anyone else thinks. I follow my conscience, and if you were so worried about what others might think, why did you make me stay during the days it snowed? I could have gone home when Pansy left. You were the one who insisted I stay."

Michael's cheeks reminded Amelia of Rudolph's nose. "I . . . ah, couldn't take care of Katie. My hands, you know."

Amelia gave him a disbelieving look. "No one else would help?"

He dropped his gaze. "No one I wouldn't have imposed on."

How cute. "And you don't think you've imposed on me? I have a mountain of sewing to finish, you know."

Again his forehead pleated. "You've always managed to sew while at the farm."

Amelia rose to her knees. "Michael, this is ridiculous. You've even said my reputation could cause difficulties for Katie." She'd never forget Mildred's attitude. "I know there are those who consider me beneath the fine folks in town simply because I don't shun the vaudevillians who perform at the Opera House. That should make you reconsider your offer. You wouldn't want to be looked down upon because of me."

Michael stood. "That's ridiculous."

Up she went, too. "That's just the point. Those who want to see it that way will say my reputation is already tattered. We can forget this conversation even happened."

He narrowed the space between them by a step. "Not at all. There's what happened that one night at the farm. That's what I'm discussing. I never shirk responsibility, and there could be unplanned consequences. Since your reputation has been damaged by my *actions*," he said, making his meaning only too clear, "I must do what is right. I must restore your good name. You have no choice but to marry me."

How dare he bring that up? And as a tool to make her accept his proposal!

How could he do that to her after he'd made such tender, passionate love to her? Yes, what about love? What about roses and candlelight and vows of forever? Didn't she deserve those, too?

Then she noticed the silence. Not a sound could be heard in the room full of people. Amelia peeked around Michael and confirmed her worst fears. Their argument had entertained those gathered there. Shock colored some expressions. Avid interest others. One thing, however, remained constant: All eyes were fixed on them.

Everyone had heard Michael's statements. No one could have missed his meaning. They awaited her response.

Why did this have to happen to her? Why couldn't she have a normal proposal? Why couldn't she find love, joy? Hope for a future?

Humiliation began in her middle, then spread to her face. Her cheeks burned. She didn't know where to look. Before her, arms crossed over his broad chest, Michael didn't give an inch. Determination fixed his features in lines of steel.

Across the room, Pansy made no secret of her efforts to miss nothing.

"I *did* say she'd come to no good hobnobbing with those loose-moraled vaudeville sorts," offered Mildred in her piercing voice.

Suddenly it became too much. Amelia choked out a wordless cry, then picked her way through the room. She ran for the coat room, gathered hers, and flew outside. She had no idea where she would go, she only knew she couldn't stay a moment longer inside that building with all those eyes staring at her. Not when Michael's less than romantic proposal had broken her heart.

Tears spilled from her eyes, but they froze on her lashes. She shouldn't be out in the cold. It could be dangerous. But she couldn't go back inside, either. She couldn't bear to have everybody there judge her for making love with Michael. That night remained the single most beautiful moment of her life—past, present, or future—and she wouldn't let anyone's sense of offended decency mar its beauty, the perfection of her first experience with love.

By brilliant moonlight, she made her way around the various sleighs in the schoolyard and found the one she'd come in. Now, if she could only find Michael's horses, then she could figure out how to harness them and drive the darn thing away. She had no idea where she'd go. She just had to get away from those people.

She had to get away from Michael and his poor excuse for a proposal.

Heading toward the barn where the horses had been led, Amelia soon noticed the cold seeping through the soles of her heavy boots and the layers of woolen socks. While they'd been inside the schoolhouse, a firm wind had kicked up and now, as she fought it, blew away the steamy puffs of her breath. She wriggled her nose, cracking the thin crust of salt her tears had left on her cheeks. Hugging her coat to her chest, she suddenly realized that Michael was right about one thing. She really needed all those layers of clothes.

But she'd left them in the schoolhouse.

And nothing would make her go back.

So she struggled on, finally reaching the barn. Grateful for the shelter, she collapsed onto a haybale in a corner, breathing the relatively warm, musky air.

A horse nickered softly. Amelia felt welcomed.

Then she heard the commotion outside. Various voices called out. Others mumbled a backdrop of chatter. The creaky sound of footsteps on dry, packed snow could be heard as someone approached the barn. Above it all, she made out a flood of expert, extravagant profanity.

In a too-familiar voice.

That voice came closer, keeping up with the squeaky snow.

And she had nowhere else to go. She'd have to face all those people again, embarrassed by the intimate things Michael had revealed in the schoolhouse. What on earth prompted him to propose in the middle of a crowd? Especially when they'd been alone at the farm for a number of days and she planned to return home with him and Katie later tonight. Why didn't he wait until then?

Why had he proposed the way he did?

A mother for Katie, he'd said. A partner at the farm. Someone to keep house. They didn't need to marry for those reasons. In fact, the only reason for them to marry were the feelings she'd thought they shared, those he'd used to try and force her acceptance. But manipulation wasn't part of what she thought love should be. And Amelia loved Michael Hayak.

She'd thought the man who'd pleasured her that night had loved her, too. Or at the very least, would come to love her with time.

She still thought so.

But, yes. There was that matter of time. That mundane commodity she didn't know if she could count on. Amelia wanted forever. Forever at Michael's side. But fate could all too easily rip her away to that lonely time she'd come from. That time she no longer wanted any part of.

The barn door screeched on its hinges. "Amelia!" Michael roared. "Have you gone mad, woman? You'll freeze out here. I hardly think my proposal merits suicide. I have your things. We're going home."

"I'm not going anywhere with you."

"What do you intend to do? Live here with the horses and the cows?"

"I like it here. There are no mules."

"Meaning?"

"Meaning that you're a stubborn mule. Insensitive and unfeeling, too. Probably half blind."

"That's nice," he answered, his tone belying his words. "Come and get your woolens before you get frostbite. You can insult me all the way home."

"I can insult you just fine right here."

Michael sighed. "You know damn well you're not staying in this barn much longer. I know, too, that having everyone overhear our . . . disagreement in the schoolhouse proved embarrassing and unpleasant, but it can't be worth risking frostbite. Let's go back to the house, forget tonight happened, and as you said before, pretend we just met. We're merely getting acquainted, Miss Baldwin. And my daughter's sleepy and cold. Shall we go?"

Not at all happy with how matters stood, but aware that she couldn't stay in the barn much longer, Amelia left her bale of hay and approached Michael. Without a word, she gathered the padding she'd worn to the disastrous event and piece by piece wrapped it around herself again. Once sausaged, she allowed herself a glance in his direction, then immediately looked away. A strangely soft, amused gleam shone in his eyes, and his lips curved in a tender smile.

A man who smiled like that had no right proposing the way Michael had. Amelia's heart wept.

But Katie was waiting. And the weather could turn dangerous. They had to get home, so she pulled herself together and pushed the barn door ajar. Head held high, she walked into the frigid night, not looking at any of the various folks loading their sleighs with fresh hot coals from the schoolhouse stove.

"Now, Amelia," she heard Pansy call, "you have no idea how fortunate you are. You shouldn't be so hasty to reject Michael's excellent offer. I shall come by as soon as the weather allows me to travel to the farm. We can have a cozy chat then."

Amelia's eyes widened in horror. The last thing she wanted was to dissect Michael's proposal, her feelings, his lack thereof, and her uncertain future with Pansy Pritchard, gossip par excellence. She waved dismissively. "Don't worry, Pansy. There's nothing to discuss. Have a safe ride home."

A few scattered titters rang out, but with everyone intent on the business of preparing for the sleigh ride home, nothing more came of it. Determined to avoid further discussion of Michael's proposal, she sat next to Katie on the bench and curled her arm around the little girl's shoulders. "Tired?"

"Mm-hmmmm . . ."

After securely tucking the heap of covers around Katie, Amelia pulled the child close to her side. At least Katie's affection was real. As real as the love Amelia felt for the little girl. A love she knew wouldn't be used to manipulate her.

Then Michael climbed in, dropped onto the seat, and tugged the robes over himself. Amelia caught her breath. Because Katie shared the seat with them, Michael's body pressed against hers, all the way from her right foot, up the length of her leg, and all along her right side. They sat as close as he'd kept them on the earlier ride, but this time they sat stiffly, the tender sense of comfort and closeness Amelia had felt replaced by the awkwardness of a rejected proposal.

The entire ride was effected in stony silence. Amelia stared out over the snow-enshrouded landscape, wondering how she'd thought it magical earlier that day. With the moon hanging high in the Prussian blue sky, she saw clearly and far. What she saw struck her as stark, empty, bleak. Lonely, and she knew too much about loneliness to ever mistake it for anything else. Only when they stopped briefly as others in the caravan reached their homes did she see anything that didn't leave her feeling empty and sad.

Even the jingling of the sleigh bells failed to cheer her up.

Finally they arrived at the Hayak farm. As soon as the sleigh came to a stop, Katie's eyes popped open. "Katie s'eepy," she said, rubbing her eyes with thickly mittened paws.

"I'll help her to bed," Amelia offered, knowing Michael still had to see to the horses.

With a nod, he began to undo the harnesses. The bells continued to peal, making Amelia long for the joy and expectation she'd felt earlier in the day. But none remained.

With a sigh, she took Katie's hand and helped her out of the sleigh. Together they crossed the barnyard and entered the house through the kitchen door. Quickly and with relief, they stripped off the layers of damp wool.

" 'Melia? Katie's thusty."

After a cupful of water and a muffled "Thanks you," Katie placed her hand in Amelia's, and both went upstairs. In no time, the child lay in bed, snug under blankets and a green and rose quilt. Amelia leaned against the doorjamb, reluctant to leave. Little by little, Katie's eyes closed, and her breathing deepened. Amelia approached the bed, leaned over, and dropped another kiss on the baby-soft forehead. "I love you," she whispered, a catch in her throat.

"I know you do," said Michael from the doorway.

Amelia flinched, then turned. "I didn't realize you'd come inside."

"I know that, too." He moved aside, waiting for her to

walk out of the room. "And that's why I can't understand why you refuse to marry me."

"I thought that matter had been laid to rest in the barn."

"I refuse to accept your rejection."

"But I didn't reject *you*! I just can't *marry* you."

A nasty twist changed Michael's expression into something Amelia had never witnessed. "Oh, I see. I'm like a horse. Fine for stud, but you wouldn't want to marry one."

Amelia's cheeks blazed. "Of course not! That's not what I said, and you know it. Besides, dwelling on a lady's lapse in judgment is unworthy of a gentleman. And you've done enough of that tonight."

"Perhaps I'm not a gentleman."

Amelia waited for him to call her something besides a lady.

"Perhaps I'm just a man," he said instead, "with a man's needs and a man's wants. Since I have found both in you, I see no reason to deny myself—or my daughter."

"So, I'm a convenient backscratcher. Except that your . . . *itch* isn't in your back but in your—"

"Amelia!"

"Yes, Michael?"

"Why are you speaking like that again?"

"What's the matter? You can dish it out, but can't take it?"

Michael sputtered, objecting without words to yet another of Amelia's twentieth-century expressions.

Too bad for him. "Sorry, Michael. It's not enough for marriage. Not for me." Shaking inside, Amelia strode down the hallway toward the room she'd been using. At least she'd found a way to put him off. She hadn't been forced to explain what she didn't think she could.

As she walked past the open door of his room, the room where Christina had spent her final moments, Amelia felt led to glance in.

Suddenly she felt dizzy. A chill swept through her. Her eyes blurred. Through a veil of white, Amelia saw Christina's room, the bed scarcely rumpled by the frail body beneath the blankets. Toward the end, Christina had always been cold. The weaker her heart grew, the more futile grew her efforts to keep warm. The figure on the bed was only a shadow of the woman she had once been.

At the head of the bed stood a large man, tense, appearing ready to leap into action, should it be needed.

At the foot of the bed sat a woman, her back toward Amelia. But even if she'd faced her way, Amelia couldn't have identified Christina's companion. The sheer mist clouded the scene before her, making it impossible to discern details of the tableau.

As seconds turned to minutes, Amelia remained where she stood, pain crushing down on her. She hurt, as if her soul wept for the people frozen in that slice of time. None of them moved. Neither did she.

Still, the sense of unreality scared Amelia. Something about the scene before her made her want to flee, but she stood in place, almost as if an otherworldly hand kept her there. Feelings rioted inside her, anguish the one sensation she could most easily identify.

Something terrible lay just beyond the sheer barrier between her and the trio in that room. And although Amelia wanted to learn what that was, she found herself helpless to push through the gossamer wash of white.

Someday she would make it through. Because she had to. Amelia didn't know how she knew that, she simply recognized it as fact. Whatever lay in the mist-filled room would affect her irrevocably. Although she wasn't ready for that, she found a certain comfort in knowing it would come to pass, regardless of what she did to stop it. She had to wonder if she'd prefer to remain in the darkness of ignorance. There was a lot to be said for knowledge.

With a shudder, the fog cleared from her gaze, and her knees buckled. She sagged against the wall between Christina's room and hers, but even with that support, she continued melting down.

Then Michael's arms swept under her failing legs, around her slumped shoulders. He picked her up, and the warmth of his body began to take the chill off hers.

Gazing into his eyes, Amelia suddenly knew that whatever lay beyond the cloud she'd seen would affect her relationship with this man. Would it draw them closer?

Or would it tear them apart?

Chapter 13

WAKING EARLY THE next morning, Amelia tried to recall exactly what had happened the night before. Her memory failed when she tried to go beyond the vision of Christina's deathbed. That image would stay with her forever.

Although she remembered Michael placing her on her bed, she remembered nothing more. She didn't know if he'd questioned her strange behavior or tried to draw her into conversation. She didn't even know if she'd told him what she'd seen. But to what purpose would she do that?

As frightened as Amelia was, she didn't think alarming Michael would help matters any. He'd probably think she'd gone nuts and kick her out of his home. Although that would solve any number of problems, Amelia wasn't ready to say good-bye to father and daughter.

When she examined what she remembered, it made absolutely no sense. What she saw hadn't actually been there. They'd buried Christina the morning Amelia arrived in 1900 Winona, so Michael's wife couldn't have been sleeping in his bed last night. Michael, Katie, and Amelia were the only ones in the Hayak home, so who had she seen through that strange milky blurring? What did it mean? More importantly, why? Why had she been given a peek at the other side of death?

Amelia had never been particularly impressed by tales of near-death experiences or other paranormal occurrences. Although she seemed to be living one of them, she still found it hard to accept her apparent time-travel. As if that weren't difficult enough, now she had to try to explain . . . what? A vision? Ghostly manifestations?

What had she seen in Michael's room last night?

For the first time since she woke up under the Winona Opera House stage floor, Amelia had to seriously consider the ramifications of all that had happened to her. That she'd lived in the latter part of the twentieth century was a given. So, too, was the fact she no longer lived in that time. She couldn't deny the reality of her presence in the year 1900, not when the evidence surrounded her at all times.

Amelia had for the most part accepted time-travel as the explanation for her existence in two eras separated by a void of nearly one hundred years. But her sudden bursts of knowledge, of advance understanding, remained a mystery. How did she know about the meat grinder? And all those other details she had no plausible way of knowing.

More importantly, what did she see last night? Did she hallucinate? Was she delusional?

Michael had been at her side while she stared at the figures in that mist-shielded room. Had he seen them, too? Dare she ask him? Or would that simply trigger another of his bouts of anger at what he called her feigned amnesia?

More off balance than she ever remembered feeling, Amelia dragged herself out of bed. She had no idea of the time, but judging by the position of the sun outside her window, dawn had long ago come and gone.

Silence caved in on her, thick and hollow. She didn't hear Katie's chatter, and Amelia knew the child hadn't serendipitously slept as long as she had. That could mean

one of two things. Either Michael had risen as early as he
always did and had his daughter under control, or Amelia
would soon be facing a disaster of prodigious proportions.

Either way, she had to get out of the uncomfortably
wadded clothes she'd worn since yesterday afternoon. Obviously Michael hadn't bothered freeing her from her damp
wool dress. Amelia didn't know how to take that.

Should she feel pleased that he hadn't taken the liberty?
Should she feel affronted by his sudden lack of interest in
her body? Or should she go for broke and worry about her
vanishing sanity?

"Oh, Amelia, you've really gone and done it this time,"
she muttered, stripping. "You can't tell what's real and
what isn't, much less what you want and don't want."

A door slammed downstairs, startling her. She chuckled.
She hadn't imagined that. From the sounds of it, Katie and
Michael were as real as she remembered them last night.

"Oh, sh-ooot!" she muttered, remembering the scene she
and Michael staged for a substantial number of neighbors.
How would they bridge the breach her refusal had dyna-
mited between them? Could she hope Michael would forget? And did she want him to forget he'd asked her to
marry him?

Her pride kept her from treating him fairly. She couldn't
marry Michael unless he fully comprehended what he was
getting into, and she doubted she could make him understand. In her situation, " 'til death do us part," could mean
any number of things far removed from the usual defini-
tions. Although marriage wasn't an option at the moment,
forgetting his proposal—clumsy and ill-timed as it had
been—didn't sit right with her, either. She didn't want
Michael to forget the night they'd spent together. She
wanted him to remember forever, just as she would.

She wanted those memories to nourish the germ of caring she knew had already sprouted within him. His actions
didn't strike her as indifferent. Simple caring, however, no
longer satisfied. She wanted Michael Hayak to love her as

she loved him, but in good conscience she couldn't do a thing to encourage his feelings. Not without telling him the truth.

So that was that.

Her decision made, Amelia went downstairs to Katie's boisterous delight. " 'Melia!" the child cried, throwing herself at Amelia's legs. "Katie holped Papa!"

"And did Papa survive Katie's 'holp'?" she asked, cocking an eyebrow at Michael.

A crooked grin split his face. "Just barely."

Amelia sighed in relief. He hadn't fed his injured pride during the night and didn't seem ready to continue their argument.

Ruffling Katie's curls, she looked around the kitchen. A scorched enamel pot sat on a crumpled towel on the table, a lava-like spill of lumpy oatmeal erupting over the edge. Two bowls, liberally covered with oatmeal at the dry-cement consistency, still awaited clearing, and the coffee-pot lay sideways and empty in the sink.

"I see you made breakfast," she said to Michael, dismay and laughter in her voice.

His chin hiked into so-what territory. "We were hungry."

"Why didn't you wake me?"

Michael averted his gaze, first glancing at Katie, then out the pane of glass in the back door, finally focusing on his sturdy brown boots. "Last night was hard on you. You even swooned in the hall. I figured you needed rest more than we needed you to cook for us."

Her pride piqued, Amelia shot him a glare. "What do you mean, I swooned? I *never* swoon!"

A broad shoulder rose, then fell. "You wilted like a patch of lettuce in the summer sun, and if I hadn't caught you and carried you to bed, you'd probably still be on the hall floor. I call that a swoon."

He had a point. From his words Amelia concluded he'd seen none of what had caused her sudden weakness. Since he had no idea that anything unusual—more unusual than their ludicrous proposal—had taken place, she could see where he might think she'd fainted. Aside from telling him what she'd seen, she had no defense. Besides, since she could recall nothing after she'd felt herself falling, maybe she *had* fainted, but not because of their argument or delayed humiliation.

Another conversational tack seemed prudent. "I thought we decided to forget last night ever happened."

Something flashed in Michael's eyes, and his nostrils flared. He flattened his lips as if to rein in his temper. "If you insist, then I have to agree. No more mention of last night's farce. You're a newcomer to Winona, and we've just been introduced." He extended his right hand. "Pleased to make your acquaintance, Miss Baldwin."

For a moment she stared at his hand. Was this the right thing to do? It felt right, so she placed her fingers over his. Despite the formality of their contact, Amelia again felt the jolt of energy she'd come to associate with Michael's touch and had to clear her throat to answer.

"A pleasure indeed, Mr. Hayak."

From that moment on, Michael bombarded Amelia with attention. After seeing to the animals, he returned to the kitchen and took up a dish towel. "Since I helped Katie make the mess," he explained, "it's only right for me to see to the cleaning." And, whistling crystal-pure melodies, he halved her chores.

Chivalry became the order of the day. On her next wash day, Michael carried a basketful of clean clothes upstairs for her, then later used the stove shovel to remove excess ash built up in the range—a dirty task, to be sure.

As time went by, Amelia became privy to more and more of Michael and Katie's conversations, ones meant specifically for her ears.

"We must be extra nice to 'Melia," he said.

Katie's enthusiastic "Yeth" followed.

"We want 'Melia to be happy with us, right?"

Another "Yeth" chimed out.

"We don't want 'Melia to leave, do we?"

"No!" Katie yelped. "Never, never, no!"

The King of Rats strolled past Amelia, whistling sweetly, an innocent smile plastered on his beaming face.

Seconds later, Katie charged Amelia, hugged her knees, raised her arms, and begged, "Up." Amelia's cheek received a toddler-sweet kiss. "Katie lubs 'Melia."

Exasperated by the father but touched by the child's honest affection, Amelia rolled her eyes for his benefit and hugged the stuffing out of the little girl. " 'Melia loves you, too, Katie."

When she chastised him for using the child to batter her defenses, he asked, "You question her feelings for you?"

"Of course not! But it's wrong to use her like that."

Unrepentant, he searched the room. "Who says I'm using her?"

"*I* say you are."

He chuckled and shook his head. "I'd be using her if I sent her to press my suit. I'm only reminding her how important you are and how much we need you with us."

"B-but, she's just a child—"

Michael placed a finger on her lips. "That's right. A child who loves you. One you love, too. The child who needs you now."

"I thought we'd agreed to forget the proposal."

"I don't recall that agreement. I remember agreeing to forget a number of things, but I don't believe the proposal was one of them."

"Of course it was. We agreed to become new acquaintances."

Triumph brightened his handsome features. "That's precisely what Katie and I are doing. We're getting to know you, and letting you get to know us."

A few days later came the episode with the apples. Thanks to all of Michael's help around the house, Amelia found time to try the recipes Pansy had left for her. One morning, she woke up craving apple pie. Michael had shown her the bushels of apples in the root cellar, and immediately Amelia had begun her plans.

With care she prepared the crust and lined the pie plates. Next she mixed sugar, flour, and cinnamon, sprinkling the mixture over slices of fruit. After dumping the resulting filling into the bottom crust, she applied the top one and crimped the edges with the pinching motion Pansy had demonstrated.

As Amelia set to cleaning the sprinkles of sugar and flour that dusted the table, Katie ran to the laundry tub where Amelia had washed the apples. Three red-cheeked fruits remained in the water. Giggling, she began dunking them, just to watch them pop right back up. " 'Melia, look!"

Katie bounced one apple, rippling the water with her chubby hand. The other ones danced across the surface, too. Amelia joined in the fun. Katie's giggles multiplied.

"What's going on in here?" asked Michael from the kitchen doorway.

"We're playing," Amelia answered, glancing his way. She caught her breath. Michael stood propped against the jamb, arms crossed over his chest, a smile on his lips. A dark brown lock fell over his forehead, and his eyes sparkled with life. Amelia had never seen a more attractive man.

"May I join you?" he asked as he came to their side.

"Of course."

"Yeth!"

In a graceful move, he sat across the tub from Amelia, and plunked an apple beneath another. Katie giggled, then chased her own piece of fruit, sailing it straight toward Amelia. Amelia sent it right back where it came from.

"Hmmmm . . ." Michael murmured. "This reminds me of something I haven't done in years." He dipped his head, mouth open, and tried to capture the fruit.

Amelia watched, remembering a lifetime of Halloweens

at the orphanage and foster homes. "I've never bobbed for apples."

Startled, Michael looked up. *Oh, no!* Amelia thought, worried he might bring up the amnesia problem again.

But he shrugged. "It's time you did, then."

"What should I do?"

"Watch!"

She did, and laughed as he went too far, dunking up to his hairline.

"How dare you laugh?"

"You should see yourself!"

"Think you can do better?"

"Of course!"

"I dare you."

"You're on!" Moments later, she wiped dripping lengths of black hair from her face. She hadn't caught her apple yet.

"Again!" she cried, determined to win.

"Very well." They went down at the same time.

Their foreheads bumped, and they both laughed, raising their heads in unison. The laughter stopped. A breath separated their lips. Blue eyes sought green. A current of . . . something flew between them. At least Amelia felt something sizzle through her.

He whispered her name and came closer, his lips grazing hers.

"What doin', Papa?"

Amelia jerked back as if stung by a bee. Michael smiled, winking. "Kissing Amelia's ouch away."

"Me, too!" Katie cried, and wrapped sodden arms around Amelia.

"I think it's time to end the game," Amelia said, sounding as disappointed as the two suddenly long faces before her. "You can taste the pies when they're done," she suggested. The smiles returned.

A few snowy days later, after Amelia talked Katie into taking a nap, Michael joined her in the parlor, where she kept the rocker swaying as she worked her way through the pile of sewing she'd brought along.

"You've done a lot for us, Amelia."

She lifted a shoulder, not knowing where his comment would lead. "I've been glad to help."

"I'd like to do something for you, but I don't know quite what. I can't escort you to a party—not after the sleighing party turned out so bad—"

"Hush! We agreed not to talk about that."

He studied her face. "Fine. But I'd still like to do something for you."

"Like what?"

"Well, in Winona we could go to a restaurant for a special meal. Or perhaps to a theatrical performance—one of those given by your vaudeville friends. But we're out on the farm, and Winona is far to go in weather this cold."

Amelia smiled but didn't comment.

He exhaled a noisy gust. "What I'm trying to say is that I'd like to offer you a special evening. I'll make a meal, wear my Sunday suit, we can chat, especially since we've only recently met . . ."

She thought her heart would burst, it felt so full of love. "Oh, Michael—"

He leaped up, shaking his hand before her face. "No, Amelia. I won't let you 'Oh, Michael' me again. The last time you did that, you rejected my suit, and we ended up embarrassed before everyone in town. Who knows how wild the talk about us has grown."

"I have no intention of turning down this lovely offer."

"You mean that?" he asked, eagerness in his voice.

"I wouldn't miss it for the world."

Whistling again, he left the parlor, and took up his post in the kitchen. Strange noises rattled Amelia's calm every so often, but despite occasional bursts of expletives, she figured he'd call her when he conceded defeat. After all, she'd seen his version of oatmeal, and it hadn't inspired much confidence in his cooking skills.

Hours later, well after Katie had risen from her nap and the sun had dipped beyond the horizon, Michael gave out the bellow she'd been expecting. "I need your help!"

She found the kitchen virtually demolished. It looked as if Michael had failed to control a herd of elephants intent on tap-dancing through. But he hadn't called her for clean-up duty as she'd supposed. Holding the back door open with his shoulder, Michael was wrestling a washtub full of steaming water out to the porch.

"What on earth are you doing?" Amelia asked.

"Open the door before I scald myself!"

She hurried, then watched him empty the basin into the shiny japanned bathtub on the porch. He ran back to the kitchen, pumped more water into the washbasin, then set it on the stove to heat. He lifted a steaming kettle out of the sink, and poured that into the bathtub as well.

"Are you going to tell me what you're doing?" she asked.

"What does it look like I'm doing?"

"Boiling enough water to kill another pig."

He made an exasperated sound. "I'm trying to take a—"

"Yuck! Baff," offered Katie as she joined them.

"You're going to take a bath? Now? Out there?"

"Only tub big enough for me is there."

Just the thought of bathing in the evening cold sent shivers of misery through her. "Better you than me. Hurry, though. That water won't stay hot for long."

Michael went to work on his shirt buttons. "That's why I put the washtub to heat. You can bring out a kettleful when I yell."

Amelia wasn't sure about this latest idea. The dinner . . . well, that had been a nice proposition. Since she had fresh bread, cheese, and apples, they wouldn't go hungry because he'd given up on his meal. But bathing on an unheated back porch? In the middle of a frozen tundra?

"All right," she said, questioning his sanity. They were a good pair, all right. Amelia with her visions; Michael with his crazy ideas. Poor Katie, caught in the middle, depending on them.

After more curses, she heard a splash, and assumed that Michael's bath had begun. Curiosity getting the better of her, she began nosing around the pots on the stove's warming shelf. Fluffy mashed potatoes filled one pan, butter-glossed green beans another. The third one held gravy, and a wonderful scent escaped the oven.

"Hmmmmm . . ." Here she'd gone to great lengths and learned to prepare the most basic foods, and Michael turned out to be an accomplished cook. A sloppy one, though. That last trait had misled her the first time she'd seen the messy Hayak kitchen. She'd assumed he was hopeless in that room and had immediately pitched in to help. All he'd needed, however, was a servant to clean up after him. "We'll see about that!"

"Amelia!" he roared.

More hot water. With the smaller kettle he'd used, she dipped steaming water from the washtub, and asked Katie to open the door. The blast of frigid air slapped her cheeks, and she hurried to keep Michael from getting chilled. When she reached his side, though, she came to a complete standstill.

The wretch sat naked—he was bathing, after all—feet dangling over one end of the tub, wide shoulders rising above the other. Occasional wisps of steam curled up from the water, but only when he moved. Seal-sleek hair dripped onto the floor. His shoulders had dried, but his chest hair still harbored drops. Glorious in his masculinity, he knew it too damn well.

Stop it! she ordered herself, disgusted to have let him witness his effect on her, then dumped the hot water in the tub. The resurgence of heat must have shocked him, since he bolted to a sitting position, and regaled her with another effluvium of profanity.

"Watch your language," she warned, "your daughter's listening." As she started back, she thought better of it. For a moment. Just long enough to plunk the empty kettle over his groin. "I'd be careful if I were you. It's cold enough out here to freeze your—"

"Amelia!"

"Yes?"

"What are you saying? After all, you did say that Katie could hear."

"I was only going to mention your . . . extremities." She sashayed back inside.

Not long after his bath, Michael returned to the kitchen wearing a crisp white shirt, its collar stiff and upright, its waist tucked into black wool trousers. At his neck he wore a black silk bowtie, and plain pearls held his cuffs closed.

Amelia could only stare. Michael's good looks were undeniable, but his appeal ran deeper than symmetry of features, well-built body, and pleasant smile. Michael wore self-confidence with the ease of one who knows who he is. Amelia envied and admired that in him, feeling the lack within herself, especially as a result of her orphanhood.

As she studied him, she remembered she still wore the simple skirt and shirtwaist she'd put on first thing in the morning. Since she wasn't about to bathe out on that frosty porch, she refilled the kettle he'd brought back in and headed for the stairs. "It's your turn to watch Katie. I'll only be a few minutes."

"Take your time," he answered, his voice rich and persuasive. "I'll feed Katie and tuck her into bed. Supper tonight is for grown-ups only."

As she went up the stairs, Amelia found her logical self battling her fanciful self. She'd decided she couldn't encourage the attraction between them, but she certainly couldn't control Michael's behavior. His actions indicated growing interest. She couldn't fail to be flattered by his attention.

He'd even dressed in his Sunday best!

She could do no less. Quickly filling the hipbath with hot water, she undressed and washed up. Then, choosing a soft, forest-green wool dress, she put herself back together. Instead of braiding her hair as she did mornings, she pulled it up, approximating a Gibson-girl look.

The mirror reflected her excitement. Her cheeks glowed rosy, her eyes sparkled, her lips smiled. The hairstyle suited her, as did the dress with its simple ecru-lace trim at the neck.

Michael was waiting for her. Every time she thought about it, her heart beat faster. They were going on a date— even though they weren't *going* anywhere. The scene he'd set wore the hallmark of a date, a special evening to enjoy, to treasure in her memory.

Excitement bubbled in her. Although she'd dated in that other, far-off life she once lived, Amelia had never felt like this. Surely something wonderful would happen. She could feel it in the fast flutter of her pulse, the glow Michael's actions lit within her, the effort both put forth to ensure a moment of beauty.

With a final pat to the wisps of black curls on her forehead, Amelia went to meet her escort.

Chapter 14

WHEN AMELIA CAME down the stairs, and as she headed for the kitchen, Michael called to her from the rarely used dining room. "Tonight is special," he said, indicating the table dressed in an exquisite, ivory cut-work tablecloth, and set with flickering tapers in silver candlesticks, gold-rimmed china, and stemmed crystal glasses.

Amelia couldn't believe her eyes. Not even at the finest of Chicago restaurants had she seen a more elegant or more beautifully done table. "Michael! This is . . . I don't know what to say! I'm stunned."

Pleasure showed in his smile. "All this came from Bohemia with my grandparents. I don't have many more treasures, but what I have suits for special occasions."

Another shimmer of excitement ran through Amelia's middle, and a flush warmed her cheeks. Subtle he wasn't, but he certainly knew how to treat a woman—when he wanted to.

"Why don't you sit here?" He pulled out a chair.

Amelia accepted and sat, then shook open her intricately

embroidered napkin. A moment later she felt Michael's
presence at her elbow again. "Apple cider?" he asked.

"Mm-hmmm."

He poured the golden beverage into her glass from a
faceted crystal pitcher whose sides caught the candlelight
and broke it into rainbows.

As he walked to the other side of the table, Amelia
glanced around the room. Both brightened and shadowed
by the glow from the candles, its dimensions seemed generous if full of carved mahogany furniture. Above a massive
sideboard hung a painting depicting harvest's plenty. In a
tall china cabinet she saw more of the gold-trimmed dishes,
even though the flanking wall lamps hadn't been lit. A pre-
dominantly garnet-and-cream-flowered rug cushioned the
floor, its colors repeated on the striped wallpaper above the
oak wainscot.

"This is a beautiful room, Michael."

He smiled again, reaching for a covered platter. "It was
my grandmother's pride and joy." He pointed to the sliced
meat. "A piece of—"

"Not that poor pig!"

Michael chuckled. "No, the Kleinschmidt boys brought
us venison."

Bambi! Amelia nearly screamed the name, restraining
herself with effort. What was she going to do about her recent reluctance to consume dead animals? It hadn't bothered her in that other life, probably because she'd never
seen an animal slaughtered.

"In that case, just a small bit." This matter merited more
thought, but later, well after she'd stored in her heart every
last, glorious memory of this unforgettable night. She took
up her glass and tasted the cider. "Oh! This is wonderful.
Did you make it?"

Michael lifted his glass and studied the beverage, its
clear amber color backlit by candles. "I'm afraid I couldn't
begin to approximate Herbert's apple cider."

"Herbert?"

Michael lifted a querying eyebrow, but responded, "Yes, Weidel's Apple Orchards are well-known in these parts."

"*Herbert* made this?"

Michael gave a wry laugh. "Astounding, right?"

"I'll say." Amelia sipped some more. "Talented man."

"And generous. He gave me two kegs of last fall's product. I'd say it was his finest year yet."

Amelia drank some more, replaced her glass, and took up her fork. "Supper smells wonderful."

"It's not as fancy as the table, but it should taste good."

Amelia took a mouthful of gravy-laden potatoes and closed her eyes. "Delicious," she murmured once she'd swallowed. "You're too modest."

Red crept up Michael's cheekbones. "It's a meal."

As they ate, they kept the conversation on the food, the day's happenings, Katie's latest antics. The room looked beautiful, they both had dressed up, the food satisfied, and the talk resembled that of a happily married couple. It felt right. As if it fit. Suddenly Amelia feared the possibility of all this ending when fate claimed her again.

When she grew quiet, Michael frowned for a moment, then stood. "I planned a treat for us."

Amelia glanced up. "There's more?"

For a moment deviltry danced in his gaze. In the golden candlelight, a rogue's smile made him handsomer still, and Amelia prepared herself for a suggestive remark. But he only said, "Plenty."

Leading her by the hand, he went to the coatrack in the entryway and held out her coat.

"We're going outside?" she asked.

"Mm-hmmm."

"This late?"

"It's the best time."

"What about Katie?"

"She's sleeping," he said. "If you want, I'll make sure she's covered."

"No, I'd hate to disturb her. Where are we going?"

"To wonderland."

"My name's not Alice, you don't look like a rabbit or a mad hatter, and I'd rather the Queen of Hearts didn't take my head!"

"What do I look like?"

The man I love. Amelia fought to silence her words, words that formed as she looked at Michael, as she admired his smile, his bright eyes, the determination he displayed. He was going to entertain her, even if it meant dragging her along in his wake.

She smiled. "You look like a child on Christmas Day."

Michael cocked his head. "You know, I feel that way. This is a special night indeed."

His words echoed her feelings, and Amelia stored them as a treasure in her heart. Without further question, she followed him to the back porch, where he insisted she sit on the old chair he kept there. "What are you doing—"

"Here!" he said, brandishing a pair of what looked like handleless tennis rackets. "Let me put these on you."

"Are those . . . snowshoes?" she asked.

"That's right. Give me your foot."

She wasn't sure she'd seen snowshoes before, but a vague recollection of pictures in old books came to mind. She supposed she'd best not bring up her lack of memory, lest it ruin an otherwise perfect evening.

Making short shrift of it, Michael strapped her to the oval frames with leather thongs much like the ones that formed a netting across the center of the oval. When she tried to rise, she collapsed back in the chair, overcome with giggles. "Whatever gave you the idea I'd be able to go anywhere wearing these, Michael?"

"Oh, let's say your . . . *determination* comes to mind."

"Are you calling me stubborn?"

"If the shoe fits. . . ."

"Oh, that's *awful!* What a terrible pun!"

"Very well, then, let's go!"

Only then did she notice that while she'd studied the

contraptions on her feet, he'd donned a pair of the same.
With a shuffling gait, he led her to the stairs and helped her
step onto the snow in the backyard.

The wind blew briskly, making Amelia glad Michael had
thought to wrap a thick woolen scarf over her head and
around her neck. Her gauntlet mittens, unwieldy though
they were since they reached well over her wrists, were just
as welcome.

"Michael! I can't walk in these things," she wailed.

"Watch," he answered, picking one foot well off the
snow, then setting it back flat on the white surface. He repeated the maneuver, and held out his hand for her to grasp.

Amelia tried, she really did. "I can't do it!" she insisted.
"My skirt gets in the way."

"Bend your knee as you pick up your foot."

She did, and found she could set the snowshoe back
down a few inches ahead of the other one.

"That's it! Do it again."

"You were right!"

"This way!" he urged, taking her hand and leading her
away from the house.

With a nod she followed, wondering exactly what was
the point of this frigid excursion. Then they arrived at the
protected side of the barn. Out of the direct path of the
wind, Michael paused, took an audible breath, and waved.
"Take a good look, Amelia. There's very little as beautiful
in the world."

Amelia did as he asked. "You're right!" she exclaimed in
an awed whisper. She'd never seen a sight as perfect as
this.

The rolling countryside extended endlessly, pristine-pure
in its gown of white. In parts, the play of moonlight and
midnight gave the impression of fine silver plate, as if to
emphasize earth's perfection. Here and there stands of pine
broke through the snow to add texture to the glistening
sheen. From the distant vista to just beyond the shadow of
the barn, minute flakes caught the brilliant moonglow and

tossed it back into the air. Those tiny stars mimicked the larger ones hung on a deep, deep blue sky above, twinkling, blurring the distinction between heaven and earth.

If ever she'd questioned God's existence, Amelia knew at that moment she would never doubt again. Only a benevolent Father provided His children with beauty so exalted they'd know His love and goodness forever. For if He'd thought enough to give pleasure in something as insignificant as a beautiful view, how much more would He not be willing to give in matters of importance?

For the first time, Amelia allowed herself a moment of hope. A prayer formed in her heart, and she held it close, wishing, hoping, placing all her awakening faith in that plea. She skimmed her gaze again over the perfect Minnesota midnight she'd been given, and released her request, sending it to that all-powerful Maker, certain He'd receive it and listen in love.

Amelia dared hope in tomorrow, a lifetime of tomorrows with Michael and Katie to love.

Almost as if he'd heard her thoughts, Michael led her a few steps forward to stand directly before him. He widened his stance so that his snowshoes bracketed hers, and wrapped his arms about her. With a sigh of obvious contentment, he pulled her back into the shelter of his body and rubbed his cheek against her temple.

Not a word was said. Not one was needed.

Never had Amelia felt such peace, such complete joy, such a current of excitement, such a sense of belonging.

She caught her breath. It was true. For the first time ever, she knew she stood where she had to be, with the person she most needed to be with, living a moment precious only to them. Could this sense of rightness be the beginning of an answer to her prayer? This soon?

As she mused on the possibilities, she realized she wouldn't know a thing about the future until it came to pass. She also realized that tonight held too much promise to waste in worries about tomorrow. For now, she'd trust in the God who'd allowed her this moment in time, this life-changing, defining incident of pure contentment and love.

Then she felt Michael stir. "Is something wrong?"

He chuckled. "Don't ask. But, here," he said, grasping her hand. "Let's take a walk. It's so beautiful, I don't want to waste even a second."

"That's just how I feel," she murmured and earned a smile.

He led her back around the barn. "Come this way."

Amelia stumbled along at Michael's side, her feet unwilling to surrender to the demands of the large, despotic snowshoes. She wondered what Michael thought, since she knew she had to resemble a drunk unable to communicate with tipsy limbs.

Her right snowshoe then snagged the left. Amelia lost her balance. She pitched headfirst into Michael's back, knocking him down, too. "Watch out!"

Laughter shook her. The snow on the ground cushioned their fall like the giant feather mattress it resembled.

Sprawled over Michael's back, she immediately felt him laugh. At the same time, she realized he lay face-first in the snow—not good, since the powdery stuff would probably stifle his breathing. She rolled off him, still chuckling. He did the same.

Their shared laughter rang out into the peaceful night. It sounded happy, warm, just right for this picture-perfect moment. On her back, admiring the starry sky, Amelia knew true happiness. As the thought crossed her mind, Michael took her hand in his.

She turned her head. Her gaze met his. Something special, private, meaningful, passed between them. He squeezed her hand. She returned the pressure. Both smiled.

Moments later, he called her name. "Look!" he said, and began flapping both arms in the snow. Up, down, up, down. Then she noticed his legs moving in the same way. "Come on," he urged. "You do it, too."

Hesitant at first, Amelia spread her arms and legs as far

as her skirt would go. Then, since no one else could see their silly play, she flapped in earnest, mirroring Michael's actions.

He stood, reached out his hand, and helped her rise. After steadying her on the snowshoes, he pulled her into the curve of one arm. "Angels in the night," he murmured, holding her at his side.

She glanced where he indicated, and saw the figures in the snow. "Angels in flight," she corrected.

"Where to?"

"Heaven, surely Heaven," she said, referring to the majestic feelings this night inspired.

"Heaven on earth, perhaps?"

Amelia thought for a moment. "You may be right."

They studied the shapes joined at the wings for a few, quiet minutes longer. In such sweet silence, Amelia failed to banish thoughts of marriage to Michael. This comfort, this joy, would come with such a union. This was what she'd always needed, what she'd never found in that swiftly fading life in another time. This was real, the emotions strong and vital, the closeness between Michael and her powerful, moving, the passion, although only an ember right now, potent and consuming.

She belonged. Right here.

The sudden flash of certainty startled her. What did it mean? Did it answer her prayer? With just a feeling of "it's right"?

No, more than likely it reflected her deepest longings, the most essential cravings of her hungry heart. And she didn't feel particularly noble. She felt a longing, a yearning, a consuming need. She also felt Michael's responding want.

What about the future? her conscience asked.

What about it? she retorted.

What if she again stumbled across the warp in time that brought her here? What if she married Michael and shortly afterward was ripped away? What if Katie's second mother vanished as irrevocably as her first had done?

Amelia had no answer.

But, argued her desires in a tempting tone, if she hadn't had this strange experience, if she hadn't plunged through time, she would still have no assurance that she wouldn't suddenly die, just as Christina had. No one faced their future with any more certainty than she had right now.

What difference would the outcome make? she wondered, her heart picking up its beat. Time warps, faulty hearts, accidents, and plagues all ravaged equally. They stole loved ones from those left behind. The grief would be no different.

If she refused Michael's proposal, she might live forever a neighbor and acquaintance, wanting what she'd once refused. If she accepted, she could die or be dragged back to where she'd come from. The difference in both possibilities lay in the present, what it could bring if in simple faith she stepped forward and grasped it with both hands.

A family. Joy. The love of a man and a woman, brought together by some unseen plan.

As she contemplated the possibilities, everything within her strained toward that dream, knowing she was a "Yes" away. She'd do it. The profit was well worth the potential cost.

Amelia Baldwin would marry the man she loved.

In the cold breeze, Michael pulled Amelia closer, relishing the rightness of the moment. He'd never seen a more beautiful night. The curve of the white-frosted hills looked as lush as the woman in his arms. Icy moonlight shone off the snowflakes on the ground, resembling Amelia's sparkling eyes. The vast silence of the night made him think of the years to come, rich and beautiful, filled with . . . love.

He allowed himself to admit it. He loved Amelia. He loved her with a love he'd never imagined, with a passion that overruled his common sense, with a need that burned within him, making it all but impossible to live without her.

That need had driven him to keep her at the farm the morning Pansy came to visit. He should have let Amelia go, return home to her life and her work. She'd given nearly two years to his wife, his daughter, himself. The honorable thing would have been to let her leave.

But Michael feared he had very little honor when it came to Amelia Baldwin. He'd fostered an adulterous desire for her while his wife lay dying. He'd kept that desire stoked after Christina's passing. He'd finally yielded to the needs of his body at the first hint of Amelia's surrender.

His actions displayed little honor indeed.

Why? Why had he found forbidden love and passion only after marrying a perfectly wonderful wife?

Just as he couldn't have guessed how little time Christina had, Michael could never have known that Amelia would enter his life when he couldn't court her, when he shouldn't think of her, when his desire for her would burn as an illicit, sinful flame.

Although he hadn't touched Amelia until the very end, he knew adultery consisted in more than simply satisfying the flesh. Scriptures he'd read long ago said, ". . . whoever looks at a woman to lust for her has already committed adultery with her. . . ."

Although plucking his eyes out, as Scripture also recommended, was out of the question, Michael didn't deserve the happiness he could find with Amelia. After all, he'd damned himself with two long years of wanting her.

He regretted the betrayal of his marriage vows. He also regretted not loving Christina as he should have. But love didn't seem to be commanded by worthiness or determination. Love grew unexpectedly, irrespective of any number of shalls and shall nots. The one who loved, however, held the power in his sometimes weak hand to choose which course to take.

That fleeting moment in the kitchen, just an hour before

Christina's death, continued to haunt Michael even now. If only he hadn't given in to his desire, then perhaps he would feel less guilty now. If he hadn't touched Amelia before Christina died, perhaps he could forgive himself the weakness that made him want her before he had that right.

Loving Amelia wasn't necessarily a sin. Touching her while his wife still lived was.

He'd wondered—incessantly—if Amelia's pretense of amnesia sprang from the guilt she might feel over that one stolen moment as her friend lay dying. She hadn't done a thing, though. He'd caught her by surprise, taken what she'd never offered. Then she ran away, disappeared for days, and when she returned she refused to acknowledge what had happened. In fact, she'd persisted with her fictitious amnesia rather than allow a recurrence of that caress.

Then came that exquisite night, a night filled with passion the likes of which Michael hadn't known could exist. And Amelia had met his desire with a fire all her own. He'd wondered since that night if her feelings for him were new. Had they grown in the recent past? Had they been born of his single lapse of control?

Or had they existed as long as his for her had?

He didn't know. He didn't dare ask.

She'd left after the loving, but she had come back. Now she stood with him, leaning into his support, sharing a moment of happiness.

As he mulled over his painful thoughts, Amelia remained quiet, clearly deep in thought, as well. Michael again wondered what troubled her. He didn't dare ask this, either. He wasn't yet ready to discuss his actions or the feelings that had brought them about. He doubted he'd be ready to discuss them until he understood them, until he found the peace he feared would never be his.

Michael wished he could read Amelia's thoughts, he wished he knew what she felt for him, what tonight meant to her. She didn't give him long to speculate. Moments later, she whispered his name. "Yes?" he answered.

"Will you marry me?"

"What did you say?" he asked, turning, grasping her shoulders, seeking her gaze.

Her green eyes danced with mischief. Her lips curved like those of a siren. Her cold-reddened cheeks revealed her excitement, and Michael knew he loved Amelia Baldwin more than he'd ever love another soul. "Yes," he said. "Yes! Yes, yes, yes!"

Her smile broadened, and he suspected it mirrored his own. He went to embrace her, but found his efforts thwarted by the wide front of their snowshoes. Taking her hand, he said, "Let's go back inside. It's much too cold out here, and besides, I think this bargain must be properly sealed. The snowshoes don't help."

Impatient, he started off for the back porch, pulling his bride in his wake. *His bride*. Amelia had agreed to marry him.

He shot her a glance over his shoulder, and caught the look of earnest concentration as she maneuvered the ungainly snowshoes. Everything she did she did carefully, with all the considerable energy and determination she possessed. Amelia would be the perfect wife, the perfect mother.

At the steps, he slowed, helping her place each snowshoe, one at a time, on a step. Then he led her to the wobbly chair he kept on the porch to take his workshoes off or put them on. Refusing even to glance at her until both were back inside the house—he feared he might yield to the need to kiss her, hold her, beg her to repeat herself—he removed her snowshoes first, then his own. Holding the door for her, he let Amelia in, then closed it after himself.

He sought her gaze, found it somewhat hesitant, then knew exactly what to do. "Come with me to the parlor," he asked. "I want this part to be as perfect as the rest of the evening."

When he placed his hand at the small of her back, he felt

her quiver from his touch. Satisfaction welled in him. He affected her as much as she did him.

The lamps in the darkened parlor took but seconds to light. Michael then led Amelia to the wide camel-backed sofa. In true chivalric style, he knelt at her feet, clasped her slender hand between his, and sought her gaze. "Will you marry me, Amelia?"

"Yes," she whispered, smiling through the veil of tears in her eyes. He kissed the back of her hand as a tear ran down her cheek.

"What's wrong?" he asked, worried.

She shook her head, smiling. "I'm happier than I've ever been. You don't know how much this means to me."

Her words reminded him that this wasn't his first proposal. "What makes tonight right and the last time wrong?"

She looked at their clasped hands. Her fingers tightened their hold. "I . . . came to a decision. It took some time to get there. Finally I decided to accept what I wanted most."

"Me?"

Her smile returned. "You."

Michael stood and pulled Amelia with him. As his arms went around her, she pressed herself against him, her arms sliding around his neck. She parted her lips. He took her invitation.

Her lips were warm and sweet, responsive as always. Addictive as well. Michael found himself returning to them, kiss after kiss, unwilling to release the source of his pleasure. As surely as a cotton wick catches fire, his body heated, passion urging his caresses.

When he slipped his tongue into her mouth, he felt her tremble, her arms tighten around his neck. Her tongue met his, dueled, then danced along the secret corners of his mouth, taking as he had taken, giving as he had. Her hands came up to cup his cheeks, holding him still as she delved in his mouth with as much passion as he had shown her. He moaned, running his hands up and down her back, skimming her hips, cupping her bottom, pressing himself into her softness.

Amelia's hands explored, too. Her fingers raked through his hair, tiptoed over his shoulders, stroked down his chest, rounded his waist. All the while, she pressed closer to him, imprinting her every curve, every valley on him, as if she sought to meld them into one.

Which was what Michael needed most, to join them intimately, to plunge into her, over and over again. He needed to ensure their unity, their closeness, make them one.

Amelia made a sound of passion, husky and hungry, against his lips. Her hands fluttered up and down his back, coming to his chest again, his neck.

She'd agreed to be his. That thought, although it stoked his hunger for her to a fever pitch, also brought him to a halt. He slowly released her lips, placing tiny kisses at the corners, on her cheeks, the tip of her nose.

Bewilderment filled her eyes. She mouthed, "Why?"

Since he knew she'd felt his arousal, and since he read the evidence of hers in her heightened color, her uneven breaths, the tightened tips of her breasts, he gently pulled away.

"Because," he explained, "the next time I have you, you will be my wife."

Chapter 15

THE NEXT FEW days took them to Heaven and Hell. Anticipation felt like Heaven. The waiting was Hell.

As though in response to Amelia's prayers, the temperature began to rise, and the snow outside to melt. Michael hadn't wanted to travel to Winona for a quick, quiet wedding at the church until the snow melted. The snow and cold posed any number of dangers.

But as soon as the road became passable, if muddy, Michael hitched the horses to his buggy, and the three of them drove in to town. They first stopped at the home of an older lady, a woman Michael introduced to Amelia as Mrs. Tomicek, his mother's closest friend.

"Mrs. Tom," he said, "I'd like you to meet Amelia. She's agreed to be my bride."

A pair of wary black eyes studied Amelia, inscrutable in their effort. She wriggled uncomfortably.

Mrs. Tom finally said, "I know who she is, but I didn't know you intended to marry up so soon."

Michael's eyebrows gathered close. "Neither did I. It just seemed the most expedient thing to do. I can't run the farm alone, and Katie needs constant watching. A mother, too. Amelia helped us through Christina's illness. We're all used to each other. I feel this is the best solution to our needs."

Amelia felt every ounce of her joy evaporate. *Expedient.* She was an expedient thing to do. After the night in the snow, she'd begun to believe that Michael could come to love her, just as she loved him. Hearing him now, cold-heartedly describing their wedding as an expedient thing to do, punctured a hole in the balloon of happiness she'd been hanging from for days. The landing in reality came with a jolt of despair.

Mrs. Tomicek continued to stare at Amelia, adding irritation to her pain. She didn't know how much longer she could stand before them and not reveal her wounded heart.

Then the older woman gave a nod and looked at Michael. "Son, marriage isn't all business, you know. You married once because you thought it was the most intelligent thing to do. Although it failed on account of illness, I hope you've learned that more than practical matters must be weighed before saying 'I do.' "

Michael's cheeks colored slightly, and he shot a guilty glance Amelia's way. "I . . . know, Mrs. Tom. Amelia and I . . . we get on well. I think we'll do fine."

Get on well! Heck, they came close to incinerating the farm every time they so much as touched, and he could only say they got on well? Amelia's temper began to boil. "I must go home and see about a number of matters," she spit through clenched teeth. "I'll be there until you're ready to speak with Father Charles."

With that, she pivoted and opened the door. Cold, damp air met her, cooling the heat of anger on her cheeks. It did nothing to soothe the misery inside.

"Amelia!" Michael called, following her. He grasped her elbow as she strode toward the street, and with a firm tug he swung her around to face him. "What on earth's gotten into you, woman?"

"Oh, I don't know, Michael. Maybe this is the way *expedient things* behave. I wouldn't know. I've never known one, much less suspected I was one before today."

"What the Hell did you want me to tell her? That the minute I scent you I get hard as rock? That I can't touch you without wanting to strip you bare? That I don't dare kiss my future wife for fear I'll take her right where she stands?"

Ineffectually *shh-shing* at Michael, Amelia cast fearful looks all around, worried that his graphic words might be overheard. "Of course you couldn't say that! But *expedient,* Michael? You couldn't come up with a better word than that?"

His lips tightened and flattened to a thin, straight line. "I'm sorry if my choice of word has injured your fine sensibilities, but you should know, Miss Baldwin, I'm a private man. What is between you and me is just that: private. I truly thought to spare you embarrassment by not alluding to more intimate matters."

Amelia resumed her walk, teetering between anger, hurt, and appeasement. He had a point. But somewhere inside, where her most secret longings lived, she needed to hear him say he cared, that there was more than convenience and sex between them, that she mattered to him, in a special, magical way.

Perhaps she wanted too much.

Her anger somewhat deflated, she stopped. "Thank you for explaining. And apologizing. During the last few days many different feelings have risen to the surface and kept me off balance. I'm sorry I lost my temper. I'll try to stay calmer, be more circumspect."

A sharp nod came with a troubled look. "Amelia, I know there is more than convenience between us. A lot more. I . . . don't quite know what it is, though, I just know that . . . it *is*. It burns inside me and urges me toward you."

With every word, he seemed to plunge the knife deeper. "Fine, Michael, I'll be the scratch for your itch. And the dutiful housekeeper. Katie's mother, too. Tell me, please, what *you're* willing to be for me."

His blue eyes widened. His jaw dropped. He stared at Amelia as if he'd never seen her before. She took advantage of his shock to bring her point closer to home. "Marriage isn't only about what Michael needs, you know. I'll be a partner in this union, and I have needs as well. Exactly what will I gain by marrying you?"

He blinked once, twice, shook his head. He opened his mouth to speak.

"And I don't want to hear a word about my reputation," she added, cutting him off.

When he again failed to formulate an answer, Amelia knew it was time to leave. "Don't follow me," she said. "Think about my questions. You want a quick wedding, but I think you'd best decide what you have in mind for the marriage, since it should last longer than the ceremony or a night in your bed. I'd suggest you do your thinking *before* you say 'I do.' "

Amelia turned westward, heading home, determined to reach its safety before the tears began to fall.

Amelia's eyes now swam in a salty sea. Michael didn't doubt it for a moment as he watched his intended stalk away. But what could he say? That he'd fallen in love with her as she nursed Christina? That he'd lusted for her for two years? That at those moments when Christina's suffering became an agony to witness he'd wished his wife dead? That he'd harbored the desire for freedom—freedom to pursue Amelia and make her his?

God help him, it was true, but he couldn't say those things to Amelia. His words would only make the breach between them wider, more impossible to bridge.

And he loved her. More each passing day. If giving her up was the honorable thing to do, then Michael wanted nothing of honor. He'd gone too far to turn back. He couldn't give up the taste of Heaven he'd found in Amelia, damning though it might be.

If she wanted pretty actions, pretty words, he'd give them to her. In time, he'd confess his love—once he could own up to his many sins. For now, Michael Hayak would marry Amelia Baldwin, even if it meant eternal damnation.

Although Amelia knew she'd made herself perfectly clear, Michael seemed determined to ignore the questions she'd posed. He'd come for her, treated her with almost cloying attention, complimenting even her choice of boots.

They'd gone to St. John Nepomucene Church—Michael's church—spoken with Father Charles Preis, or rather Michael spoke with the priest while Amelia watched and listened, wondering if Michael was suffering lapses of memory, too.

Selective memory. That was it, what Michael had. And although Amelia wasn't about to back down from her questions, she wasn't about to refuse to marry the man she loved just because he was a blind, insensitive, stubborn, *male* mule!

Surely as Mrs. Hayak she'd get those answers, perhaps even better than as Miss Amelia Baldwin.

Preparations for the wedding began in earnest. Amelia spent the next few days sorting, packing, and storing her belongings, organizing her little home. For the moment, the house would remain vacant, but she would consider offers to buy. She would, of course, be moving to the farm.

After years of dreaming of a wedding dress, Amelia found that simplicity appealed more than ruffs and frills and fussy trims. A quick trip to Choate's Dry Goods Store, however, left her reeling again. Not only had Michael replaced Mrs. Stoltz's ruined fabric, he'd also ordered an equal length in pale mint-green for Amelia. The satin moiré would make an exquisite wedding gown. When she got it home, she found she had enough to fashion a miniature version for Katie.

The little girl had been ecstatic since the moment they broke the news to her. "'Melia's Katie's mama?" she asked a million times a day.

"Yes, munchkin, I'm going to be your new mama," Amelia gladly answered each and every time. Even Michael had taken to calling her Mama when he spoke with his child.

Since she had taken her sewing out to the farm, she chose to spend the night before the wedding there, despite tradition, superstition, and old wives' tales. Her dress and Katie's needed minor adjustments, and it was simpler to do them where she now kept her tools.

Katie's excitement ran amuck with the little girl. As Amelia tried to tuck in a seam and adjust a scrap of lace, Katie wriggled and wiggled and shot rapid-fire questions her way.

"We's going t'church?"

"Mm-hmm," Amelia murmured through lips holding pins.

"P'iest be there?"

"Mm-hmmm."

"Mama, Papa, and Katie get married?"

"Mm-hmmmm."

"Whazzat?" She touched the pins poking out of Amelia's mouth.

"Katie-angel," Michael said from the kitchen doorway. "You talk too much. Let your mama finish what she's doing so you can go to bed. Tomorrow will be a busy day."

"Papa!" she called. "Looky dreth!"

"Lovely!" He came close and asked Amelia, "Are you done?"

"Mm-hmmm," she managed through her mouthful of pins. Running a final one through the last loose bit of lace, she spit the remaining pins into her hand. "Time for bed, munchkin."

Moments later, Katie's fancy dress lay over the arm of the rocker in the parlor, and Amelia tugged a pink-and-white-striped flannel nightgown over the child's head. "All ready?"

Katie ran to kiss Michael goodnight. "Nigh-night," she said as he held her close.

"Pleasant dreams, angel."

"Katie's weady." She slipped her fingers into Amelia's hand.

Up the stairs they went, and well before Amelia finished reading the story she'd promised, Katie slept. As usual, she made sure the blanket covered little arms and legs. A kiss on the child-round cheek followed.

Amelia smiled from the doorway as she paused to take another look at the child who after tomorrow would be hers. Her daughter. Emotion filled her heart. She was living her fondest dream. Life could only get better, since tomorrow she'd marry the man she loved.

As she watched Katie sleep, Michael joined her, slipping an arm around her waist. She glanced up, and saw that he, too, thought about the child. At that moment, Amelia held everything she'd ever dreamed of in the palm of her hand.

Almost everything. She didn't have Michael's love yet.

His tender kiss on her temple gave her hope. "Do you plan to finish the dresses tonight?" he asked.

"No. There's very little left to do, and plenty of time to do it in the morning. The ceremony isn't until the afternoon."

"I hope you don't mind that I've invited a few people," he said.

"Guests?"

"Some. Pansy and her husband, the Weidels, Fred and Hilda Smyser, Mrs. Tom. Not many, just friends."

"That sounds nice, but I thought we were only having a ceremony. I didn't expect guests who'd need to be fed or entertained. I have nothing prepared."

Michael chuckled. "No need to worry about that. Pansy's taking care of everything. You just need to say 'I do' at the right time."

Amelia remembered her talk with Pansy. "Between dictating the details of someone else's wedding, and controlling the arrangements, she must be in Heaven!"

Both chuckled, then Michael led Amelia a ways down the hall. He paused, both turned of one accord, and in silence they gazed into each other's eyes. The spark of passion was there, smoldering, but something else shone in Michael's eyes, something deeper than desire, richer than companionship. Although her practical side told Amelia she saw nothing more than the play of light on his eyes, her romantic side suggested it might be love.

"Good night," he murmured, then brought his lips to hers.

A gentle rocking, a tender touch was all he allowed them. Amelia felt cherished, precious to this man. If these kisses hadn't sprung from love, then surely she didn't know what love was.

"Good night," she answered, running her hand along his jaw.

Tonight would be the last lonely night Amelia would spend. From tomorrow on, for as long as God gave her life, she would sleep in Michael's arms. She couldn't wait for tomorrow to come.

Excitement thrummed through her as Amelia went toward her room. She heard Michael's footsteps on the stairs again, and she cast him a glance. "Aren't you tired?"

"Yes, but there's one last thing I must do. I'll turn in afterward."

That sounded strange, but he certainly didn't need her permission to do anything he wanted. "Good night, then."

"Good night."

With a glance around the upper floor, Amelia again felt that sense of rightness, of belonging. This cozy farmhouse would be her home, filled with Katie's laughter and Michael's voice, with triumphs shared and troubles halved, and maybe, if God so pleased, one day the laughter of more children would join Katie's and ring through the house.

Nearing the door to Christina's room, Amelia vowed she

wouldn't look in. She'd done this since that last time, that time when she'd caught a glimpse of . . . she didn't quite know what. It had seemed to work. She hadn't had any more disturbing visions since.

But as she walked by tonight, she couldn't help but wonder which room Michael intended for them to use. When he'd balked at sleeping in that room after his injury, she'd thought fresh bedding and removing the evidence of Christina's death would take care of his reluctance. After her own experience, however, she questioned her prior certainty. She doubted she could ever sleep in that room.

Against her better judgment, her eyes strayed in that forbidden direction. For a moment, Amelia thought she'd walk by unscathed. Then the hideous chill that accompanied her episodes of precognizance, of déjà vu, skittered down her spine and spread in waves, lodging sickly in her middle. Her palms grew damp, her breathing rough. She felt light-headed. Shivers rocked her, and she knew, she simply *knew* something awful was about to happen.

Reluctantly, but helpless to fight the impulse, she looked into the shadowed room. As before, a misty veil separated her from what she saw. This time, only the woman in the bed and the man at her side could be seen. He held a child in his arms, a child whose arms reached for the frail woman even though she failed to get a response.

Then, as if by an all-powerful hand, the mist was wiped away. Amelia saw Christina's tangled blond hair, her emaciated hands clutching the covers, the meager rise and fall of her chest. She was dying.

Amelia looked at the man and recognized what she'd known all along, but hadn't wanted to acknowledge. Standing by the bed, Michael held Katie, who cried for her mother, reaching for arms that could no longer hold her. Amelia witnessed the devastation of a family.

In Michael's eyes she saw grief, pain, and love. She also saw anger and guilt. In that moment, his every emotion was readable with an almost supernatural clarity, an other-worldly understanding.

Katie's cheeks and nose were red, her blue eyes swollen, her lips puffy from crying. "Mama . . . Mama, pleeze . . ."

But her mama was past answering.

Michael's misery clearly grew greater as tears poured down his cheeks. He held Katie closer, her head on his shoulder, both arms clamped about her as if he'd never let her go. Then the sobbing began, the weeping of a strong man who suffered, great gusty gasps that racked his frame, shook his daughter, ripped through Amelia's heart.

The grief, oh God, the grief Amelia felt was such that she could hardly breathe, couldn't even cry out. Watching Michael's misery caused her an agony all its own. She wanted to reach out, to hold him, to comfort him, but some-how she knew that her presence right then would bring him no peace.

So she suffered with him, endured the pain she saw in his eyes, felt the agony she heard in his cries, wept tears like those that wet his face.

Very gently Michael helped Katie to sit down on the edge of the bed. Katie took this as permission to pat her mother's hand, to cry "Mama! Mama—aaa!" in a more des-perate tone each time. Then the child leaned over and placed kisses on that translucent white face. "Mama . . . Mama . . . Mama . . ."

Michael knelt by his wife and child, lowered his head to the bed. His shoulders rocked with his cries, and he surren-dered to grief.

Amelia felt the urge to help him, but something held her back. Her feet remained where they were, as if frozen in the doorway to the room. Michael's anguish affected her more deeply than anything she'd ever seen before. Katie's grief moved Amelia to tears, to despair. But she didn't think any-thing she did could erase the trauma they faced.

As she stood, desolate, separated from those she loved, Amelia bitterly questioned her arrogance. What gave her the right to try to step into Christina's place? To love Christina's husband, her child?

The vision began to melt in slow ripples, the edges fading first. Finally, the only thing left to see were three figures on the bed. Christina, Michael, Katie. Then they, too, were gone.

"Nooooo. . . ." she cried and felt her legs give way.

A flood of tears, hot and stinging, washed her face. Sobs that started at the very center of her being ripped up, choking her, stealing her very breath. She curled into a tiny ball, huddled into herself to seek comfort, shielding herself from further pain, from the misery in her heart.

Loud footsteps approached. "Amelia!" Michael cried. "What happened?"

She couldn't speak. She couldn't move. She could only cry over a loss she couldn't explain. She'd never known Christina, yet here she lay, mourning the woman's death.

Michael slipped his arms under her, pulling her into his lap. Gently he smoothed the hair from her damp cheeks, dried her tears with his lips. "God in Heaven, what's wrong? You were fine just a moment ago. Amelia, tell me! Tell me, what's gone wrong?"

Little by little, her sobs turned to hiccups, and the tide of tears began to ebb. "Oh, Michael. I'm so sorry, so very sorry she died."

"Christina?" he asked, bewilderment in his voice. "Why, of course you're sorry. But . . . I don't understand. Some time has passed. Why now? Why are you crying now?"

"I don't know! It just hurts so bad . . . It's awful, horrid, and I can't get the pain to stop."

Questions dominated her thoughts. Why was she hurting so much? Why now? And why were these visions haunting her? She hadn't been here when Christina died. She never knew Christina. Holding onto those thoughts as if her very life depended on it, she tried to make sense of what she felt. Finally she gave up and shook her head.

"I don't know," she repeated. "I don't understand."

Silence descended upon them. Michael continued to caress Amelia, gently, soothingly, sliding his large hands down her back, her arms, running his rough farmer's fingers over her cheeks, her temples, her hair.

Suddenly Amelia stiffened. A thought came to her. Could this vision have come tonight, the night before her wedding, as a warning? To demonstrate the magnitude of grief her own disappearance would bring those she loved?

Dare she go through with the ceremony as planned?

Chapter 16

THE HUSH OF the nearly empty church behind her made Amelia uneasy. Although she hadn't found the courage to tell Michael she wouldn't marry him, she feared this wedding wouldn't lead to "happily ever after." The visions haunted her. They tore at her and filled her with dread. Hardly the feeling a bride should entertain on her wedding day.

Regardless, here she stood, in her perfect mint-green dress, facing the altar and Father Charles, hearing but not registering his quiet words. At her side, she felt the warmth of Michael's body. At her rear, the occasional burst of Katie's chatter pierced the numbness that surrounded her.

Amelia felt as if she were an observer at some fateful event—detached, anything but a participant in the ceremony. That is, she felt that way until the priest intoned, "Do you, Amelia Baldwin . . ."

Her temples began to throb, her heart to pound. Her breathing quickened. Her hands shook, and she felt cold, colder than she'd ever been. Colder than a Minnesota win-

ter night, colder even than the warning of a ghostly apparition. Colder than fear for her sanity.

Would it be "Yes" or "No"?

When the priest's words faded, the silence of the church
grew deafening, making the relentless beat of her heart only
that much harsher, rougher, reminding her that although she
was here—alive—right now, she could just as easily vanish
the way Christina had. Fear, that awful dread she'd fought
during the night, clutched her throat, made it difficult to
speak.

With superhuman effort, and the sustaining touch of
Michael's hand clasping her own, Amelia forced herself to
focus on the question she'd been asked. Would she marry
Michael? Would she consent to be his wife for as long as
they both would live?

"Yes," she whispered.

Michael squeezed her fingers.

Father Charles murmured, "Louder, please."

"Yes," she repeated. "For as long as we both shall live."

At that moment she could only promise that. She
couldn't promise that the future would bring no sorrow, no
pain. Only God knew what the future held. He'd only given
Amelia control of the present, this moment in time where
she lived. She couldn't change the past, and she had no idea
what the future would bring.

So for today, she promised to love, honor, and cherish
Michael Hayak. As for tomorrow . . . well, she'd leave tomorrow in God's hands.

"Do you, Michael Hayak . . ."

As the priest voiced those all-important words, Michael
again was racked by guilt. How dare he defy God by marrying the very woman he'd betrayed his wife with? The woman
he'd wanted so badly that he'd longed for freedom . . . the
freedom to woo her, court her, take her, while his wife lay
dying.

Although at the time he'd assured himself he only
thought of Christina's suffering, he'd found himself enter-

taining a wish for his wife's swift release. Now, however, Michael was forced to consider whether his wish was as lofty as he'd believed at the time. Had there perhaps been a self-serving motive behind it? Had he wished for widowhood in order to pursue what he would attain with his response to the priest today?

Had he wished Christina dead so he could make Amelia his?

Michael wanted to believe himself a better man than that. His consuming need for Amelia, however, made him question his motive. At least, thank God, he'd done nothing but his utmost to ease and prolong Christina's life. Of *that* Michael was certain. His conscience didn't have to bear the burden of possibilities unexplored, avenues untaken. He'd done *everything* humanly possible to heal his wife. And still she'd died.

At least he didn't come to this marriage as a murderer by default. An adulterer, yes; murderer, no.

But, taunted his conscience, would marrying the woman he'd sinned for somehow right that old wrong? Like a drowning man, Michael clasped the thought tightly to his heart. Once Amelia married him, his need for her would be only that which God ordained for man and wife.

". . . Michael?" asked Father Charles, and Michael realized he'd missed his cue.

"Er . . . yes! I do."

The priest, forehead wrinkled, scoured Michael's face with a probing look. Then with a sigh he made the sign of the cross and proclaimed them man and wife.

It was done. Amelia was his wife.

Turning, Michael placed a hand on her shoulder. With his other hand he reached into his pocket and brought out his gift. "This is for you."

Carefully he reached around her neck under the lacy netting of her veil. With awkward, shaking fingers, he tried once, twice, three times to secure the dainty gold chain. Finally it was done.

"What is it?" she asked.

He gathered the pendant in his hand. "Look."

Amelia did. Michael held a perfect, crystal heart. The piece had facets cut into every side and caught the subdued light in the church, breaking it into shimmers of red, blue, green, gold, bringing the spark of hope and the light of joy to her heart.

"It's beautiful. Did your grandfather make it for your grandmother?"

"No. I made it for you."

Amelia drew in a sharp breath. Michael's desire to please her was as clear as his crystal heart. Slowly, fearing what she'd find but daring to hope, Amelia lifted her gaze to his. "I'll treasure your heart forever. And keep it safe from harm."

A solemn look crossed Michael's face. He obviously took the time to weigh her words. And his. With a finger, he caressed her cheek. "I'll treasure *you*, and keep you safe from harm."

Then Pansy's vigorous sobbing broke into their private world. Katie ran up and hugged their legs—one chubby arm around Amelia's, the other around Michael's. "Mama! Papa!" she cried. "Katie wub you."

Michael leaned down and picked their daughter up. Even with the recent spate of best moments of her life, Amelia recognized that none rivaled this. Before God and man, they'd become a family. Her dreams had come true. Now, if only she could keep on dreaming, and seeing her dreams come true, one by one. . . .

Only God knew.

After that, thanks to Pansy's marshaling talents, Amelia was left with not a moment to think serious thoughts. The small party followed their dauntless leader as Pansy directed them through a delicious meal, the opening of various gifts, and finally an applejack toast—courtesy of Herbert—for the future of the bride and groom.

Then they were on their way back home—minus Katie,

who'd been left in Mrs. Tom's more than capable care. Mrs. Tom, aided and abetted by Pansy, had insisted that the newlyweds needed at least a night or two of privacy. Somehow, and Amelia didn't know quite how, the two older ladies had persuaded Katie to stay behind. So now she and Michael drove toward the farm while the last golden rays of the sun kissed the edge of the world and faded into night.

Their first night as man and wife.

Although Amelia recognized the anticipation she felt, her nerves were taut as a violin string, leaving her hesitant, unsure of herself. It wasn't as if tonight was their first time together. They had been intimate once before. It was just that . . . tonight she was his wife. Amelia wanted more than anything to be his love as well.

She hoped and prayed their physical union would serve to bind them closer.

Michael drove in silence, apparently deep in thought, too. Amelia wondered what he was thinking, but didn't dare ask. She was far too worried that it might not bode well for their marriage, as he could be thinking of his first wife.

She wanted to be the only one on his mind tonight.

During the ride she kept quiet, giving him the opportunity to mull over his thoughts. But as they pulled into the drive at the farm, Amelia decided she'd had enough of this not knowing.

But before she could formulate a comment, he led the horses to the barn, and called out, "I'll be right in."

"I'll be waiting," she responded, making her meaning clear.

He turned his head for a moment, and in that flash of time Amelia saw a spark in his eyes and a smile curve his lips. She thought his steps quickened, too.

Amelia ran upstairs to her room. She knew exactly what she would wear. The 1900 Amelia had loved delicate feminine nightwear, and one of the treasures she'd found in the cherry-wood wardrobe at the little house in town was a fine lawn nightgown, its bodice a cobweb of floral lace. Amelia had tried on the special garment only once, as it struck her as the sort of thing a woman would save for the man she loved. The gown had been created for a night like tonight.

In seconds, Amelia had lit a single candle, then stripped and pulled the whisper-soft gown over her head. The sheer fabric settled over her like twilight flowed over the world outside. It covered her, yet at the same time revealed much by virtue of its muted touch.

Glancing in the mirror above the washstand, Amelia smiled at her reflection backlit by candleglow. If she remembered their first intimate encounter correctly, Michael would think of nothing but her the moment he laid eyes on her.

Downstairs, the kitchen door opened then clicked shut. Michael's footsteps rang out in the silent house. A flush warmed Amelia's cheeks, desire filled her, and anticipation made her heart speed up. The footsteps climbed the stairs.

Her bedroom door swung in. Michael stood in the doorway, his eyes landing unerringly on her. Amelia felt the most delicious shiver run through her at the heated contact of that gaze.

His eyes feasted on her face, then slowly slid down her throat. When he reached the lacy edge of her gown, something flickered in those eyes, making them darken, deepen more than they'd ever done before. His appraisal evoked a sensation so powerful that Amelia could have sworn she felt its touch on her breasts when her husband's eyes lingered there. Her nipples tightened, and she knew he saw the pointed tips through the flowered lace that cupped them.

As if he'd been using his hand, Michael's scrutiny stroked the rest of Amelia's body, riding in at her waist, curving out at her hip. He followed the flow of the nightgown's silky skirt, lingering on her thighs, her calves. Then, deliberately, he looked back up to focus on the shadowed area between Amelia's legs.

His gaze narrowed. A dangerous smile curved his lips. He stepped toward his bride.

Amelia took a deep breath. "I want you, Michael."

As if a damn had burst, Michael's breath rushed out. His hands flew to the stiff collar of his white shirt, removing first the tie, then the restrictive celluloid piece from his neck. Pearled buttons flew apart in the wake of his rushing fingers, and then his chest was bared.

"Amelia," he murmured, reaching for her. "God in Heaven, Amelia . . ."

Michael's hand hovered over her shoulder, almost as though he feared the contact. Amelia caught her bottom lip between her teeth and wondered if she hadn't spoken out of turn.

Michael closed his eyes, placed a finger on a lace blossom, adding "Thank God," in a reverent voice. With a light but stirring touch, he traced the edge of the petal, closing in on its very center, homing in on the budded crest of flesh beneath.

Amelia sighed, a fluttery, trembly sound. "Michael," she said again and caught his gaze when he glanced up at the sound of his name.

Then a rich, deep, masculine sound answered her call, and he reached for her, drawing her near. Tender kisses touched her lips, her cheeks, her chin. "It seems I've wanted you all my life."

At his confession, Amelia reached up around his neck, ran her fingers through the thick hair on the back of his head, and brought him to her lips. He covered her mouth with his. His lips moved against hers, seeking, tasting as if he'd never get enough to quench his thirst. Large warm hands roamed her back, pressing her to him, bringing her closer still. Unsatisfied, he cupped her bottom and brought her flush against his heat. Through the negligible cloth of her gown, Amelia felt the thickness of his arousal, the heat his need had stoked. She clasped both arms around his back and strained against him, wanting more of him than even this.

They kissed again, tongues dipping, dancing, the sensations so heady Amelia felt giddy, transported to another plane. Her breath came hard, sharp, interspersed with nips and nibbles, as she tasted Michael, savored his touch.

Then he pulled away. Amelia whimpered. He slipped an arm around her shoulders, the other under her knees, and carried her to the side of the bed. There he sat with her on his lap, then lifted her chest closer to his mouth. Through the lace bodice, Amelia felt his tongue, his lips, tease and taunt her nipple, refusing her the fullness of his mouth. "More," she asked, bringing her hand back to his head.

He complied. Drawing the tight tip deep into his mouth, Michael suckled at Amelia's breast, setting up a tugging at her core. She murmured her pleasure as the flood of feeling her husband unleashed swept her away.

For a second, he let go, then he returned, bent on treating the other breast the same. Amelia had never known that rapture could be had on earth, but it seemed right now that Michael promised just that with every passionate, tender touch of his mouth.

With gentle care, he placed her on the bed, then straightened. His hands went to his belt, and Amelia's eyes followed. Holding her breath, she watched him unfasten his trousers, tug them and his drawers down, then stand up straight again.

The perfection of his build struck her again. The rippling muscles he'd honed by working his body, the length of limb God had given him, the ready jut of flesh desire for her had wrought. He was hers, her husband, her lover, her mate.

Knowing she held his interest, she reached down to her ankles and began to smooth the nightgown toward her thighs. She rose onto her knees, crossed her arms, and took hold of the fluid fabric again. With a sensual stretch, she pulled it up over her head, then dropped it on the floor by the bed.

She smiled and held out an inviting hand. Taking hold, Michael came down on the bed at her side. The heat of his body warmed her, making her passion burn hotter. With a smile, he brought his hand to cup her breast, his large palm filled with the soft globe, his thumb rubbing the hardened tip.

Keeping her in his embrace, he brought them both down, placing her head on the pillow, his lips at her throat. He wove a chain of kisses around her neck, then sleeked his tongue over the curve of her collarbone.

Shifting farther down, Michael returned to kiss both breasts, first one, then the other, pulling the nipples into his mouth, rolling his tongue around each bud, biting softly. With a touch like fire, he ran a hand down her belly to the curls at her mound.

Propping his weight on a bent elbow, Michael watched her, unwilling to miss even the slightest subtlety of Amelia's response. Black-velvet curls cloaked her most private secrets and lured his hand to where those secrets hid. He cupped her gently, then slipped his fingers down to caress her slick folds, gently touching her pleasure points until she gasped and tightened her thighs around his hand.

Silky dampness, lush and ripe, lay at his fingertips. Amelia felt so smooth, hot, and wet. Michael stroked her from the tight nub to the heated depths of her, summoning her reaction, testing her readiness, preparing the way for himself. Each long stroke, deliberate and slow, evoked a keening sound from her, as well as the tossing of her head, the arching of her back, the trembling of her thighs. His wife was a flame in his hands, his lightest touch wringing from her the most astounding response. Michael had never felt so much a man as he did loving Amelia tonight, their wedding night.

Leaning over, he caught a nipple in his mouth while keeping up the play of his hand. Then, as her trembling intensified, he parted the quivering layers of her flesh and again dove deep inside. Amelia gasped, opened her eyes wide in amazement, then cried out as shudders racked her body and her pleasure pulsated in his hand.

Michael watched, awed by the power of her release. When the tension of her climax began to ebb, he lay down at her side and wrapped his arms around her. What he had witnessed was so sensual, so erotic, he was afraid that if he plunged into her as he desperately wanted to do, it would be all over much too soon. So he held Amelia close, pressed flush up against him, his erection cradled by her thighs.

But she didn't lie there for long. Soon, she placed her hand on his chest, forcing him onto his back. Then the torture began. Her fingers danced over his skin, exploring him as he'd explored her. Her lips followed, kissing, tasting, nipping. She latched on to a nipple, suckling him. Michael's eyes shut tight, and he experienced bursts of sensual fireworks detonated by his wife.

She slipped up and kissed him full on the mouth, her tongue sparring with his as her hand followed the trail of hair to where his shaft blocked her path. Curling her fingers around him, she murmured her approval. He, in turn, moaned. He was hot and stiff, and only seconds away from exploding. Her delicate hand squeezed him, then moved up and down. Again. And again. Michael bit his lip, feeling the pleasure build inside him, feeling himself throbbing in her clasp. He wouldn't survive more than moments of her touch . . .

He jackknifed up, clapped his hand over her talented fingers, and muttered, "Enough!"

In one swift motion, he covered her body, balancing on his forearms, pressing himself against her moist flesh. "My wife," he whispered.

"Husband," she replied.

Then slowly, and with his gaze holding hers, Michael entered her. Amelia moaned, wrapping her arms around his shoulders, her legs around his hips. Still, he kept his pace slow, deliberate, torturous. It was a claiming, total and absolute. She was his.

Another sound slipped past Amelia's lips, and she quivered and quaked. Michael altered his pace at her cry, taking her first slow and soft, then hard and fast, and slow and soft again.

Amelia felt the ribbon of passion tighten within her, the approach of another climax imminent. She shivered, shuddered, dug her fingers into his skin. His hair-covered chest chafed her breasts. The strength of his hips brought him deeper and deeper inside her. Then she took flight. She clung to him, gasped, soared. Dying, she could hardly breathe. She went to heaven in a burst of fire.

From the heights of her climax, she felt Michael's arms cradle her, felt his hips speed up his thrusts, felt him strive within her in fierce abandon. He cried out her name, stiffened, his arms tightening their hold on her, binding her so close she knew they were one.

Later—she didn't know how long—Michael whispered her name. "Mm-hmmm?" she answered.

"You're beautiful, you know."

"You make me feel that way."

Wrapping an arm around her waist, Michael pulled her against his front. Then he reached up and followed the golden links to where the crystal heart lay nestled between her breasts.

"I'm glad you kept it on. You wore nothing but my heart."

She smiled. "While we . . ."

He chuckled, and she felt the vibrations on her spine. A tingle of awareness ran through her, catching her unprepared.

"Yes, Amelia, while we—"

"Never mind!" she gasped out. "I get the point."

"Tell me, wife—"

"Say it again!" she demanded.

Michael rose on one bent arm. He studied her face. "What?" he asked. "Wife?"

Amelia sighed and smiled. "Precisely that."

Again he laughed. "I'm afraid you'll soon tire of hearing me say it, since I've done nothing but think it since we said 'I do.'"

Craning her neck, she sought his gaze. "Never, Michael. I'll never tire of hearing you call me wife."

A satisfied look softened his features. "Good, but . . . could you return the favor?"

She winked. "What favor?"

With a light touch, he tapped her rump. "Tease!"

Amelia sobered. "Not at all, husband. You are that, you know? My husband."

Slowly, Michael nodded. "Sounds good. Right."

They grew silent, each fighting disturbing thoughts. They might have dozed. Amelia wasn't sure. Later, when the candle she'd lit to set a mood in the room had gone out, and a ray of moonlight entered the window and pooled on the bed, she turned to study the dear face at her side.

Michael seemed younger in his sleep. The crinkles at the corners of his eyes didn't appear quite as deep, and the lines that frequently marked his forehead weren't there. Deep breaths lifted his chest, tickling her with the hair there.

She didn't know how long she gazed at him. She might have slept again, but she knew the very second his fingers covered the crystal heart between her breasts. "Perfect," he whispered against her lips.

"I'll never take it off."

At her words, a spark caught fire in his eyes, and his fingers stroked the rounded side of her breast. Sliding his palm beneath its fullness, he cupped the soft flesh, brought the tip of his tongue to the top, and tasted her again. Then he blew on the nub he'd just kissed, and Amelia felt a fierce tug through her body, from her breast to her womb, leaving trails of fire and ice in its wake.

Michael rose over her. He straddled her hips, and both hands molded her breasts as if they were a precious offering. "They're beautiful, like you."

As Amelia began to answer, he tipped his hips and filled her to the hilt. A rough moan escaped her lips. She lost track of what she'd been about to say, lost the train of her thoughts. She only knew he pulsed hot and hard inside her, his hands on her breasts, passion in his gaze.

Amelia gave herself up to the pleasure. She met his every thrust with a lift of her own. She ran her hands over his chest, circled his nipples, whispered how she felt.

"You're mine," he said. "All mine. And my heart is now yours."

Amelia remembered the look in his eyes when he'd studied the crystal heart between her breasts. Possessiveness had glowed there, but instead of threatening her, it thrilled her. She recognized the feeling since she felt it, too.

Rhythmically tightening inner muscles, she dragged a groan from him. "Look at me," she asked. When he did, she said, "You're mine. All mine."

Then there were no more words, just two bodies joined as one, giving and taking, loving and pleasing all through the night, until the eastern sky began to bloom with light.

In the morning, after an exuberant sponge bath that left more water on the bedroom floor than in the basin they'd used, Amelia and Michael dressed, knowing that otherwise the day would fly by, and they'd never leave the bed.

They laughed like children. They held hands. Their gazes caught, and private messages were sent and received. Refusing to allow dark thoughts to intrude, they both concentrated on the joy they'd found.

After he saw to the animals, Michael returned to the kitchen and poured himself another cup of coffee. "I'd like you to put on your coat. There's something I want to show you."

Amelia furrowed her brows. "And I need my coat to see it?"

"We'll only be a minute. It's out in the barn."

A dreamy memory made her smile. "The last time you took me out to the barn I saw one of the most glorious nights I'd ever seen."

"So . . . are you saying you trust me?"

Amelia paused. "Why . . . yes, I think I'm saying precisely that."

"Well, you needn't sound so astonished, madam!"

With a wry smile she stood and came to his side. She placed her hand on his wide shoulder and rubbed. "Dented your pride, did I?"

"Some."

"Even after last night?" Mischief bubbled in her, and she knew he saw its glow.

"Last night wasn't about pride, woman!"

Amelia laughed out loud. "Well, I certainly stroked your—"

"Amelia!"

Innocence was easy to don. "I *was* about to say your ego."

"Mm-hmmmm," he offered dubiously.

"Really! I was."

He pushed his chair away from the table. "Put on your coat before I show you just what you stroked last night. This morning, too."

Heat blazed all the way up to Amelia's forehead, and she hurried out, knowing Michael quite capable of doing just as he threatened. Although . . . the thought of all he could show her didn't frighten her one bit. In fact, it made her hurry, so they could do whatever he wanted, then return to his version of show and tell.

"Goodness!" Where had that little phrase come from? It had been days since Amelia had even thought of that far-off life she'd once led. But here, now, a few words brought her back to her senses.

Why had she been brought to this time? Had it been to bring that smile to Michael's lips? She remembered the sadness in his expression when she'd first seen the portrait on the Opera House wall.

Perhaps.

Shaking off the thought, Amelia wrapped herself in her coat, and ran back to her husband's side. "I'm ready."

"Let's go."

They avoided the puddles that a tenacious drizzle had left in the backyard, then headed straight for the barn. Michael let Amelia in, and she breathed the spicy smell of hay mixed with the musk of farm animals. "Is something wrong with one of the cows?"

Michael chuckled. "Nothing's wrong at all. I just want to show you something that is mine, all mine. Like you."

Amelia experienced a thrill at his words but had no idea what he meant. She silently followed him through a door in a corner of the building. Dark and windowless, the room smelled of smoke and something else, Amelia didn't know what. She heard the *skritch* of a match, and a lamp went on.

What she saw stunned her. In one corner, a small furnace yawned widely, its fire at the moment unlit. A number of metal pipes protruded from the blackened mouth. A collection of different-sized steel pots rose in a stack at one side of the oven, and a few feet away, a large wooden block with a hollowed crevice in its top made a worktable of some sort.

As the flame in the lamp flickered, Amelia saw light dance over a number of sparkling items gathered on the shelves that lined the walls. Vases, pitchers, platters, cups, birds, fish, deer and dogs, all came alive in the golden glow of the lamp. Magical crystal pieces invited her to come and touch, admire and marvel.

"Michael, they're beautiful. Was this your grandfather's workshop?"

He nodded, a flush tinting his cheekbones, a smile curving his lips. "Mine, too."

Amelia's hand flew to her throat, and she pulled the heart out from her dress by the chain. "Is this where you made the heart?"

"Of course."

"All those times you disappeared from the house . . ."

He nodded.

Indicating the collection on the shelves, she asked, "Which are yours?"

He beckoned her close, holding out his arm. Amelia walked right into its haven. "I'll show you," he said after kissing her lips.

Time flew as Michael proudly displayed the work of his grandfather, his father, and himself. The exquisite craftsmanship, the eye for detail, the instinctive capture of beauty left Amelia breathless. What an astounding man her husband was!

"Is this something you do during the slower winter months?" she asked.

"Not really. I come and work on the glass whenever I can, regardless the time of year. I wish . . ."

His voice trailed off, and a longing crept into his eyes. Amelia waited, but he said nothing more. Too bad. He'd started to tell her something, and she'd be damned if he'd quit before he did! "You were saying something about a wish?"

He ran a hand through his hair, rubbed his forehead, then pinched the bridge of his nose. "I wish there was a way I could start a glassworks factory. But as you can imagine, that has to remain an empty wish. I have a farm to run, then there's Katie, and now you."

Suddenly Amelia remembered a day in another time. A young woman's voice—Wendy, her name had been—telling the tale of a man by the name of Michael Hayak, a widower who had raised his daughter alone while farming his land. A man who had set aside artistic talent, traded in his dreams of working with glass for the hardship-filled life of a farmer. An honorable man who'd met his responsibilities at the expense of his heart.

In that moment, Amelia knew why she'd been brought back to this time. She was here to see that Michael pursued his dreams. She was here to replace Michael's sadness with joy.

Chapter 17

SURELY THAT WAS why she'd come to 1900. To relieve Michael's loneliness with her presence and to give him the opportunity to follow his dream. To love him and bring him the joy he'd otherwise lack.

Amelia liked that role. The belief that her husband needed her so much warmed her insides. She'd found a purpose to her life, something she'd missed in that other time, something she hadn't been able to find since she'd arrived in this one.

After her moment of revelation in Michael's workshop, they returned to the house discussing what it would take to give Michael his chance. Once inside, Amelia threw out their cold coffee, percolated another pot, and they now sat at the table warming their hands as they held the china cups.

Michael continued explaining what it would take to make his dream come true. "I need to make sure I can afford regular shipments of silica—sand, you know," he said. "It's what you melt to make glass."

Amelia thought for a moment. "For that we'd need to run the farm at its most profitable."

"Precisely. And, since I'd have to spend so much time working the glass, I would need to hire a farmhand."

"You know . . ." she murmured, hesitant to bring up a potentially charged topic. "I could help."

"How so?"

She sat up straighter, squaring her shoulders. "I have made my living for years now with my sewing."

"And . . . ?"

"There's no reason why I couldn't continue to sew. It would bring in additional money, maybe enough for the sand."

Michael frowned. "I'm not certain I like the thought of my wife having to work. It would seem that I couldn't keep my part of the marriage bargain."

"Oh, for crying out loud! I didn't marry you so you could support me. I can do that by myself."

"Then why *did* you marry me?"

Amelia bit her lip. This didn't seem the best moment to confess her love, but he appeared to need an answer to his question, as was evident by the intensity of his gaze. "I married you for . . . you. Not because you could feed and clothe me, not to salvage a supposedly ruined reputation, not even because your daughter—*our* daughter—needs me."

Michael leaned closer across the tabletop. "I asked you *why?*"

Amelia blushed. She waved her hands vaguely. "That's not what we're discussing now, Michael. Later, when we've finished with the matter of the glassworks, we can talk about that."

He frowned. A stormy look appeared in his eyes. He *really* hadn't liked her response. His fists closed tight. His troubled gaze narrowed, sharpened. "I asked you why—"

"I know you did, so tell me this. Why did *you* marry *me?*"

At her words, a flush covered his cheekbones, and suddenly his hands grew busy, twisting and turning a kitchen towel she'd left on the table earlier in the day.

He cleared his throat. "So . . . you propose to give me your earnings for the sand?"

"I just figure that between the profit from the farm and the money I earn, we should be able to give the glassworks a try."

Michael fell silent. Amelia could almost see his mind churning the possibilities. Finally he slapped his hands on the tabletop and, standing, pushed his chair back. "I'll have to think on this some more."

"You'll tell me what those thoughts are?"

"Once I figure them out."

"That's fine," she answered, satisfied for the moment.

The rest of the day passed uneventfully. They resumed their routines, keeping as busy as usual. Amelia took the opportunity to give the house a fair cleaning during Katie's absence. By late in the afternoon, however, she found herself chuckling. This wasn't a typical honeymoon!

But Michael had animals to care for, and besides, he'd told her he wanted to review the numbers from the farm's performance last year. That would be a tedious, time-consuming task, and she had been the one responsible for igniting his flame of hope. She had no reason to complain.

When Michael came in after milking the cows, Amelia had supper ready. Only after they'd sat to eat did she pause to marvel at her growing expertise in the culinary arts. Funny how she'd never thought to learn to cook in that other life she'd lived. She was beginning to enjoy the more creative parts of the endeavor. Like adding and subtracting ingredients to invent brand-new dishes.

As he scraped the last crumb of pumpkin-and-spice-flavored piecrust from his dessert plate, Michael grinned. "That was delicious. You've always been capable in the kitchen, but it seems you're improving as time goes by."

His praise lit a glow in her heart. "Thank you," she said. "I'm glad you enjoyed it."

A roguish gleam appeared in his eyes. "I believe you will find I also enjoy *you*."

The glow in her heart turned to heat in her cheeks. "*I* believe I've seen that spark in your eyes in the recent past."

His smile tipped up one side. "Oh, perhaps a time or two."

Amelia chuckled. "Are you hinting again?"

"Not at all! I'm expressing my intentions."

"Then it's to my advantage to finish in here quickly."

"I'd say so, Mrs. Hayak."

"Hmmm . . . I'd say I agree, Mr. Hayak."

They laughed, anticipating the delights to come. Amelia rushed through her cleaning, making sure everything in the cozy kitchen gleamed. Since Michael wanted to wrestle numbers for a while yet, she'd have time to prepare herself for his arrival in their room.

Feeling buoyed by the outcome of her first day as a married woman, Amelia ran up the stairs as soon as she'd hung her apron on the hook by the kitchen door. Eagerness had her body tingling. She'd never considered herself a particularly sensual creature, but she had a suspicion that had been due to the absence of the right man.

Humming softly, she approached her room. But as she hurried past the door to Christina's room, she again felt the horrid cold that preceded the hated visions. Her feet froze in place, although her every fiber screamed for her to leave, to run as far away from that room as she could ever get. Still, something kept her there against her will.

Although the door was only partly ajar, Amelia could again see the bed through the cloudy whiteness that accompanied her visions. As before, Christina lay on the bed, hands clenched around wads of blanket. Michael stood at the head of the bed again, holding Katie in his arms. The child sobbed, Michael's cheeks shone with spilt tears, and Christina struggled to breathe.

This time, however, Amelia saw another person, the woman she'd seen sitting at the foot of the bed in that first apparition. Tonight, the woman stood before Michael, one hand on his forearm, the other offering comfort to Katie.

As minutes trickled by, the milky veil began to dissipate as it had the last time, and Amelia sucked in a sharp breath at the sudden influx of grief. She felt tormented, anguish crushing her heart, fear and horror mingling there, too.

When the last of the mist vanished, Amelia could make out more detail in the scene. The woman at Michael's side wore a simple, high-necked blouse, a plain navy skirt, and her black hair had been piled in a loose knot on her crown. Wispy curls lay at the nape of her neck, and when she turned toward Katie, Amelia saw more of those soft locks at her temples.

Then she saw the woman's profile. *The woman was her!*

Amelia felt her legs weaken, her breathing stop. The misery in the vision reached out and lodged in her heart, twisting, tearing at her, ravaging.

Panic-stricken, she realized she had just assumed the feelings of the woman in that room. How? She didn't know. Why? Even less. She only knew something was terribly, terribly wrong.

Then she knew nothing more.

Through the icy darkness, Amelia heard her name. "Amelia . . ."

Warm hands patted her cheeks, rubbed her fingers, cradled her close. Nonsensical endearments filtered through the haze around her, and gently insistent kisses deposited more of the warmth she craved on her icy face and hands.

Finally, with effort, she opened her eyes. Michael's fear-filled face appeared in her line of sight. "Please wake up," he murmured. "Amelia?"

Her lips were dry, so she tried to moisten them with her tongue, but her whole mouth felt like cotton, making it difficult to answer even the simple "Yes?"

Michael's arms tightened about her, and Amelia knew she never wanted to leave the shelter they offered. She burrowed deeper into his warmth.

"Hold tight," he urged, then stood.

Amelia clasped her arms around his neck. A few paces later, he placed her on her bed—thank God, *not* in that other bed.

Michael hurried to the washstand, poured some water in the basin from the pitcher there, then moistened the corner of a towel. "Here," he said, "this should feel good."

"Not as good as your arms did."

A crooked smile appeared on his lips. "Thank you, Mrs. Hayak."

"Welcome, Mr. Hayak."

"I'm glad to see you coming back to yourself. Will you tell me what happened this time?"

Amelia's eyes flew open wide. She couldn't tell him what she'd seen! She'd have to tell him *everything*, and after tonight's frightening mirage, she realized how little she understood about her situation. "I'm not sure what happened. I . . . blacked out."

"Could you . . ." he started, then blushed. "Ahem! That is . . . could you possibly be . . . increasing?"

"Increasing?"

The red on Michael's cheeks intensified. "*You* know!" he answered, staring pointedly at her belly.

"Oh! You mean pregnant." She thought back a moment. "Anything's possible . . . that first time . . . but I don't think so."

Disappointment replaced his embarrassment.

Amelia found *that* intriguing. "Would you like me to be?"

His eyes met hers. He nodded. "Yes, I really would."

Amelia reached for his hand and laced her fingers through his. "You know, I would, too." She tugged lightly, and he joined her on the bed.

They held hands for a silent while, both contemplating

the prospect of another child. After a sigh, Michael turned sideways and wrapped his arm around Amelia's middle, spreading his big hand over her belly. Filling his hand with the mound of their child would be one of the greatest joys of her life.

Lives. . . .

No! She would not think about that now. She was tired, exhausted, and the oblivion of sleep would suit her just fine. Besides, thinking and more thinking had gotten her nowhere. She wriggled to a sitting position. "Get up a moment," she asked Michael.

"What are you going to do?"

"Nothing much, I just thought we'd like the quilt over us rather than under us."

"You stay right there! I'll get your nightdress."

And he did. With tender care that spoke of love, he helped her undress. To his credit, despite his obvious hunger for her, he only kissed the valley between her breasts where the crystal heart lay. Moments later, he had her white cotton gown buttoned to the throat and the quilt tucked in all around.

She watched as he stood and stripped down to his drawers, then turned out the lamp. "We need some rest," he murmured as he joined her on the bed.

Amelia scooted closer. "Mm-hmmm . . ." If it wasn't love inspiring her husband's actions, she truly had no idea what love was.

Later, much later that night, Amelia woke up to find her face bathed in tears and her heart pounding hard enough to feel as though it would burst. She couldn't remember what she'd been dreaming; she only knew it had something to do with the vision she'd seen.

Again unnerved, she reached for Michael's warmth, curling up tight against him. He felt so strong . . . she felt so fragile, her emotions all in a dizzy whirl.

It wasn't fair. Here she finally found what she'd always

needed, and she couldn't even enjoy the beginning of the discovery, the start of her married life. All she wanted was to be with Michael, share his life, love him to distraction. But she found herself agonizing over some crazy waking nightmares featuring his first wife—a woman who'd died before Amelia had even arrived.

"No." She wouldn't let herself think those thoughts right now. Now she was going to indulge her need to kiss her husband. She only wanted life, strength, hope, and love.

With a light touch, she placed kisses on Michael's broad chest, on his chin, his cheeks, his lips. She murmured appreciatively when his mouth moved under hers, returning her kiss.

Growing bolder, she caressed his chest, his back, the line of his thighs, the hard curve of his rear. She opened his drawers and, with a hesitant touch, she found him hard and ready. As she curled her fingers around him, he chuckled, tossed her nightgown upward, and began his own study of her choicer parts.

With a moan, Amelia gave herself to the delights of their lovemaking, rejoicing in the power of their passion, the expression of their need, the evidence of life in their responsive bodies.

Filled with an unnerving sense of desperation, Amelia gave and demanded more. Michael complied, and their touch grew wilder, their caresses frantic. She needed this. She needed to feel the frenzy of passion, to feel Michael deep inside her. She needed the madness of completion to banish the specter of death from her thoughts, her dreams. "Now!" she urged.

"Now!"

He again joined them as one.

As everything in life does, the lusty exploits in bed came to an end when morning arrived, and they had to get out of bed. To her dismay, Amelia found that her fear remained intact, and her anguish continued. Physically sated, she found her emotions in as much turmoil as they had been when she'd collapsed outside Christina's room.

And that was another thing. They were going to have to do something about that room. Although Amelia didn't believe in ghosts, that room held an abundance of pain, too much sorrow. Obviously, stripping the sheets and pitching the sickroom supplies hadn't done the trick to vanish the grief that hung there as solidly as the curtains at the window. She didn't think building a new house was an option, but neither was living with the constant fear of what might appear there next.

Fear. Paralyzing and stifling, it followed her wherever she went, whatever she did. Dread. Cold and distracting, it consumed her with its hold on her thoughts.

The increased frequency of her visions frightened her. The greater clarity did, too, as did the pain she felt, the horror, and yes—incomprehensible though it was—the waves of guilt that pressed down upon her. What did she have to feel guilty about?

In numb silence, Amelia took care of her chores, finishing quicker than ever. Her efficiency made more real Katie's absence from the farm. Although she'd agreed with Pansy and Mrs. Tom that she and Michael needed time alone, Amelia could no longer tamp down her anxiety. She needed Katie where she could reach out and touch her sturdy little body, where she could listen to her baby chatter, where she could wrap her arms around her daughter, hold tight, as if she'd never, ever let her go.

When Michael came in for his noon meal, Amelia broached the subject. "I miss Katie. Terribly. Would you object if I went to town and brought her back? I know we'd agreed to spend some time without her, but we have done just that, and . . . well, I'm ready to have her home with us. After all, that's how we'll continue from now on."

Michael pinned her with his bright blue eyes. It seemed he searched her very soul with that piercing look of his. Then he shrugged. "I don't object, Amelia. I did think you might want a holiday from chasing the little scamp around."

"At the time I thought so, too, but it's just not so. I want her home, close to me."

Her husband slanted her another questioning look, but Amelia wasn't about to elaborate on her fears. Not when the thought of being forced back to the 1990s was their direct cause, even though she hated to admit it. That possibility had the power to bring her to her knees in prayer. Amelia found herself pleading constantly, begging God to spare all three of them that wrenching loss, agreeing to any bargain He might offer, if only He'd consent to let her stay.

Michael's deep voice broke into her disturbing thoughts. "I had planned to go to town tomorrow and fetch her home. I see no problem with going this afternoon. We can leave as soon as I finish what I was doing."

Amelia would have expected her anxiety to abate once they were on their way in to Winona. But it seemed she would find no respite. During the trip back home, Katie securely held against her, Michael pressed flush up against her other side, Amelia trembled at the possibility that this might be their last drive home together.

Something was happening to her. What, she didn't know, but the ever-clearer visions, and especially her presence at Christina's bedside during the latest apparition, had her mentally seeking possible explanations.

Just what did it all mean? The ghostly sightings. The misery she now felt. The growing sense of guilt with no apparent cause.

Amelia tightened her grasp on her husband and child, as if by doing so she could anchor herself at their side and never be taken away.

Once they were back at the farm, they went about their chores. Amelia prepared supper while Katie offered detailed descriptions of all she had done with Mrs. Tom. "Katie cookeded."

"Really?"

Golden-brown curls bounced. "Yeth. Katie cookeded cookies."

"What kind of cookies?"

"Th'good kind!"

"Mmmmm, I see. And did Katie help clean up afterward?"

"Katie holped. Katie broomded th'floor. Katie holp Mama?"

Amelia chuckled, then scooped the little girl up into her arms. "I should have seen that one coming, munchkin! Yes, I think you can 'holp' Mama. Before cooking, though, Mama needs a big hug and kiss. Mama missed Katie while Katie visited Mrs. Tom."

Watching the expressions flitting over the little girl's face, Amelia tried to seal the memory in her heart. She might need to pull it out in the future, just to help her make it through a lonely day.

Katie pressed her chubby hands against Amelia's cheeks, holding her in place for a barrage of sticky kisses. Then little arms wrapped around Amelia's neck, and a flood of love rushed through her. "I love you, munchkin," she murmured through the knot in her throat.

"Katie wub Mama, too."

That's how Michael found them when he returned from settling the horses for the night. Although the sight of his wife embracing his daughter didn't fail to move him, Michael felt a niggling twinge in the deepest part of his heart. Something was wrong with Amelia. He couldn't quite place his finger on it—whatever it was—but as well as he knew he loved her, he knew something was seriously wrong.

There was that fainting spell last night. The look of fear in her eyes. Then she'd woken him with fiery caresses that, although arousing, brought more worry in their wake. Amelia's passion had been tinged with desperation, and Michael couldn't understand that at all.

Finally she'd insisted on going for Katie. While that in

itself didn't worry him, the way Amelia had held the child the entire way home, and the way she'd clutched his thigh as he drove, disturbed him mightily. He'd never seen her— or anyone else, for that matter—behave quite that way.

Now, in the kitchen, with everything presumably back to normal, Amelia stood before him, arms latched around Katie, tears spiking her black lashes. He knew what she'd answer should he ask her to explain.

"I don't know," she might say. Or, *"It's nothing, really."* She would again evade his questions with more of her vague responses, even though he knew perfectly well that something was terribly wrong.

Before he could demand yet another explanation, Amelia kissed Katie one more time, then placed her in a chair at the table. "Here we go," she said, her voice weak, "help me stir milk into the potatoes."

When she looked at Michael, he felt like calling her bluff. Although a patently contrived smile curved her lips, her green eyes still wore a haunted look.

All evening long, he watched her closely. Her determined cheer never lagged, driving him to new heights of frustration. When they put Katie to bed, Amelia read the child a story, as she had always done. Then, after their daughter slept, Michael wrapped an arm around her waist and led them to their room.

As kindling reacts to a match, Amelia burst into passionate fire at his very first kiss. Together they reached heights of physical satisfaction he'd never imagined possible, but for all that his body felt sated, that edge of frenzy again seemed to drive Amelia's touch, leaving him with a hollow feeling inside.

Michael feared she harbored deep-rooted feelings of guilt over that fateful moment they'd shared just an hour before Christina's death. And, dear God, he feared that if he broached the subject, even to assume what guilt she thought she bore—as he rightly should—Amelia would again abandon him, leave him with his guilt to face once again the fact that he'd run roughshod over his wedding vows, that he'd betrayed his wife.

He was too selfish to let her go. He couldn't do the honorable thing, release her from the bonds of guilt, seeing that she really bore none. He couldn't do what would surely drive her away. He couldn't say what had to be said.

The next few days passed, and Michael saw no change in Amelia's behavior. She remained jumpy, nervous, and she refused to let Katie stray more than a few steps from her side. He couldn't count the times he found her, fear on her pretty features, her green eyes drowning in a sea of tears.

At the same time, she often murmured in the stillness following their spent passion, "I'm so happy." But the hitch in her voice remained doggedly there, belying her words.

Michael had a very difficult time coming up with joy each time he examined the bizarre manifestations of his wife's "happiness." One thing he knew without a doubt: things couldn't go on like this much longer. Amelia had begun to push aside the food on her plate, and her face now looked thinner, her sweet features acquiring an unfamiliar sharpness.

Still, Michael remained unable to unburden himself. He had yet to come to grips with his own troubles. Besides, he didn't know for certain that her behavior came from guilt over that momentary slip. If that wasn't her problem, he'd hate to add more weight to whatever burden she bore. He just wanted to help her, wanted to see the bright smile he'd grown to love, the energetic way she'd always tackled her chores, the light and life that had always sparkled in the emerald depths of her eyes. Each day that went by, Michael grew less able to banish the suspicion that he was losing yet another wife.

Was this slow loss to be the punishment for his sin?

Michael had already lost one wife, and Amelia felt herself slipping deeper and deeper into a world all her own. Her

fears and worries dragged her farther from her husband, her
child, her life. The agony of not knowing what would happen next kept her off balance, always wondering if this
would be her last day, her last hour with those she loved.

Desperation became Amelia's constant companion. How
much longer would she have to live with this worry, this
fear? Surely Michael's penetrating stares came as a result
of his suspicions. She had been acting strangely, after all.

Had she truly gone mad? Delusional? What did it all
mean?

Every time she brooded over her circumstances, Amelia
came up with more questions and no answers. So she
fought to deflect the troublesome thoughts. She tackled her
work with a vengeance, obtaining impressive results. She
finished all of Myrtle's costumes—those the woman hadn't
been able to retrieve since Amelia had spent days snowed
in at the Hayak farm. The farmhouse soon took on a verita-
ble glow, not a speck of dust could be found, and the mingled scents of yellow soap and lemon oil proclaimed her
industry.

Each meal she prepared, she concentrated on improving
and perfecting her abilities. Michael complimented her efforts lavishly, and Katie always begged to "holp" Mama.

On the surface, everything might have seemed normal,
but deep in her heart, Amelia knew something was wrong.
She just had no idea what it could be. Only two things
stood out in her mind. For one, she loved Michael and
Katie more than ever. And, two, she had changed; she no
longer saw herself as simply a woman who'd been thrust
into an unfamiliar, long-past time. She wasn't just the
Amelia Baldwin who'd lived in the 1990s—she was also *this*
Amelia Baldwin who lived in the year 1900. But . . . what
did that mean? Who was she? Aside from Michael's second
wife and Katie's stepmother?

Amelia's questions seemed fated to remain unanswered.
At least, no answer seemed imminent. So she fought her
fears and continued with her daily work.

*   *   *

One blustery late-November afternoon, as Amelia busied herself with Thanksgiving baking and supper preparations, she paused before entering the pantry to review the scrap of paper where Pansy had written the recipe for chicken pot pie. From here, she needed flour and lard for the crust, and small jars of peas and corn for the filling. She'd have to get carrots, potatoes, and onions from the root cellar, and the chicken had been stewing on the stove for the better part of the day.

As she checked off items, she glanced out the kitchen window and noticed a denuded oak quaking in the wind. the low, dull-gray sky indicated the approach of snow.

Without any notice, a warm pair of male arms laced around her middle, and she felt Michael's strength at her back. "I missed you," he murmured.

"Don't you have enough to do . . . ?" Amelia's voice died as the hideous chill of her visions knifed through her again.

The familiar, hated cloudiness formed before her, and she struggled to escape. She found she couldn't move from where she stood, and her paralysis wasn't due to Michael standing behind her. Some unseen force, a power unknown, forced her to stay rooted in place.

As she tried to focus on the shapes that formed before her, Amelia felt panic rise to her throat. A scream welled up, but impending hysteria stifled the slightest utterance. The mist began to clear, even though Amelia didn't want to see what lay before her. The other visions had been bad enough.

She closed her eyes. It didn't help. The veil continued to lift. She made out the lines of the kitchen sink and the small square window directly above it. In front of the sink, a man and a woman embraced, sharing an intimate kiss.

Despite her reluctance, Amelia grew more certain than ever that these visions happened for a reason. What that could be she had yet to find out.

Minutes crept by, and the couple before her took the kiss deeper, waves of passion cresting around them like a tide surging over land. On and on they kissed, each one's hands moving, touching, caressing the other. Mixed in with the passion, Amelia sensed grief, fear, and guilt.

Then, as had happened before, the wispy veiling vanished, and what she saw rocked her very soul. Before her stood Michael, holding her, Amelia Baldwin, passionately to himself, kissing her as if he'd never stop, as if his life depended on the expression of his need. To her horror, Amelia saw herself returning the kiss, matching Michael's urgency, his need.

Unlike the kisses they'd recently shared, a dark and ominous sensation accompanied this embrace. That feeling, although different, affected her as much as the thought of being pulled from this time, being taken from Michael's side, losing Katie as well as the man Amelia loved.

As she watched in horror, something deep inside her shifted, causing her mind to blank out, her body to crumble into Michael's waiting arms.

Chapter 18

Hᴇ ᴡᴀs ʟᴏsɪɴɢ her. As surely as a whisper rides a breeze, Amelia was slipping away from him. Michael didn't know what to do about it. These strange spells came more frequently now, and with each frightening episode, he felt her closing in on herself, shutting him out.

As she lay on the parlor sofa, still unconscious, still in the grip of whatever had made her faint, he rubbed her hands between his, patted her cheeks, opened the buttons of her cotton shirtwaist. She remained inert, pale, scarcely drawing breath.

He'd seen another woman lie this still—Christina had died.

Katie's footsteps tapped down the stairs. Michael was torn. He knew the child shouldn't see Amelia like this. She'd had enough nightmares during her mother's protracted illness and after her death. At the same time, Amelia shouldn't be left alone. Not until she came to and he made sure she was as well as could be expected.

"Mama?" Katie called.

"She's busy," he answered. "But I'm coming. Wait for me."

He met his daughter partway up the stairs. With a final worried glance at Amelia, he picked Katie up. "What have you been doing today?"

" 'Sploring."

"And what were you exploring?"

"Twunks."

"Trunks?" Michael frowned, then placed Katie back on the hallway floor. "You'd better show me these trunks."

With a nod and bouncing curls, Katie took off. She skidded to a stop before the door to the attic. Michael scratched his head in bewilderment. "I thought I'd locked it . . ."

Obviously Katie had found a way to get inside the attic. As he bent to enter the low-ceilinged storage area, he caught sight of the havoc his daughter had wreaked. "Oh, Katie-angel. This is not good, not good at all."

To his dismay, the trunks Katie had torn apart were the ones in which Amelia had packed Christina's things. Dresses, books, shoes, brushes, and a hand mirror littered the rough, wood-plank floor. Everything wore streaks of dust.

He bent to pick up a lavender dress Christina had loved, and sadness tugged at his heart. He hadn't been the best husband. He regretted that. Christina had deserved better.

Folding the rose-scented garment, he approached the trunk. He dropped the gown into the case, then heard a scraping sound downstairs. It almost sounded like the back door closing. Since Katie stood at his side, and Amelia hadn't been moving when he last saw her, Michael grew curious.

"You wait right here, Katie," he instructed. "Don't touch *anything* in those trunks. Do you understand? Nothing!"

"Yeth, Papa."

Michael ran down the stairs, only to pull up short. Amelia no longer lay on the parlor sofa. "Amelia!"

He rushed to the kitchen and found it deserted. Opening the back door, he called out again, then headed for the barn.

"Amelia!"

His voice faded into the cloud-shrouded afternoon. The cold seeped in under his flannel shirt and wool trousers, but Michael paid no attention to his comfort. He had to find Amelia.

Then he heard a vehicle clatter on the road out front. Glancing that way, he saw Amelia's old wagon turn off the farm driveway, headed for Winona. "Dammit, woman!" he bellowed. "Where do you think you're going?"

But she was already too far away to hear. He turned on his heel and ran back to the house. This couldn't be happening again. Not now, not when he'd finally admitted to himself how much he loved her, how much he needed her. She couldn't abandon him again.

He couldn't face a future without Amelia. It would be the most cruel of punishments. Surely God wouldn't flay him that way.

Unable to deal with his panic, he clung to a veneer of anger. Heart pounding so hard his chest ached, he flew up the stairs, yelling, "Come, Katie. We must find your runaway mama."

On the way to the attic where he'd left her, Michael grabbed Katie's coat, mittens, hat, boots. Pausing to regain his breath, he whispered a prayer. He couldn't lose Amelia. Not now. They needed her, they loved her.

He loved her.

Lowering his head, he stepped over the mess. To his surprise, he found his daughter where he'd left her. "That was very good, Katie. You did what Papa told you to—"

He stopped. Katie held out a slim, cloth-covered book with a dried rose and a folded sheet of thin letter paper sliding out from between the pages. Christina had once told him she'd pressed the roses she'd worn on their wedding day.

Again, the sense of guilt, of having failed his wife, hit

him in the gut. That carefully preserved blossom spoke of
dreams, hopes. He'd betrayed the woman who had thought
to keep forever that token of their wedding vows. Grief
pressed in on him, but he took the volume anyway.

When he carefully extracted the rose, the book cover fell
open, and he realized he held a diary. Christina's diary. Her
rounded script covered every page, and although he wasn't
as fluent in Bohemian as his parents would have liked, he
could make out the gist of her entries.

> . . . I wish I could say something to them, but they do
> not even let me mention the end. I know it is coming. I
> am only counting days until I am free of this pain.
>
> They belong together. Even though neither one has
> revealed their feelings. And neither one would think to
> speak to me of the future. They are too busy denying
> that soon I will be gone.
>
> Michael is a good man, kind, a good worker, decent
> and sober and proud. That pride stands in his way too
> often. He needs a strong, sensible woman at his side,
> one who will not fear standing up to him, making him
> see more than just his side of a situation. Amelia is
> ideal for him.
>
> I often think he should have married her instead of
> me. She is stronger than I ever could be. She can hold
> her own in any disagreement they might have.
>
> Katie needs Amelia, too. Especially since Amelia
> has been more mother to her than I have. I could
> never imagine a better woman to raise my precious
> angel.
>
> Or a better woman to love Michael as he should be
> loved. I never achieved a deep and abiding passion, a
> romantic love for him. I fear my heart died when my
> darling Peter did four years ago. At that time, So-
> phie's offer to come and help her with the children
> after Heinrich's passing seemed a better choice than
> reliving memories of Peter, as I had been doing. When

*I met Michael, after Sophie married her Irish man,
one husband seemed as good as another. Since
Michael proposed a convenient, practical marriage
when I had no other alternative, I agreed.*

*Despite how well Michael and I have gotten on, and
the joy that is our beautiful Katerina, I have lived to
regret my decision. Not because of anything he has
done or failed to do, but because he has had no
chance to pursue the love that came unbidden, grew
unexpectedly. I am certain he loves Amelia, just as I
am sure she loves him, too.*

*Perhaps once I am gone, they will find the courage
to confess their feelings. Nothing would make me happier or give me more comfort as the end comes near,
than to know that the three of them will become the
family they deserve to be. I can only hope that my
legacy is a life filled with love and joy. . . .*

Michael wiped the tears from his cheeks. She'd known.
Christina had known all along that he'd fallen in love with
Amelia. Yet she hadn't said a word, and he was to blame
for that. Each time Christina tried to speak of the future,
he'd hushed her, not letting her speak of death. He continued to contact doctors right to the very end.

He would never have abandoned his ailing wife, no matter how much he loved another. But that didn't change
facts. The kiss he and Amelia shared remained as wrong as
always. Regardless of his feelings for Amelia, at that time
he'd been a married man. But perhaps Christina's words
might have helped ease his guilt, since he hadn't betrayed
her. In fact, in a strange sort of way, he'd brought about the
very thing she'd most hoped for. He'd married Amelia, the
woman he loved.

Christina forgave him.

Could God perhaps forgive him, too?

But Amelia had again fled, and he didn't know what had
caused her flight. After reading Christina's diary, however,

he knew precisely what he had to do. He had to find Amelia, he had to share with her Christina's final wishes, he had to say those words he'd never said before.

He tucked the diary in his coat pocket. "Here, Katie," he said. "We're going after Mama. We're going to bring her home to stay."

Nothing, absolutely nothing, would keep them apart.

A short while later, as evening approached, Michael brought his buggy to a stop in front of Mrs. Tom's house. He scooped his sleeping daughter in his arms and strode up the walk to the front door. Careful not to jostle Katie, he knocked and soon heard Mrs. Tom's sprightly steps.

"Michael! What brings you back?" A frown pleated Mrs. Tom's brow. "And with Katie! Here, give me that baby. Tell me what is wrong."

"Amelia had a strange swooning spell today. It wasn't the first one, either. I left her on the sofa, went to fetch Katie, and when I came back to the parlor, Amelia had disappeared."

Mrs. Tom's frown deepened. She pursed her lips. "What is wrong with that girl? Again, she does the same thing. Did she tell you where she was going?"

"Not a word! I left her unconscious. I came back, and she was gone. I have to look for her. I must find her."

Looking troubled, Mrs. Tom started toward the back of the house. Over her shoulder, she called, "I'm putting your daughter in bed." Moments later, she returned, worry tightening her motherly features. "Yes . . . you must find Amelia. This time, make sure you learn why she runs away."

Michael sighed and pressed the heels of his hands to his eyes. "I intend to, Mrs. Tom. Believe me, I want to know why. I need to understand."

As he drove down silent streets, light poured from the windows of the homes on his either side. Michael felt a twinge of envy, since most folks would be gathered for supper, while he remained alone. Alone and searching for Amelia.

He had to find her. He would let nothing take his wife from his side. He and Amelia belonged together.

Turning onto her street, Michael was shocked when he saw no lights in the windows of her little home. Surely she wasn't sitting in the dark? No, that was too strange, even for a woman who'd been suffering from . . . what? He only knew that Amelia had suffered four swooning spells.

He pulled hard on the reins, then jumped down from his rig. Approaching the front door, crisp, determined footsteps came his way. Turning, he saw Mildred O'Houlihan, one of Winona's most accomplished gossips and critics.

"Michael!" she cawed. "Michael Hayak, you wait a moment for me. I'll have a word with you."

Michael stifled a groan. This was not the time to put up with Mildred. "What could that be?"

"Why, it's that hussy you have taken for a wife! How you could have done such a foolish thing, I'll certainly never know."

Michael's studied interest vanished. In its place came irritation and annoyance, and he wanted more than ever to be on his way again. He had to find Amelia.

Since Mildred seemed to expect a response, Michael indulged her. "I'd be careful what you call a man's wife, Mildred."

A gasp echoed her look of horror. "Are you threatening me, you upstart?"

"No, ma'am. Just mentioning that a man doesn't want to hear his wife abused with ugly words."

Tipping her chin up, Mildred sniffed. "Well, Michael Hayak, that man should be more careful who he takes for a wife. Why, with that tiny child you have to raise, I can't imagine why you'd marry an audacious chit who spends her excessive leisure time with the vaudeville troops that come to town."

"It's none of your business why I married Amelia, but I will tell you that I'm more than satisfied with my choice."

Mildred waved frantically before her face, as if warding off a swoon. "I should have known! Men are all the same, only interested in satisfying their baser, more prurient impulses."

The throbbing in Michael's temples grew to an unbearable pounding. He'd had enough. "Mildred, I have to find my wife. There's . . . something we have to do tonight, and I'm afraid she's running late." His conscience offered not one twinge at the white lie he'd told. "I'm growing concerned, especially since she's not here," he added, indicating the dark house.

Mildred squared her shoulders. "Well, Michael Hayak, if you're so satisfied with a woman who cavorts with riffraff, you should know where to find her when she strays from home."

Through clenched teeth, Michael asked, "Meaning, madam?"

"She's likely at that Opera House," she said. "The Huntleys are in town for a performance, and Amelia's friendly with Myrtle Huntley."

So? Michael thought. Nothing wrong with that. "Tell me, Mrs. O'Houlihan, why didn't you just say where Amelia was? Why did you have to make such ugly comments about my wife *and* her friend when they aren't even present to defend themselves? I've only heard good things about Mrs. Huntley's performances, and since she travels with her husband, I find no impropriety in that."

Again Mildred sniffed. "Your wife's unreliable, flighty. Here one day, gone the next! She promised to have my traveling suit ready for my Thanksgiving trip to Rochester, and now I'm leaving, and she hasn't even cut the cloth yet."

Suddenly Michael understood the woman's problem. She was peeved that Amelia had finished sewing for Myrtle Huntley but hadn't worked on Mildred's suit. What a mean-spirited biddy! "Buy yourself a suit, Mrs. O'Houli-han. I'll be happy to pay for it. Now, I must be on my way."

"B-but—"

"Nothing. Amelia hasn't been well recently. I'm worried, and your insults stick in my craw."

"Oh . . . oh!" Mildred pressed a hand to her heart. "Why, you're just as bad as that Amelia Baldwin! I pity your poor little girl. Why, Christina—a lovely woman—must be turning in her grave."

That did it! Michael grasped the old crow by her black-coated shoulders and moved her out of his way. "Amelia was Christina's closest friend, and the person my late wife wanted to raise Katie after she was gone," he said, as he climbed into his vehicle. "There is only one reason why Christina might be horrified right now, and that reason is you. Your unfinished suit isn't worth the hurt your words can cause Amelia and Mrs. Huntley. If you'll excuse me, I have a wife to find."

With a smart snap of the reins, Michael left, pleased to notice Mildred's mouth hanging agape. Seems she'd finally found herself at a loss for words.

Although . . . she was probably right about one thing. Amelia had worked on Myrtle Huntley's costumes at the farm, probably finished what needed to be done. Returning the garments fell within the range of possible reasons for her departure. But somehow Michael felt certain that simple explanation was just that, too simple. It didn't explain why she had left without a word.

What could possibly have sent her running from the farm at a time when she had to have been at her weakest? Would he ever get her back?

She had to get away. The moment she came to on the parlor sofa, Amelia knew she had to leave. She had just kissed Christina's husband, and Christina not yet dead.

She ran outside, hitched old Bess to her wagon, and

headed to Winona. How could she have allowed the situation to escalate to where Michael kissed her? True, she'd had powerful feelings for him for a long while now, but . . . a kiss? One she'd returned just as passionately as he'd given it.

As the conveyance clattered down the road, Amelia suddenly drew a sharp breath. That kiss hadn't just happened. Christina had been dead a while now. She, Amelia, had married Michael in the interim, and was now his wife.

In a kaleidoscopic whirl, memories shot at her. She remembered the days she'd spent helping Christina just after Katie was born. She remembered the stream of physicians who had come to examine her friend. They'd all left shaking their heads in regret.

She saw years of her life go by in the form of crisp, detailed memories. She remembered the first day she looked at Michael Hayak and saw the man, rather than her friend's husband. She remembered crying herself to sleep nights, the guilt of loving a married man tearing her to shreds. She remembered running after that kiss, blindly rushing away from the longing to repeat the caress.

She remembered going home, gathering two of Myrtle Huntley's costumes, and proceeding to the Opera House. She'd hoped to find her friend, to talk about the new skits the Huntleys were working on, to talk about vaudeville, always so jolly and lively and fun. Anything to take her mind from what had just happened.

At the Opera House, she'd gone to Myrtle's dressing room but found it empty. She'd left the garments hanging from the top of a painted screen in a corner of the cramped room, then gone to look for her friend. No sooner had she stepped onto the stage floor, than floorboards cracked and gave way beneath her.

With her coat sleeve, Amelia wiped fresh tears off her face. She was nearly home. But she wasn't sure she could cope with the loneliness she'd be sure to find there. She needed time to come to grips with all she now knew.

Because, together with the memories of Christina's illness came the even more disturbing recollections of a future life. Amelia now knew without a doubt that she'd traveled through time. Not once, but twice.

The first thing she remembered after falling through the darkness was the loneliness she knew as a child at the orphanage near Chicago, the series of foster homes. She still remembered the Beatles, Smashing Pumpkins, Presidents Reagan, Bush and broccoli, Clinton and burgers. She remembered movies, the space shuttle Columbia, and the Gulf War. She even remembered working her way through college and being hired to costume the vaudeville revival.

She recalled coming to Winona and falling through the stage one more time.

Most of all, however, she remembered the horror, the guilt of loving her best friend's man. After that kiss, Amelia knew she couldn't live with herself. No matter how much she loved Michael, and all the promises she'd made to Christina, she remembered planning to leave town. To go far, far away from the temptation to covet that which she had no right to want. Far from the temptation to steal the forbidden, sinful caresses she so longed for.

She'd planned to leave the man she loved for his own good. She didn't want to tempt him to sin again.

As her past, present, and future melded into a vast panorama in her mind, Amelia fought to make peace with her memories, her friendship with Christina, the love she felt for her new husband, and the fear that suddenly she might be dragged back to the twentieth century.

"What am I going to do?" she cried out, begging God to answer her prayers, and to do so decisively. She was now married to Michael, but she had no idea why she'd gone through time. That first time . . . perhaps a merciful God had taken her from a morass she'd been unable to ford. Every essential part of her, her integrity, her principles, her honor, had been unable to cope with her love for a married man. The man married to her closest friend. But, once she'd arrived in the future, once she'd made her way through that life, why had she been brought back?

That glorious day after their wedding, she had thought she'd come to ensure Michael's happiness, to make possible the dreams he had otherwise been forced to set aside. Marrying Michael had been a joy, it had felt so absolutely right. But was that marriage an act of defiance against fate?

Against a God who had decreed theirs a forbidden love?

As she approached downtown Winona, Amelia went straight to the Opera House. There, she'd keep the troubling thoughts at bay a little longer. She'd always enjoyed the theater, those who worked there.

Outside the Opera House, Amelia tied old Bess's reins to the hitching post, then lugged out the box full of costumes. Barely able to see above it, she headed for the door.

"There you are, missy!" she heard Mildred O'Houlihan announce.

Damn! This was no time to deal with that woman. Amelia tried ignoring her.

Determined footsteps came closer. "Amelia Baldwin! You wait for me right this minute."

Panting, Mildred came to a halt between the box Amelia held and the door to the theater. Unless she either walked over the battle-ax or shoved her out of the way, Amelia would have to listen to whatever was on Mildred's mind. And she had a sinking suspicion just what that was.

Mildred took a dainty handkerchief from her reticule, and although the temperature hovered right around freezing, she made a pretense of dabbing perspiration off her face.

"You should be ashamed of yourself! Making an old woman run to catch you. You have deplorable manners, missy!"

Amelia felt like stuffing one of Myrtle's dresses into Mildred's squawking beak, but then Myrtle would be one costume short. She'd wait Mildred out.

Mildred wagged a gloved finger at Amelia. "And it's not

just today that I refer to. You show great difficulty with keeping your word. Where's my traveling suit? Hmmmm? Ten days, you said."

With a sigh, Amelia set the box down. "There isn't much I can say, Mildred. Circumstances have been such that I wasn't able to do as I promised. And, what's more, I can't have the suit done in time for your trip. I . . . had other matters to see to."

Mildred's eyes narrowed nastily. "Yes, I'll say you did! You had to make sure you married that Michael Hayak, didn't you? And such a scandalously short time after his wife's passing. Tell me, Amelia, how long have you been tempting that man with your . . ." Mildred raked Amelia's figure, pausing at her breasts. ". . . assets? Did you start while you pretended to care for his wife? As I always say, a person who can't keep her word can't be trusted. Not in business or in personal matters."

Mildred's words flew straight to the more tormented part of Amelia's heart. Dear God, did everyone think she'd been plotting and planning to marry Michael all the while she took care of Christina? Did they think she'd indulged in adultery all those months?

Although Amelia knew she'd tried to keep from loving him, the facts remained. She'd loved Michael all that time. Suddenly she couldn't stomach Mildred and her accusations any longer.

Certain the woman would consider her actions rude, Amelia picked up the box of costumes and elbowed her out of the way. Pushing open the heavy door, she turned to face Mildred, who stood gasping like an over-boiled teapot, hissing and spitting and whistling away. "If you will excuse me, Myrtle's waiting for these. I'll make sure you have your fabric back tomorrow at the latest."

"Hummph!" Mildred snorted. "Who can trust a thing you say or do? For all I know, tomorrow you'll be gone again, and no one will have a clue where you've gone."

Those parting words clutched at Amelia's heart, heightening her fear. While she couldn't change the past, and her present teetered on shaky ground, Amelia feared her future the most. After all, she'd been ripped from this time once before.

Now, however, she was married to Michael. Katie had become her child. She stood to lose so much more than before. What was to become of her?

Tears welled in her eyes. Grief clouded her thoughts. Was she about to be taken?

Would a caring God spare her the agony of an adulterous passion, only to give her a taste of happiness before taking her away again?

Chapter 19

"MYRTLE!" AMELIA CALLED as she went backstage. The auditorium was silent, unusual for late afternoon before a scheduled performance. She turned toward the dressing rooms to look for her friend, but her troubled thoughts diverted her.

That stage floor. She'd fallen through it twice. Was there some strange weakness to the oak boards that allowed you to escape a difficult existence and suddenly find yourself living a brand-new life? Had it only happened to her?

Hesitantly she walked toward the stage. Pushing one of the heavy ruby velvet curtains aside, she examined the expanse of floor. From where she stood in the wings, it looked deceptively normal. But Amelia knew too much about those pieces of wood to be fooled.

She approached warily, her steps careful, her eyes focusing on the spot where she next intended to tread.

For a moment, she questioned her motive. Why on earth had she returned to such a frightening spot? Was she trying to tempt fate? Did she want to run the risk of being taken away?

Or did she want to learn if she was here, in 1900, to stay?

No more than eighteen inches ahead, she noticed a patch of different-colored floor. That must be where it happened. Even though the auditorium wasn't lit, from where she stood she saw that a substantial amount of wood had given way when she went through. Someone had repaired it by installing sturdy new planks.

"There you have it . . ." she murmured. What an extraordinary thing! And it had happened to her. Too bad she hadn't known about her adventure during her stay in the future. She might have paid more attention to everyday things, life in general.

And now? What would happen next, now that she knew the entire story? Would she be taken away from Michael again in punishment for her once-forbidden love?

"Amelia!" she heard Myrtle exclaim right behind her.

Amelia turned, but caught the toe of her boot on a ribbon that had slipped out from the poorly closed box of costumes. She stumbled, lost her balance, and felt her feet go out from under her. As she flew through the air, the only thing she saw was that lighter patch of flooring come straight at her so fast there was no escaping her fate.

The moment she struck her head, she saw black . . . a void. "Nooooo . . . !"

As Michael entered the Opera House, he heard his wife's strangled scream followed by a series of sickening thuds. Something had happened to Amelia.

In the dark, he headed down an auditorium aisle, his heart beating painfully hard. She had to be all right, she just *had* to. Katie needed her. *He* needed her.

Now that he'd learned of Christina's wishes, and realized that his love for Amelia had indeed been a forgivable sin, he was more certain than ever that they belonged together. He only had to find her, show her Christina's words, prove to her that she could stop rushing away from the memory of an ill-timed kiss.

As he approached the stage, shadows materialized. The lack of light in the vast chamber made it difficult for him to make out who was kneeling near center stage, but he thought it looked like Myrtle Huntley.

Then he noticed the woman's distress. Urgent murmurs could be heard, too low for him to make out, but it seemed as if someone lay prone on the stage. Leaping up the three steps to the platform, Michael caught sight of the body on the floor.

"Amelia!" he cried, his heart breaking at the sight of her, pale as death, still as a marble statue. A sob ripped past his throat. "No . . ."

Dropping to his knees, he turned to Myrtle. "What happened?"

"Oh, Mr. Hayak—"

"Michael."

She nodded. "I saw her standing on the stage and called her name. The next thing I knew, she tripped and landed hard on the floor. Her head must have struck those boards they used to repair the spot where she first fell through."

Michael had by now unbuttoned Amelia's coat, removed her hat and the scarf she'd worn around her neck. Frantic, he felt for a pulse at the base of her throat. Because he'd left the farm in such a rush, he'd forgotten his gloves. His cold, numb fingers couldn't find the slightest beat.

"Amelia," he whispered, unable to utter another word. Tears filled his eyes, dropped onto her face. A gentle touch to his wife's cheek caressed them away.

Myrtle placed a hand on his forearm. "I'll go for Dr. Wilhite. You stay with her. She'll need you more than she needs me."

The knot in Michael's throat twisted tighter, and he could do no more than nod. Then he went back to search for signs of life.

Amelia couldn't be dead. Not now that she was his.

He opened wide the lapels of her coat, and unfastened the two top buttons on her soft green flannel blouse. As he

parted the pieces of fabric, a light flickered on at the foot of
the stage. A brilliant flash caught Michael's gaze, and he
saw the crystal heart in the hollow of Amelia's throat.

*I'll always treasure your heart. And keep it safe from
harm,* she'd said. That day had been magical. She'd become his wife. Another wrenching sob tore through him,
and he laid his head on her chest, hoping against hope to
hear the flutter of her heart.

The moment he pressed his cheek to her breast, he felt
the slightest rise, then fall. Through his fear, he grasped at
that sudden ray of hope. "Amelia . . ."

But there was nothing more. He went back to her neck,
determined to find that pulse. She was going to be fine.
Katie needed her mama more than ever. And he couldn't
consider living without her any longer.

As he felt for the action of that tiny vein, he saw the
crystal heart give a wobble. "Amelia . . ."

The softness of a sigh caressed his wet cheek. "Amelia?"

Another footlight went on, giving Michael a better view
of the throbbing spot at the base of Amelia's neck. She was
alive!

"Don' mind me, son," called Herbert from the general
area of the footlights. "I'm jist preparin' fer tonight's
show." He clucked sympathetically. "Ain't that sumpin'
how that liddle Baldwin gal keeps on fallin' at the same
spot?"

Michael tried to smile, still keeping his gaze fast on the
flickering evidence of Amelia's life. "She's Mrs. Hayak
now. And it's something, all right."

"Don'cha worry, son. She's gonna be jist fine. Only,
keep 'er off that there stage, will ya? It don't seem so
healthy fer 'er."

". . . angels . . ." whispered Amelia. "Herbert . . ."

"Amelia," Michael murmured. "Can you hear me?"

"Michael?" she asked.

"Yes! Yes, love, I'm here."

"You're . . . an . . . angel . . . ?"

He couldn't have heard right. Had she called him an angel? She usually called him a mule. But she had received another bump to the head. God knew what this one would do to her. "Are you hurt? You fell down again, you know."

She moved her head up and down, then moaned. "I'm . . . down there . . . again?"

"Down where?"

One eyelid rose. The other one followed. Emerald irises peeked out. A wobbly smile curved her lips. Then she groaned and closed her eyes again. "Under the . . . stage . . . floor."

"No, of course you're not." He rapped hard on the fresh planks. "See? They fixed the weak spot. These are strong, solid oak. Hard enough to give you a good bump."

Again she tried to smile. "Feels more like . . . a Mack truck . . . ran me down."

"Truck? What truck? Amelia, you're in the Opera House. There are no trucks in here."

A soft chuckle, and she lifted her head. "Ooohh! This is some headache." She raised her hand to the back of her head. "Hmm, no blood."

Michael sat down at her side, sighing in relief. "You're going to be fine."

The green eyes he loved opened all the way. "You're really here!"

He frowned. "Of course I'm really here. Where would I be? After all, you're the one who keeps disappearing. I'm the one who has to look for you."

Suddenly she paled. Michael grasped her by the arms, afraid she'd faint again. In turn, she gripped his shoulders with surprising strength. "What's the date?"

"The date?" he asked, puzzled. "You want to know the date?"

She nodded, her eyes intent on his face.

Michael shook his head. "I'll never understand you. It's Wednesday, November—"

"Not *that*. The year. What year is this?"

"The same as it was yesterday, this morning, and will be tomorrow! We're nearing the end of 1900."

A radiant smile broke out across her lips. Her eyes opened wider. A tender look caressed his face. "A miracle . . ." she whispered.

"A miracle?" he asked. "The only miracle is that you haven't done yourself in yet running away like this. It simply must stop. No more running. You have to tell me what's wrong, no matter what it turns out to be. I might even be able to help."

"I daresay you could. Here and there." She placed her hand on his forearm. Her expression turned solemn. "Michael, about my running . . . well, it has to do with Christina."

To Amelia's surprise, he nodded. "I suspected as much." He pressed his lips tight, worry lined his brow.

"But—"

He pressed a finger to her lips. "It's my turn to speak. You just had an accident. Listen, and let me hold you."

It was the second most wonderful offer she'd ever received. As she wriggled into a more comfortable position against him, Michael pulled a small blue book from his coat pocket. "What—"

"Hush! Just listen." He began to read. Moments later, she realized it was Christina's diary.

By the time he finished the last entry, both had fresh tears on their cheeks. "She knew," Amelia whispered.

"Yes, she did."

"And she forgave," she added.

Michael nodded. He squeezed his eyes shut, and two more tears rolled down his face. "Will you tell me now what happened to you? Those times you fainted? Why did you run away the day Christina died? Why did you miss her funeral?"

Amelia sighed. Seeing that she hadn't been ripped to the turn of the next century, she felt fairly certain that she was here to stay. And since they were now married, Michael deserved some answers. Only . . . some questions had simpler answers than others.

"You know why I ran away that day," she said. "You'd kissed me, and you were married. To my dearest friend." Amelia lowered her gaze. "I'd wondered about . . . about you . . . wished for your kisses, for a very long time before that. Wrong though it was, I kissed you back." Her voice broke. "And I wanted . . . more."

"You, too?"

"Too?" Her eyes flew open. She scoured Michael's face.

He nodded. "I'd come to have . . . feelings for you over those two years. It felt as if I'd wanted to kiss you nearly forever. When I finally did, it wasn't planned. It . . . just happened. I knew it was wrong. I was married. I'd betrayed my wedding vows."

"I couldn't face the guilt," Amelia confessed. "So I ran away. And I planned to continue running."

"Where did you go?"

She was going to have to tell him. Everything. But not here. She'd tell him what she could here. Then, once they were home again, she would tell him the rest. "Under the stage."

"You mean . . ." Horror filled Michael's eyes. "You spent two days in that hole?"

"This is as far as I went." She shrugged. "I'd brought Myrtle's costumes, left them in her dressing room. Since she wasn't there, I went to look for her, tripped, and fell through the floor."

He narrowed his eyes. "And the amnesia? No more secrets now. I have to know the truth."

Amelia smiled and brought her right hand to her chest. "I can swear that when I finally came to, I knew nothing, absolutely *nothing* that happened before that very moment."

"You weren't pretending?"

"No."

"You weren't . . . lying?"

"Watch it, buster! I don't lie!"

Michael laughed. "Sound more like yourself by the minute, feisty and sharp-tongued. But, for Katie's sake, would you please do something about those strange expressions you've been using?"

Uh-oh! She wasn't out of the woods yet. "What strange expressions?"

"Oh, the ones like, 'Watch it, buster!'" He ran a finger down her cheek, cupped her jaw in his palm. He fell silent, gazed at her as if she were the most precious thing on earth.

"I thought I'd disgusted you," he finally said. "You'd always appeared so self-assured, so responsible and upright. I figured that an adulterer's attentions would offend you."

Amelia shook her head. "No, it wasn't you that horrified me. It was the feelings I had for you. That I'd allowed a moment of such weakness to happen." Placing a hand on his chest, Amelia looked into Michael's eyes. "You could never disgust me. I'd been secretly . . . loving you for too long."

"What did you say?" Michael's index finger and thumb captured her chin, holding her in place as his eyes sought his answers.

She lowered her eyelids momentarily, but then—again—met his gaze. He deserved as much. "I fell in love with you from the very first. Even though I knew it was wrong."

Michael pulled her close. "Thank God! I couldn't stand thinking I'd offended you. You see, Amelia, I, too, fell in love. With you. During those two hellish years of watching a good woman fight a losing battle against death. You were the brightest part of my life. You and Katie."

"You love me?"

He nodded. "I love you, wife."

"Can we go home now?"

Footsteps rang out in the auditorium. "Now you wait just one minute there, young lady!" cried out Dr. Wilhite. The portly, white-haired and bearded gentleman rocked from side to side in his penguinlike walk, making his way up the steps to the stage. Plopping down his voluminous black bag at her side, he immediately pushed Michael's arms out of the way.

Amelia giggled at the outrage on her husband's handsome face.

Myrtle came and stood to the side. "I really think you should spend a few days in bed," she suggested, concern in her voice. "This is the second time you've hurt your head in recent months."

Michael's chest bounced beneath Amelia. Glancing up, she found a gleam of mischief dancing in those brilliant blue eyes. "Michael," she warned.

"What dear?" he answered in an innocent voice. "I'm merely in agreement with Mrs. Huntley. Remember when I hurt my hand? You took *very good* care of me while I was in bed. I do believe we're going to have to keep you there for quite a while. I must make sure you're—"

"Yes, yes," she cut in before he embarrassed them any further. "I promise! I'll make sure I get a lot of rest."

"In fact, dear," Michael went on, wicked glee in his grin, "I think this is a perfect time for Katie to spend a few days with Mrs. Tom. I'll have to keep a very close eye on you at all times—just to make sure you recover completely, you understand."

Amelia found it difficult to keep from laughing. She knew exactly what her husband meant. And . . . she couldn't help but agree with his intentions. Now that she knew he loved her, that Christina had, oddly enough, given them her blessing, that she believed a loving God had forgiven her and Michael, and given them another chance.

After tapping and peering, jabbing and prodding, and finally palpating the sore spot on the back of Amelia's head, Dr. Wilhite turned saber-sharp eyes on her while addressing Myrtle. "I believe, Mrs. Huntley, your friend isn't as seriously injured as you first thought." He winked at Amelia, but continued speaking to Myrtle. "I agree with her husband's plans. A few days in bed, and Mrs. Hayak will be right as rain."

Amelia felt the heat of her blush all the way to her hairline.

Michael burst out laughing.

Myrtle stared at all three, then shrugged. "I must get
ready for tonight's performance." She began walking off-
stage, then turned around. "Amelia, you wouldn't be up to
staying for the show, now would you?"

"No!" Michael leaped up. "Er . . . I mean, no, I don't
think she should linger another minute. Like Doc says, I
must take her directly to bed."

"Too bad," said the attractive, red-haired actress. "Some
other time."

Amelia stopped laughing long enough to answer. "Another time, perhaps, Myrtle."

Michael shook Dr. Wilhite's hand, then helped Amelia
stand. As the doctor left, Amelia donned her scarf and her
hat. Michael distracted her with a shower of kisses.

"Now d'ya see that, son?" piped in Herbert.

Michael turned and found the busybody perched on a
piano banquette, a benevolent smile illuminating his broad
face. "See what?"

Herbert waved expansively. "Jist like I tol' ya. Ya
needed yerself a woman. *Real bad.* An' the one ya needed
was right there at hand."

Amelia blushed again.

Michael laughed.

Again.

"Herbert," Michael suggested good-naturedly, "why
don't you get back to your apples and the rest of your business?"

With a chuckle, Herbert winked. "That's what ya said
the last time, but if I hadn'a tol' ya, ya might still be itchin'
somethin' fierce!"

"Herbert!" Amelia exclaimed.

"Sorry, Missus Hayak, but I tells 'em how I sees 'em.
An' I seen the two of ya needed a liddle push." He hooked
his thumbs in his suspenders and stood. Approaching, he

went on. "Way I figgers it, ya oughta name yore first one fer me!"

Amelia's eyes nearly popped in horror. Name a child of hers after Herbert? Herbert Weidel? The unlikeliest of angels?

"We'll see," answered Michael in a choked, yet polite voice. "But don't hold your breath. It could always be another girl."

"Oh, hush, Michael! I'm not even expecting."

"Good night, Herbert," Michael said to the "angel." Leaning toward Amelia, he whispered, "Yet."

As they hurried outside, Herbert called out, "Won't be long now, Missus Hayak!"

They laughed, linked arms, and went for the buggy. Climbing in, they spread the carriage robes over their laps, and Michael took up the reins.

After they'd stopped to arrange for Mrs. Tomicek to watch Katie for the next few days, they began the ride home. Curled up tight next to her husband, Amelia felt a deep sense of joy, the knowledge that all was right with the world.

A perfect full moon appeared from behind a cloud. "Oh, look, Michael," Amelia said. "The moon is out."

"That's nice," he murmured.

Oh, well. *She* cared. Tonight was the start of a new life for them both. A life that would hold many blessings, but perhaps none as great as this second chance they'd been given.

"Michael?"

"Mm-hmmm."

"I know we haven't had the opportunity for many serious discussions . . ."

"Yes. And?"

"And looking at this perfect night, I have to wonder."

"What about?"

"Well . . . do you believe in God?"

"In God? Of course I do!"

"You know, I think He has some absolutely astounding ways of making things happen just the way He wants them."

"Like?"

"Well, like . . . you and me."

He remained silent for a moment. Then he looked skyward. "What about you and me?"

"It's like this. You know that scripture about a time to be born and a time to die, a time to love . . ."

"Mm-hmmm."

She was fast losing his attention. "I think it's positively right. There is a time, a *right* time for everything in our life."

"And?" he asked again.

"And since you said we should have no more secrets . . ."

He whipped his face around. Blue lasers bored into her. "Secrets? What secrets are you keeping now?"

"Well," she said, taking a deep breath, "it's not *exactly* a secret. You know how I fell through the stage floor?"

A long-suffering sigh preceded his. "Who doesn't?"

"What if I told you it happened not once, but twice?"

Epilogue

As the group of tourists entered the Opera House foyer, the young tour guide with them pointed to a portrait on a wall. Depicting a Victorian couple, it showed the man's hands clasping the woman's shoulders while a loving smile brightened his face. The woman's hand covered his, and a smile of fulfillment graced her lips.

"That's Mr. and Mrs. Michael Hayak," the young woman said. "They were benefactors of the Opera House around the turn of the century. Without the trust they established, we wouldn't be here any longer. Mr. Hayak made a fortune with a glass factory outside of town. Mrs. Hayak wore that beautiful mint-green dress at their wedding. She made the gown from fabric he gave her. They say the heart-shaped crystal pendant she wears is one of the first pieces he crafted. Mr. and Mrs. Hayak had a large family, and old-timers say they were deeply in love."

Author's Note

While doing research for another story, I stumbled upon the description of the Winona Opera House. I also learned it was torn down in 1990. As many authors often do, I began to play "what if."

What if someone had bequeathed a minor fortune to the Opera House in memory of a loved one? What if instead of dying, that love transcended the limitations of time and flourished, saving the Opera House?

I knew I had a story.

While Ben and Myrtle Huntley were indeed vaudevillians who frequently performed at the Opera House, Michael, Amelia, and Katie Hayak exist only in my imagination and the pages of this book. I prefer to think not of what has been lost, but of what might have been saved.

Let me know what you think. I love to hear from my readers. Please write to me at The Berkley Publishing Group, c/o Publicity Department, 200 Madison Avenue, New York, New York 10016. You can also contact me at GINNYAIKEN@AOL.COM